Charles Rogers

A Century of Scottish Life

Charles Rogers

A Century of Scottish Life

ISBN/EAN: 9783337330231

Printed in Europe, USA, Canada, Australia, Japan

Cover: Foto ©Andreas Hilbeck / pixelio.de

More available books at **www.hansebooks.com**

SCOTTISH LIFE.

MEMORIALS AND RECOLLECTIONS

OF

HISTORICAL AND REMARKABLE PERSONS.

WITH ILLUSTRATIONS OF

CALEDONIAN HUMOUR.

BY THE

REV. CHARLES ROGERS, LL.D., F.S.A. Scot.,

HISTORIOGRAPHER TO THE HISTORICAL SOCIETY OF GREAT BRITAIN.

SECOND EDITION, ENLARGED.

LONDON:
CHARLES GRIFFIN & CO.,
STATIONERS' HALL COURT.

1872.

LONDON :
PRINTED BY J. AND W. RIDER,
BARTHOLOMEW CLOSE.

PREFACE TO THE SECOND EDITION.

THE first edition of this work having obtained a degree of favour much beyond its deserts, I have been encouraged carefully to revise every portion of it. The entire arrangement has been altered, the department more especially anecdotal recast, and much new matter added. Besides, the present edition is produced at a price more suited to the majority of readers.

A CENTURY OF SCOTTISH LIFE is the most appropriate title I can devise for a work which includes memorials and anecdotes of remarkable Scotsmen and others during the last hundred years. For a portion of the memorials I am indebted to my late father, a Scottish country minister, and one of the best conversationalists of his time. Personally I have had the privilege of associating with many gifted Scotsmen for the last thirty years, and I have commemorated those who are departed. My sketches are short, for I have not attempted biographies. Throughout the work I have endeavoured to be succinct, preferring to illustrate my subject with anecdotes rather than with reflections of my own. The present edition is enriched with contributions from my patriotic friend Mr. Sheriff Barclay of Perthshire, and other ingenious and obliging correspondents.

CHARLES ROGERS.

SNOWNDOUN VILLA,
Lewisham, Kent.

CONTENTS.

A CENTURY OF SCOTTISH LIFE.

A COUNTRY MINISTER AND HIS RECOLLECTIONS.

My father, the Rev. James Roger, minister of Dunino, Fife-shire (1805—1849), was an eminent classical and general scholar. Born on the 24th June, 1767, at Coupar Grange, Perthshire, an estate of which his ancestors were co-proprietors, he was dedicated to the altar by his father, a pious elder of the Church. In his fourteenth year he entered the University of St. Andrews, having gained by competition a bursary or exhibition, which secured his education and maintenance for four sessions. At the close of his first session he obtained a premium awarded by the Earl of Kinnoull, Chancellor of the University, to the student who had made the greatest progress in his classical studies. During the latter years of his theological course he attended Marischal College, Aberdeen. In 1791 he was licensed to preach by the Presbytery of Dundee. Soon afterwards he was introduced to the celebrated Mr. George Dempster of Dunnichen, and, on his recommendation, was appointed to prepare an Agricultural Survey of Forfarshire for the Board of Agriculture. In 1796, he published an essay on the principles of Government, intended to correct popular notions as to the beneficial consequences of the French Revolution. In the same year he was awarded a gold medal by the Highland Society, for an essay on the best method of improving the Highlands.

My father now contemplated an extensive work on the rise and progress of Agriculture, but he afterwards abandoned the intention from lack of encouragement. He next made trial of literary life in London, but lost heart and returned to Scotland. In 1805 he was ordained to the ministerial office at Dunino,

B

where, in the hope of obtaining academical preferment, which had been the lot of his three immediate predecessors, he devoted himself to studies of a more recondite and philosophical character. In 1816 he was a candidate for the Professorship of Moral Philosophy at St. Andrews. He continued to prosecute his classical and philosophical studies with unabated ardour. Until his 82nd year he read daily in the Latin and Greek classics, and in Hebrew literature. His conversational powers were of the first order, and his information was almost encyclopædic. After a period of feeble health he died on the 23rd November, 1849, at the age of eighty-three. A few days after his decease he was thus described by an able journalist:—" With the excellent natural abilities which he possessed, cultivated by study, the fruits of which a memory of great tenacity enabled him to have always at his command, and with a varied and extensive acquaintance with the real living world, Mr. Roger was to those who had the happiness of being acquainted with him only in his latter years, an acquaintance at once delightful and instructive to a degree which cannot well be described. He had acted as a reporter in the House of Commons, at a time when its deliberations were influenced by the heavings of those terrible convulsions which afterwards overthrew the thrones of Europe, and in every country, except Britain, threw back for more than a century the cause of rational and solid liberty. Mr. Roger had noted the speeches of Pitt and Fox, and of a host of able though lesser men. Others might have had his opportunities of listening to these great men who might not have felt the influence or retained the memory of their presence, or been able to make an after generation the wiser of their experience ; but Mr. Roger was just the man whose vivid and picturesque descriptions in conversation faithfully conveyed to others the scenes which he had himself witnessed, and he could raise up before his hearers the whole figure of Charles Fox, with his blue coat and yellow waistcoat, opening his manly and simple addresses with a downcast look and an unanimated, heavy air, and gradually getting more and more carried away by the strength of his feelings, till his voice was elevated beyond the pitch to which a calm attention to gracefulness would have confined it, but never elevated so as to lose its power of impressing and ruling the hearts of the senate."

Of my father's recollections the first portion is presented in his own words.

"In November, 1781, I was introduced to the Latin and Greek professors at St. Andrews, by my relative, Mr. John Playfair, minister of Liff. This ingenious man, who afterwards obtained European fame as Professor Playfair of Edinburgh, was already in high repute for his scientific attainments. In 1772, while only twenty-four, he contested the Chair of Natural Philosophy at St. Andrews, and lost the appointment only through an excess of local influence on behalf of a competitor. Soon after, he succeeded his father in the church living of Liff, but he was still prosecuting his peculiar studies, being more ardent about success in the academy than in the Church. In after life we did not meet ; but I remember him as one venerated for his learning, and whose unaffected kindly manners caused me to regard him with affection. At the period to which I refer, the professor was in his thirty-third year. Though he had been patriarchal, he could not have administered more fatherly counsel, or warned me more emphatically against the snares which beset the inexperienced. 'Write often,' he said, ' to your father and mother. Never indulge in play till you have finished your tasks, and select only a few companions. Rise early, and revise your morning lesson before leaving your apartment. Keep your room in the evenings, unless on the appointed holidays.'

"When I entered St. Andrews University, I found that the visit of Dr. Samuel Johnson to that ancient seat of learning was still a theme of conversation, though seven years had passed since the English sage walked under the porch of St. Salvator. There was a difference of opinion about Johnson— one section of the gownsmen ' siding,' as they expressed it, with the professors, whose learning the English lexicographer had ventured to impugn. At the banquet to which the professors invited him, Johnson expressed surprise that a blessing should have been asked in English rather than in Latin ; and when the key of the library was missing, he spoke of a library of which the key could never be found. Several of the older students remembered Johnson's visit, and described the awe which he had inspired.

"John Campbell, a Highland student, was bold enough to lampoon the sage, and even to throw ridicule upon his dictionary. 'What is a window?' propounded the facetious querist. Johnson was supposed to reply, ' A window, sir, is an orifice cut out of an edifice for the introduction of illumination.' 'And how should one ask a friend to snuff the candle?

'Sir, you ought to say, Deprive that luminary of its superfluous eminence.' At St. Andrews, Johnson indulged to the full in his combativeness of talk, and the professors, while unwilling to speak harshly of one so noted, remembered his visit with distaste.

"St. Andrews, with its three colleges, had dwindled into a state bordering on decay. The modern tenements were built of timber, and the older houses were in ruins. The streets, meanly paved, yielded a crop of grass, which was mowed by sheep ; while less frequented thoroughfares had crossings of boulders, by means of which pedestrians could in wet weather avoid stepping into pools of mud. In the heart of the city a street was named the *Foul Waste,* and the name was appropriate ; it was the receptacle of abomination of every sort, and constantly emitted a loathsome smell. The Cathedral buildings were unenclosed ; from the ruins, builders took stones to rear private dwellings, and the citizens adapted the surrounding burial-ground for every purpose of convenience. The three colleges were greatly dilapidated. St. Leonard's Halls were the repositories of farm produce and winter fodder. The Common Hall of St. Salvator's College was a dreary vault, with cobwebbed roof and damp earthen floor. The lecture rooms were small, dingy, and ill ventilated. In St. Mary's College, one room, dark and dismal, served for the prelections of the four Professors of Theology. The foundation bursars resided in a wing of St. Salvator's College ; they were lodged, maintained, and taught at the expense of the institution. The entertainment provided was limited in extent, and in quality most wretched. For breakfast we received half an oaten loaf, with half a chopin of beer ; the latter was brewed on the premises, and could not have been of worse quality. Dinner was at three o'clock served in the Common Hall. Broth and beef constituted the fare four days weekly. A professor presided ; he tasted the broth, and looked on as we ate the coarse flesh with which it was prepared. Thrice a week we dined on fish or eggs. Tea and coffee were unknown. Our evening meal consisted of a twopenny loaf, with a jug of the college beer. Each bursar's apartment was eight feet square. The bedsteads were timber tressels, and the beds were rough and hard. Each room had a fireplace, but as smoky chimneys were the rule, we seldom used fire, except when extremity of cold rendered smoke with a little heat more tolerable than starvation. Each bursar provided and kept clean his knife and fork ; but the professors, in consideration of deducting from our bursaries sixteen shillings and eightpence, gave us the use of silver spoons.

"Thirteen years before my entering the United College, Robert Fergusson, the poet, occupied the same chamber in St. Salvator's which was assigned to myself. Many of his rhymes, inscribed on the walls, were still legible. There was a tradition that, by means of a poetical pasquinade, not very reverently introduced, Fergusson achieved considerable reform at the college table. Each bursar said grace by turns. It was Fergusson's turn. He rose up and expressed himself as follows :—

> 'For rabbits young and for rabbits old,
> For rabbits hot and for rabbits cold,
> For rabbits tender and for rabbits tough,
> Our thanks we render, for we've had enough.'

Hitherto rabbits from a warren in the neighbourhood constituted the chief fare, and though complaints were often made, none proved effective. The present stroke was irresistible. The professors dreaded to inflict censure on the graceless poet, who might, if reproved for his present rhymes, inflict others even more wanton. The rabbits disappeared.

"Among the more erudite Professors in the United College were Dr. John Hunter of the Latin, and Dr. George Hill of the Greek chair. As the accomplished editor of the Latin classics, Dr. Hunter became celebrated. Already he enjoyed high reputation as a teacher.* He composed Latin elegantly, and as the business of the class was conducted in the Roman tongue, we found that he always expressed himself well and neatly. But he wrote English with less skill. Imitating in some measure the Johnsonian formality, but deficient in fancy, his English composition was ponderous and uninteresting. This is apparent in his 'Treatise on Conjunctions,'† and in the article 'Grammar,' which he contributed to the seventh edition of the 'Encyclopædia Britannica.'

"If biography is intended to stimulate to industry and virtue, it is to be regretted that a life of John Hunter has not been written. Man of genius he was not; there was no

---

* Dr. John Hunter was born in the parish of Closeburn, Dumfriesshire, in September, 1746. He died at St. Andrews on the 18th January 1837, in his ninety-first year. The year before his death he was advanced to the Principalship of the United College.

† Edinburgh Philosophical Transactions, 1788.

poetry in his nature, and he had little aptitude for business. He did not excel in conversation, and in matters of science he was very partially informed. But he had the sagacity to know his *forte*, and to keep by it. At the Free School of Wallace Hall he evinced a remarkable promptitude in mastering the details of Latin grammar, while he excelled all his class-fellows in discovering the true meaning of the classic writers. His father was a poor operative, and as all scholastic appointments were then made through private influence, it seemed doubtful whether the young scholar of Wallace Hall might ever attain a post beyond that of a country schoolmaster. He left school while still young, and proceeding to Edinburgh, became clerk in a merchant's office. Recommending himself to his employer, he obtained permission to attend the Latin and Greek classes in the university. His attainments as a Latin scholar were as marked at college as they had previously been in the academy, and when Lord Monboddo applied to the Professor of Latin for a clerk who could read Virgil, Hunter was named at once. Acceptance was matter of course, and the learned judge was delighted with his clerkly acquisition. Hunter was silent when his patron spoke about the origin of mankind, but when he talked about the classics, the clerk proved equal to the judge. Monboddo began to defer to his amanuensis respecting the meaning of Latin phrases, and at his table introduced him to those who could appreciate his scholarship. In 1775 a vacancy occurred in the Humanity Chair at St. Andrews. To the patron, General Scott of Balcomie, Monboddo strongly recommended his *protegé*. The story went, that the General, on receiving the recommendation, went to Monboddo's house, and desired to have an interview with his friend. On his presenting himself, the General drew from his pocket a copy of Horace, and asked him to read. Hunter read an ode, and gave a free and intelligent translation. The General put a few questions which were answered clearly and correctly. 'Now,' said the General, closing the book, 'I give you the Professorship, not because you are Lord Monboddo's friend, but for your personal merits.'

"Advanced from the clerk's stool to the Professor's chair, John Hunter never forgot whence he had risen, and never permitted his attention to be diverted from the earnest pursuit of those studies of which the early prosecution had led to his elevation. He formed a critical acquaintance with the best Latin authors, and his editions of the classics, prepared as they were with extraordinary care, retain an honourable place.

"My Greek Professor, Dr. George Hill, afterwards attained great eminence in the Church. With the Greek Professorship he held the second ministerial charge of the city, and his pulpit duties were discharged with the same power which characterized his academic teaching. His habits were singularly industrious; he rose at four and prepared for his class till seven, when he took breakfast. No portion of his time was lost. He was eminently courteous. By his agreeable manner he charmed all with whom he came in contact. He had the art of pleasing. 'Laugh, laugh,' said he to his little daughter, as a blockhead at his table was relating some silly anecdote at which he himself laughed vociferously. 'What a becoming hat!' he said to the Rev. Thomas K ——, whose intellectual qualities did not admit of even a qualified laudation. None could easier turn away an angry word spoken in debate. In the General Assembly he had encountered a fearful onslaught from the Rev. James Burn, minister of Forgan. When Mr. Burn concluded, he said with a smile, 'Moderator, we all know that it is most natural that *Burns* should run down *Hills*.' The laugh was effectually raised against his reverend opponent. It was in the General Assembly that his oratory was chiefly displayed. He succeeded Principal Robertson as leader of the moderate party, and by his even temper, eminent tact, and enticing eloquence, he maintained his position to the close. He died in 1819 in his seventieth year, after attaining nearly every honour which a minister of the Scottish Church could enjoy. His Theological Institutes published posthumously, are a monument of his learning and industry. The work has been used as a text-book in various theological seminaries.

"In St. Mary's College, the chair of Church History was occupied by the Rev. William Brown, a man of considerable scholarship, strong will, and some odd ways. He composed his lectures in Latin; and during the first two weeks of the session his prelections were entitled *Res Gestæ ante mundum conditum.* As he did not pretend to any acquaintance with geology, which indeed had scarcely taken its place among the sciences, his introductory lectures were not very interesting. As he did not examine, few cared to listen, and the business of the class passed on without any work being done. A curious history attended Mr. Brown's appointment to the Church History chair. After the battle of Prestonpans, several officers of

the royal army were carried off by the victorious rebels, and
subjected to imprisonment at the village of Glammis. Along
with some followers, Mr. William Brown, then a theological
student, rode from Dundee to Glammis, and by overcoming the
detaining party, rescued the prisoners. Mr. Brown's gallantry
was reported to the Duke of Cumberland, who promised to
befriend him. Soon after Mr. Brown obtained licence, and was
promoted to the church living of Cortachy. In this charge he
had not been long settled, when a rumour spread to his disad-
vantage. He was accused of seduction. The Presbytery of
Forfar were unwilling to prosecute one who had so lately distinguished himself in the royal cause, and Mr. Brown was dis-
inclined to undergo a trial, when, as he alleged, so many of his
people being lately in rebellion were disposed to testify against
him falsely. He resigned his charge, and through the influence
of the Duke of Cumberland, was appointed minister of the
English congregation at Utrecht. Through the same channel
of influence he was appointed to his professorship. He received
his commission in 1757, but did not obtain installation for
some time afterwards, his nomination, on account of the old
Forfarshire rumours, being resisted both by the University and
the Presbytery. But his cause was warmly supported by the
Government, and the General Assembly at length ordered his
induction. He was somewhat hospitable, and when he invited
his students to his house, delighted to show them the brace of
pistols with which he had encountered the Highlanders at
Glammis. Professor Brown has, perhaps, his best claim to
remembrance as the father of a distinguished son.

"That son was William Laurence Brown, D.D., Principal of
Marischal College, Aberdeen, whom, at a subsequent period, I
knew intimately. Principal Brown was an able and accomplished man, but could not be commended for his *bonhommie*.
He was always on the attack—always disposed to run some one
down. He monopolized conversation, and lost his temper if
the monopoly was interfered with. Sarcasm was his forte, and
it was cruelly indulged towards those against whom he had
conceived an aversion. Principal Hill expressed to Lord Melville an opinion that he was not sufficiently prudent to discharge wisely the duties of the Principalship of Marischal
College, and unhappily this opinion was brought to his notice.
Henceforth he pursued Dr. Hill with a relentless vengeance.
He ridiculed him in society, denounced him in the General
Assembly, and published 'Philemon,' a poem in two volumes,

in which, under the name of *Vulpellus*, he sought to exhibit him to the world as a monster of treachery. Principal Brown died in 1830. He had, I believe, long previously abandoned that severity of expression and sentiment which, in former years, disfigured a career otherwise adorned."

At Aberdeen my father studied under Dr. George Campbell, and Dr. Alexander Gerard, author of the "Pastoral Care." He remembered Dr. Gerard as a venerable gentleman, without much animation, and with only a moderate share of originality. On the merits of Dr. George Campbell he delighted to expatiate. He spoke of the excellence of his lectures, and of the vigour and dignity with which they were expressed. At the Principal's table he was an occasional guest, and he was much struck by the delightful frankness which the distinguished host extended to every member of the company. His conversation was sprinkled with a humour peculiarly his own. "We have got," said a visitor, "nearly all sects and denominations represented in Aberdeen ; but it is singular there are no Jews !" "No ;" said the Principal, "we're owre far north for them here." There was a decided point in the story, for Aberdonian traders were supposed in their dealings to exercise a tenacity of gain scarcely to be rivalled.

There was an anecdote of the Principal and the Convener of the Trades, a hairdresser, who affected superior shrewdness, and an ample acquaintance with local history. As the Convener was one day prosecuting his craft, the Principal asked him, "Do you remember, sir, when Pontius Pilate was provost o' the Al'ton ?" (Old Aberdeen). "I canna say, Principal," was the ready response, "that I mind o' him mysel' ; but I've often heard my father say that he mindit him weel."

In the class of Dr. James Beattie, author of "The Minstrel," my father was not an enrolled student ; but he was a frequent listener to his prelections. I cannot recall his sentiments respecting Dr. Beattie's professorial qualities, but he spoke emphatically in regard to the high estimation in which he was held as a poet. My father related an anecdote in connection with his becoming acquainted with Mr. Francis Garden afterwards Lord Gardenstone, a little more copious in detail than that supplied by Sir William Forbes in the Professor's "Memoirs." Mr. Garden was residing at Woodstock, in the parish of Fordoun, of which Beattie was schoolmaster. He had been told that the parish teacher was eccentric and suspected of lunacy. One day, walking in an unfrequented glen, he heard

some one speaking, and proceeding to the spot, found
Beattie seated on a stone, writing, and repeating aloud what
he had written. Mr. Garden listened, and at once perceived
that the schoolmaster was a man of genius. Introducing himself to the bard, an intimacy soon sprung up, when Mr. Garden
informed him that the country people thought him mad. "No
wonder," said Beattie, "for I've sometimes found myself
walking all night in the glen, forgetful that I was compro-
mising myself." And so he composed "The Minstrel."

At Aberdeen my father boarded in the house of Mrs. Riddoch,
née Miss Dallas, the widow of an Episcopal clergyman, and
cousin of Johnson's Boswell. During their visit to Aberdeen,
Boswell and his illustrious fellow-traveller spent an evening
with Mrs. Riddoch. To my father, who was a profound admirer of the sage, Mrs. Riddoch related the principal incidents
of the evening. She was not favourably impressed with Dr.
Johnson's appearance, and his " bow-wow manner " she held as
repulsive. Several of the professors had accepted her invitation
to meet her cousin and his friend, and the evening was spent
in controversy. Dr. Johnson seemed to cavil at everything, and
his incessant utterance of " No " rang in Mrs. Riddoch's ears
long after. " But," added Mrs. Riddoch, " Mr. Boswell would
hear nothing to his dispraise."

In 1791 my father became ministerial assistant at Cortachy.
Many of the older parishioners had, under Lord Ogilvie, been
attached to the standard of Prince Charles Edward. These
expatiated to my father on the sufferings to which they had
been subjected after the disastrous battle of Culloden. None
seemed to lament the fall of the Chevalier, whose cause they
had espoused out of attachment to their young landlord, and
from no personal conviction. Lord Ogilvie was long an exile
in France ; but having obtained a pardon, he was permitted to
enjoy the family honours. As fifth Earl of Airlie, he resided
in his ancestral mansion of Cortachy Castle. He was a singular
old man, dressed in the French fashion, and had many odd
ways. He received a weekly newspaper, but after reading it,
put it into the fire, that he might enjoy the satisfaction of
retailing the news to his dependants. For this purpose he
visited the servants' hall every evening at eight o'clock, where,
leaning against a large upright chest, he discoursed with his
principal attendants on the political aspects of the times.
They listened reverently ; but all had seen the weekly journal
before it had passed into his lordship's hands.

In 1793 my father was introduced to Sir John Sinclair, Bart., then in his zenith. With Sir John he enjoyed a little personal intercourse. He was much struck with his bustling character, and extraordinary appetite for work. Sir John's vanity, my father said, was apparent on the slightest acquaintance with him.

With Mr. George Dempster of Dunnichen, my father about this time began an acquaintance, which continued with growing respect on both sides for a quarter of a century. Hearing of my father's literary tastes, Mr. Dempster invited him to Dunnichen House, and the visit was, by his desire, speedily repeated. A steady friendship grew up, and the laird of Dunnichen rejoiced frequently to entertain a gentleman whose store of information was not inferior to his own.*

On his retirement from Parliament in 1790, Mr. Dempster began to devote his energies towards improving the natural resources of his country. He obtained an act for the protection and encouragement of Scottish Fisheries. He advanced the interests of northern manufactures, but at length concentrated his exertions in the cause of husbandry. In its agricultural concerns, the county of Forfar, more especially in the upland districts, considerably lagged, and it was Mr. Dempster's ambition to imbue the tenantry of his district with a spirit of enterprise and emulation, which he hoped would ultimately subdue the mosses, and reclaim the waste lands. In this laudable object he found a willing and experienced coadjutor in my father, who was familiar with the agricultural condition of every parish in the county, and had, by extensive reading, made himself acquainted with agriculture as a science. With my father's assistance, Mr. Dempster established the " Lunan and Vinney Farming Society," of which, at the first meeting, my father was elected honorary secretary. The society held yearly a festive entertainment at Dunnichen, and some eighty persons—landlords and tenants—were enrolled as members. On Mr. Dempster's death in 1818 meetings of the society were suspended, and the minute-book is now in the custody of the writer, as the secretary's representative. The minutes abound in curious agricultural speculations, with extracts from the

* In his *Fasti Ecclesiæ Scoticanæ* (Edinb., 1869, part iv., p. 424), Dr. Hew Scott represents my father as amanuensis or secretary to Mr. Dempster. This is an error ; my father did not have the honour of being so employed by his friend.

classic and eloquent speeches with which Mr. Dempster, the ingenious president, delighted the assemblages.

An incident which occurred at one of these agricultural feasts may be related. Mr. Dempster had one year offered an apology for drinking toast and water, by stating that he was an invalid. At the following meeting, one of his farmers followed his landlord's example of abstinence. "Why," said the president addressing him, "aren't you taking your glass, James?" "Excuse me, Maister Dempster," said the farmer, "for I'm an infidel." "Ah," rejoined Mr. Dempster, "you differ from the old infidels, who said, 'Let us eat and drink, for to-morrow we die.'"

Though for nearly thirty years a member of the House of Commons, and fond of conversation, Mr. Dempster seldom alluded to his parliamentary experiences. His sterling independence had gained him the designation of "Honest George," but it was my father's opinion that he regretted he had so long engaged in political concerns. He had achieved his entrance into Parliament as member for the Fife and Forfar burghs by a course of bribery on an enormous scale. To obtain the means of defeating his opponent he sold three estates. He sometimes alluded to these matters regretfully, and would speak of the impetuosity of his hot youth. He mentioned that a hairdresser in St. Andrews had received from him five guineas as a recompence for shaving him. By the acceptance of this gratuity he understood that he had secured the barber's vote; but on resuming his canvass, he heard that the honest hairdresser had been liberally recompensed for shaving his opponent. Meeting him one day he said, "Why, Mr. Bell, you have been shaving the opposition! I did not expect this." "Troth," said the barber, "I just wantit to pleasure ye baith." Calling at the house of another trader, he proceeded to ingratiate himself with his wife and daughter. On leaving, he made a fashion of kissing the honest matron, quietly placing five gold pieces in the hand which was modestly extended to protect her face. Contemplating her glittering prize, the delighted housewife exclaimed, "Kiss my dochter too, sir!" Mr. Dempster often related the anecdote.

Mr. Dempster was well acquainted with Mr. Macpherson, of Ossianic celebrity. He sat with him in Parliament. He related to my father that it was believed that the parchments which Becket, the London publisher, exhibited in his shop as the originals of Fingal and other poems, were Gaelic leases from the charter chest of a Macleod of Skye.

A London gentleman of fortune was visiting at Dunnichen House. My father was also there on a visit. All were seated in the library one evening, when Mr. Dempster said to his London friend, "How is Woodfall?" Woodfall was the publisher of "Junius." "Ah!" said the London visitor, "poor Woodfall is much reduced. Some of his old friends lately subscribed a small amount to help him; but he is still very poor, and at his advanced age his circumstances are not likely to improve." "Indeed, indeed!" exclaimed Mr. Dempster, "I wish, for his sake, I had been rich; but will you add these as my contribution in aid of my old friend?" Mr. Dempster handed a small bundle of Scottish notes to his visitor, and turned round to conceal his emotion. My father believed that Mr. Dempster was in the secret as to the authorship of "Junius," but he durst not venture to put questions on a theme so delicate.

At Dunnichen my father met John Pinkerton, the antiquary. Pinkerton attended a meeting of the Farming Society, and took part in a discussion on fiorin grass. He is thus introduced in the minutes:—"Mr. Pinkerton, the antiquary, had not bent much of his mind to modern things. He had only to state that Camden mentioned a field in the west of Scotland, which was cut four times a year, and consisted of fiorin grass." It was my father's opinion that Pinkerton desired to be regarded as a universal genius. He spoke of being admitted to a library abroad solely from his reputation. He was ready to debate on any subject, and in the assertion of his views was opinionative and dogged. Contradiction, even in the mildest form, he would not tolerate. He had been on a long visit to Dunnichen House, and had rendered himself obnoxious to the young people. Said a young miss of thirteen to Mr. Dempster one morning, before the antiquary joined the breakfast-table, "Grandpapa, when is Mr. Pinkerton going away?" "Hush, my dear," said Mr. Dempster, with a smile. Pinkerton spent a large portion of his time in visits to county families and others, who were content to tolerate his peculiarities. He latterly resided in France, where he died in 1825, in circumstances of penury.

Respecting the character of Mr. Dempster, my father shared the opinion of his contemporaries. A stainless patriotism was his leading characteristic. Though latterly the reverse of opulent, he was liberal to his relatives, and benevolent to the poor. Latterly he became frugal in his domestic arrangements from a delusion, incident to old age, that he was on the verge of poverty. He dismissed his valet, who had been in his employment for forty years. The disconsolate old man applied to my father to intercede for him. "It is unnecessary," said my father ; "return to your duties, and Mr. Dempster will at once relent, if he has not already forgotten what has occurred." The advice was followed, and the faithful valet remained till his kind master bade adieu to time resting in his arms.

Mr. Dempster died in February, 1818, in his eighty-fourth year. Some time before his death he was requested by my father to express his wishes in regard to a memoir. In answer, he wrote on the 9th June, 1816, "You joke about the life of an individual to whom nothing but *oblivion* belongs :—

> 'Vixi, et quem dederat cursum
> Natura heregi.'"

After his decease, no documents likely to be useful to a biographer could be found in his repositories. The whole had been destroyed.

Disappointed in obtaining ecclesiastical preferment, though more than one congregation had applied to " just and auncient patrons" on his behalf, my father resolved to try a literary career in the metropolis. Provided with letters from Mr. Dempster, and his relatives, Principal Playfair of St. Andrews, and Professor Playfair of Edinburgh, in the autumn of 1802 he sailed for London. There he placed himself chiefly under the guidance of Mr. William Playfair, brother of Professor Playfair, and well known as an inventor and miscellaneous writer. By this gentleman my father was strongly dissuaded from remaining in the metropolis. "As a newspaper reporter," he said, "you might make a decent livelihood ; but you are at the mercy of your employer, and an ebullition of temper on his part, or an attack of illness on yours, might throw you helpless on the world. Besides, you have influence in Scotland, which, sooner or later, must lead to your obtaining a living in the Presbyterian Kirk." My father listened, and hastened home, leaving one letter of introduction undelivered. This was addressed by Mr. Dempster to the Rev. William Thomson, LL.D., formerly assistant minister at Monivaird, but for many years a well-employed miscellaneous writer in the metropolis. Mr. Dempster's letter to Dr. Thomson proceeds thus :—

" Dunnichen, Forfar, 13th Sept., 1802.

" MY DEAR SIR,—I am glad to embrace this opportunity of inquiring how you are, and expressing my hopes that this will find you in health and prosperity. It serves to introduce to you the Rev. Mr. James Roger, who, by being assistant to our parish clergyman, has gained the good opinion and good-will of all our parish, and no small share of mine among the rest. In your time a Scotch kirk was no great object, and at present an assistant is as poor an object as ever. He has therefore accepted some proposals for establishing himself in London. He will mention particulars to you himself. I know you have a heart that disposes you to acts of kindness to others. You are a successful veteran in the career that he is about to begin. I pray you let him avail himself of all your experiences, and if possible share in your laurels. I am persuaded that you will have satisfaction in his acquaintance, and find him grateful for your attention to him. He will tell you about me. Time has altered many parts of me, but has not abated a tittle of my liking and respect for you. Farewell. My dear and rev. sir,

" Yours, &c.,

" GEORGE DEMPSTER."

A few sentences will express my father's opinion of Mr. William Playfair, whose stirring but not prosperous career is described in the biographical dictionaries. He was a laborious worker, but amidst a variety of accomplishments was incapable of discovering where his chief strength lay. He was most patriotic, but from some lack of ballast, statesmen could not utilize his powers, or reward them with emolument. He died poor—the lot of so many literary adventurers in the metropolis of Britain.

Mr. Playfair augured rightly, for in 1804 my father was presented to the church of Dunino, by the masters of the United College of St. Andrews, at the intercession of his relative, the Principal. Mr. Dempster hastened to offer his congratulations in these terms :—

" Dunnichen, Forfar, 25*th Feb.,* 1804.

" REV. AND DEAR SIR,—Ever since I heard of your being certainly provided with the kirk of Dunino, I have been confined to my room with a fit of sickness, which I mention as my apology for not having congratulated you earlier on that happy event. It does great honour to your friend Principal Playfair,

, being a vigorous act of friendship. I also ascribe your good fortune to the kind interposition of Providence in your favour, for there are few college patronages occur at a time that none of the patrons' families are qualified to receive them ; neither do I doubt that your dutiful attention to your aged parents, and your diligent discharge of all your other duties, have disposed Providence favourably towards you, and induced you to refuse the killing drudgery of a London newsmonger, and a precarious provision in the family of a Highland laird. Such are my reflections on this occasion. They are accompanied with the most heartfelt satisfaction. I now heartily wish you good health to enjoy your preferment. All this family are much pleased at your good fortune, and I remain most sincerely

" Yours,

" GEORGE DEMPSTER."

To the ministerial charge of Dunino my father was ordained in May, 1805. The parish manse was four miles from St. Andrews, where there was pleasant literary society and the well-stored university library. Among the more intimate associates of my father's early ministry were Dr. Henry David Hill, Dr. James Brown, and Dr. James Hunter, who had all preceded him in his parochial cure, and were now professors; also Mr. Thomas Chalmers, minister of Kilmany, and Principal Playfair, his relative and patron.

Dr. James Playfair is entitled to remembrance. At a period when astronomy, geography, and the kindred sciences attracted little attention among Scottish scholars, he diligently prosecuted those branches of learning. His work on Geography, extending to six volumes quarto, with a folio atlas, constitutes the basis of many less costly geographical publications ; while his folio Chronology is known as a work of great research and respectable authority. It afforded my father peculiar satisfaction to prove serviceable to his relative when he was exposed to some serious hostilities. These he honourably surmounted, and died in peace with all mankind in May, 1819, in his eighty-first year. Of somewhat unbending manners, and not particularly sociable, Principal Playfair preferred the quiet retirement of his study to any displays of eloquence or learning, whether in the pulpit or in the academy. But he was both an orator and an elegant scholar.

Through his marriage with Miss Margaret Lyon, who was

nearly related to the noble family of Strathmore, Dr. Playfair became father of four sons, who all attained positions of distinction. Colonel William Davidson Playfair, the second son, after a successful military career in India, spent many years of honourable retirement at St. Andrews. Colonel Sir Hugh Lyon Playfair, LL.D., the third son, was distinguished as an artillery officer, and as the constructor of the great military road between Calcutta and Benares, and more especially in after life as the greatest city reformer of his time. He was many years chief magistrate of St. Andrews, and he changed that place from the condition of a mouldering hamlet into a well-constructed modern city. For his praiseworthy exertions at St. Andrews he was knighted in 1856; he likewise received every honour which the citizens or the University could confer. Sir Hugh died on the 23rd January, 1861, in his seventy-fifth year.

Principal Playfair's eldest son George became Inspector-General of Hospitals, Bengal. A son of this gentleman, Dr. Lyon Playfair, LL.D., C.B., at present represents in Parliament the Universities of St. Andrews and Edinburgh, and is highly distinguished for his scientific attainments and his interest in the cause of education. Dr. Playfair's youngest son James prosecuted in Glasgow a successful mercantile career, and became one of the magistrates of that city.

Dr. Henry David Hill was a younger brother of Principal Hill, formerly noticed. He was ordained at Dunino in May, 1785, but demitted the cure on being appointed Professor of Greek at St. Andrews in October, 1789. Professor Hill published a work on " The Institutions, Government, and Manners of the States of Ancient Greece." He was remarkable for his social qualities and ready humour. Dining one day with the Presbytery of St. Andrews, a joint was found to be imperfectly cooked. " Come," said Dr. Henry, " let us not grumble. We can easily hand it to the cook, who will pass it to the kettle, and all will be made right." Dr. Cook and Mr. Kettle were two of the brethren present. The laugh which followed restored the clerical equanimity. Professor Hill found Mr. Kettle seated on a large boulder at his manse gate as he chanced to come up. " Seated so lowly, Mr. Kettle," exclaimed Dr. Hill, " when your brother Pan was a heathen god!" A humorist of this ready stamp was an acceptable visitor at the manse of Dunino. Dr. Henry David Hill died in February, 1820.

C

Of an entirely different mould was Professor James Brown. He held the living of Dunino from 1790 to 1796, when, on the recommendation of Dr. John Hunter, he was appointed Professor of Natural Philosophy at Glasgow. For this office he was eminently qualified, but an unhappy affection of the nervous system soon incapacitated him for performing the professorial duties. For some years he discharged his duties by proxy, but afterwards resigned his chair on an allowance. He long made St. Andrews his head-quarters, and his remarkable powers of conversation drew around him not only all the lettered society of that neighbourhood, but learned and distinguished persons from a distance. My father frequently invited him to his table, where the brilliancy of his conversation contrasted not unpleasantly with the more solid talk of other learned persons, who were frequent visitors at the manse. Professor Brown died in November, 1838, in his seventy-fifth year.

Dr. James Hunter was my father's immediate predecessor; he was minister of Dunino for six years. Son of the celebrated Dr. John Hunter, Dr. James inherited his father's tastes, and was expert in discussions connected with classic literature. In 1804 he was elected Professor of Logic and Rhetoric at St. Andrews, an appointment which he held till his death in 1845. As an instructor in metaphysics and *belles lettres* he did not excel. Formal and precise in manner, he failed to impress his students with any philosophic ardour; and some even doubted his personal interest in those branches of knowledge which it was his duty to inculcate. In private life he was kind and sociable. He had read much, and aided by a powerful memory, he could use promptly what he knew. He indulged in a species of repartee which fell somewhat heavily on the object of it; but he never left a company without, by a corresponding compliment, compensating for his unpleasantnes s In the pulpit his manner partook of that freedom which characterized him in private life. Preaching for my father on the evening of a communion Sunday, he failed to discover his text. After a pause, he exclaimed, "This is extraordinary; I cannot find my text. I marked it on the top of my sermon last night, and I thought that it was in the Epistle to the Hebrews, the 13th chapter, and 22nd verse; but that's a mistake. The text is, 'Suffer the words of exhortation,' but where these words are I can't tell you. But your minister has a good knowledge of passages. Ho!" proceeded the doctor, looking towards my father, who was seated in his family pew, "can you tell me where the text is?" "You're quite right," said my father; "look at the passage you have named.". "Well, brethren," said the preacher, "your minister says that the text is in Luke — Luke's Gospel, the 30th chapter, and the 22nd verse; if not there, it's somewhere else, for I know it's in the Bible." After service, the professor being informed that the text was in the middle clause of the verse which he had at first named, called out in the churchyard, "Holloa! my friends, the text is in the Hebrews after all; you'll find it when you get home."

No clerical neighbour was by my father more esteemed than Thomas Chalmers of Kilmany. On the occasion of every visit to his parents at Anstruther—and they were not few—Mr. Chalmers spent one or two days at Dunino manse, which stood about halfway between Kilmany and Anstruther. One of Chalmers' earliest movements was to improve the social status and domestic condition of the clergy. He came to my father on a Monday in a state of great enthusiasm. "Yesterday I preached," he said, "in the College Kirk, and inaugurated my scheme for the augmentation of stipends. I'll read to you my discourse;" thereupon taking a MS. from his pocket, and placing it on the table. "Just twenty minutes," said my father, who knew that his friend, when he entered warmly on a subject, forgot everything else; and the cook had announced that dinner was almost ready. "Half an hour," pleaded Chalmers, "and you shall have the entire discourse." My father assented, but placed his watch upon the table. The orator proceeded, as if he had been addressing a congregation. "The church bell," he said, "may ring for a century to come, but if the clergy are not properly remunerated, they will be termed 'puir bodies,' and themselves and their ministrations will be regarded with contempt." "I beg your pardon, Mr. Chalmers," said my father, "but what's your text?" "My text," said the orator, "is Luke 12th and 15th—'A man's life consisteth not in the abundance of the things which he possesseth.'" "You are not textual," said my father. "Wait a little," rejoined the orator, "and you'll see." The sermon proved both eloquent and appropriate. "He never expressed himself better," said my father, "even in the days of his greatest popularity." *

* This discourse, slightly altered, was delivered by Chalmers as his maiden speech in the General Assembly of 1809, and created no inconsiderable interest. It was published by request.

Throughout his entire career Chalmers was prone to indulge in long words and startling phrases. In a popular lecture which, when minister of Kilmany, he delivered at St. Andrews to a mixed audience, he began a thrilling portion of his address in these words,—" We are all familiar with the pleasures of intoxication." The ladies were momentarily surprised, but the speaker proceeded graphically to depict sources of frenzy other than those produced by hard drinking. When, twenty years afterwards, he sat on the heights of Ben Lomond with his friend the Rev. Robert Story, of Roseneath, and a party of ladies, he exclaimed with the unreflecting vehemence of former times, " Come, let us yield ourselves up to miscellaneous impulses."

In general conversation Chalmers was reticent. But he was an agreeable companion, and even loquacious in the society of a few. At this period he was actively pursuing his chemical studies, and making experiments in natural science. " I was much troubled in shaving," he said, " till I discovered proper cutlery. The secret is worth knowing. If you desire to shave smoothly, use razors with brown or mottled handles. I now shave painlessly." " An odd experience," replied my father, "for razors of the finest edge are mounted in ivory, and are accordingly sold at a higher price."

On a Saturday morning, the minister of Kilmany stepped in. " My dear sir," said he, " I have been detained at Anster all the week, and I am unprepared for to-morrow's duty ; so allow me to take your place, and, like a kind man, you'll take mine at Kilmany." My father consented. " I don't know what my housekeeper may have for you in the way of eating," he proceeded, "but there is very fine whisky ; and this reminds me I have discovered a method of eliminating the harsher and more deleterious particles from all spirituous liquors. I leave my bottles uncorked, and place them in an open cupboard, so that atmospheric air entering the necks of the bottles may mollify the fluid." " All very good," said my father. On a bottle of Mr. Chalmers' rectified aqua being produced next day after dinner at Kilmany, he found that other agencies than those of th atmosphere had been reducing the strength. Three-fourths of the liquor had evidently been poured out, and the remainder proportionately diluted with aqua from the well. Whisky of such extreme mildness might be drunk readily. In the evening, as my father was approaching his manse, Mr. Chalmers met and hailed him. " Got well through, I hope ? " " Oh yes."

"And some home comforts too?"　"Yes, a very good dinner, and very mild whisky."　"Glad you liked it; knew you would. I've fallen on the true secret."　"It was so very mild that I finished the bottle."　"Nonsense, my dear sir!" said Mr. Chalmers, who now began to suspect his friend's sincerity; "had you done so, you would not have been here to tell the tale."　"Oh yes," persisted my father, "I finished the bottle. The fact is, Mr. Chalmers, you're a bachelor, as well as myself, and if you take the corks out of your whisky bottles, and throw open your cupboards, your whisky will be mild enough. Yours was mostly water." Chalmers was a little crestfallen, but added after a little, "Depend upon it, sir, the air does it." *

My father induced Mr. Chalmers, in an important case, which was before the Provincial Synod, to make an oration. He was proceeding to place before him the record of the proceedings, with comments of his own. "Don't," said Chalmers, "but give me a point—one branch of the case,—and I'll work it out; I cannot scatter myself over a multitude of points." An important point was accordingly selected, and upon it the minister of Kilmany promised to be prepared in due time. The Synod met at Kirkcaldy, and when Chalmers rose to address the meeting there were thunders of applause. A number of gentlemen from St. Andrews had planted themselves in different portions of the building to encourage the young orator. "Mr. Chalmers," said my father, "acquitted himself magnificently. The sarcasm heaped upon our opponents was crushing. His eloquence seemed to bear upon the court like the onward progress of a great river." The point was gained. "You have done admirably," said my father, grasping the orator's hand. "I was vastly helped," was the reply, "by those fellows encouraging me to go on. Encouragement, my dear sir, is half the battle."

One winter afternoon Chalmers called at Dunino manse, uttering expressions of distress. "I am come to crave your assistance, my dear sir. Have you a spare suit? I have suffered a terrible disappointment. Some friends extracted a promise that I would attend the military ball to-night, and I wrote to my mother to get me proper clothes for the occasion. I went to Anster yesterday, and at once asked about the clothes. Conceive my mortification when my mother said that, being

* This anecdote and a number of others, which I communicated at his request to my friend Mr. James Dodds, have been included by that respected gentleman in his recent work, "Thomas Chalmers: a Biographical Study," Edinburgh, 1870, 12mo.

unable to read my letter, she had put it on a shelf that I might
read it when I came." My father laughed heartily, and agreed
to lend the desiderated garments, but suggested that both might
be as profitably employed in a quiet evening talk as amidst the
excitement of a ball-room. The minister of Kilmany at length
acquiesced, and tarried at the manse.

Mr. Chalmers was chaplain and adjutant of a corps of
St. Andrews' volunteers. The members were to dine together in
the city, and my father was invited. Some time before the
hour of dinner he met Mr. Chalmers in the street, fully
equipped in military attire, including a scarlet coat and white
trousers. "How are you, my dear sir?" said the pastor of
Kilmany. "Very well, I thank you," said my father, "but
you have the advantage of me. I don't know who addresses
me." "Don't know me? You know me perfectly—Chalmers
of Kilmany." "Forgive me," persisted my father. "You
certainly resemble my friend Mr. Chalmers, but I feel that he
has too much good sense to appear in a dress so unsuited to
his profession." Chalmers took my father's arm, and some conversation ensued, which resulted in the adjutant of volunteers
appearing at dinner in clerical vestments.

Soon after the publication of his " Inquiry into the National
Resources," Mr. Chalmers presented himself at Dunino. He
was (1808) in his twenty-eighth year, and was still subject to
an effervescent ardour concerning any theme which for the
nonce arrested his fancy. "Have you read my book, my dear
sir?" he inquired, eagerly. "Yes," said my father. "Well,
have I not established my theory?" Removing from his table
the *Farmer's Magazine*, which contained a slashing attack
on the work, my father said, "You'll have my views after
dinner." When that meal was concluded, the friends proceeded
together to an eminence a few hundred yards eastward of the
manse. Having seated themselves on some boulders, with
which the little hill was covered, my father began, "Now,
Mr. Chalmers, for your political economy! You allege that as
a nation we should be independent of foreign trade, and that
if our home resources were properly economized, commerce with
foreign countries might be dispensed with." "Precisely, my
dear sir." "Well," said my father, "I don't propose to substitute another theory, nor to assail yours; but let us look
round. The estate of Dunino, on which we now are, how was
it acquired?" "Oh, you know," said Mr. Chalmers, "Mr.
Irvine made a fortune by trading in the West Indies." "Pre-

cisely so," said my father. "And Stravithie?" "Partly by foreign trade, no doubt." "And Bonnytown?" "Yes, by colonial merchandise." "And Feddinch, Lathockar, Brighton, Lingo!" naming nearly every estate which could be seen from the spot. "I suspect," added my father, "we must not quite abandon our foreign trade." Chalmers accepted the criticism very good-naturedly.

On the appearance of Dr. Claudius Buchanan's "Christian Researches," Mr. Chalmers became much interested in the conversion of the heathen, and a vigorous advocate of missions. In order to interest him in what had produced such a powerful effect upon his own mind, he presented my father with a copy of Buchanan's work. The volume occupies a place in my library. The presentation note is dated 24th January, 1813. Dr. Chalmers removed from Kilmany to Glasgow in 1814. After an interval of four years, he and my father renewed correspondence, but only for a brief period. A difference of ecclesiastical sentiments estranged them. To the last my father, while upholding a policy opposed to that of his old friend of Kilmany, yielded every tribute to his genius. He would say, "We all knew that Chalmers would become eminent. If he had not identified himself with party, he would have been the greatest man in Scotland."

Francis Jeffrey married as first wife a daughter of the Rev. Dr. Charles Wilson, Professor of Ecclesiastical History at St. Andrews, and sister-in-law of Dr. James Hunter. Through Dr. James, my father became acquainted with the Reviewer. As the General Assembly came round, he found himself at Jeffrey's table, enjoying a hospitality which was profuse and elegant. Jeffrey was singularly acute. Though entertaining company during the entire evening, he was sure to appear in court next morning, perfectly at his ease, and quite familiar with his brief. From what my father termed his "affected" English accent he did not excel in leading parole evidence; but in demolishing unfavourable testimony he was matchless.

Jeffrey discouraged litigation, and urged those who desired to try fortune at the law to make up differences in private. A widow, who had consulted him about certain claims on her husband's estate, rejected his counsel for an extra-judicial settlement of her case. "If you can no longer advise me," she said, "can you refer me to a law-book which will help me?" "Consult Darling's Practice," said Mr. Jeffrey, as he made his bow and retired. The work named was a book of legal

forms, but Mr. Jeffrey hoped that the title might be suggestive.
Though a severe critic, he was in private life singularly amiable
and beneficent.   He had advertised for a gardener, specifying
that he desired to have one without encumbrance.   A candidate
appeared who confessed that he had a family of nine children.
Mr. Jeffrey expressed himself satisfied with the applicant's re-
commendations, but stated that his numerous household was
an insuperable barrier to his appointment.   "I would," said
the learned gentleman, "constantly be hearing of whooping-
cough, &c., and that would not suit me."   "Weel, weel," said
the gardener, "that's the third situation these puir weans * ha'e
lost me.'   Melted by the speech, Mr. Jeffrey said feelingly,
"I'll take you and your weans."

Mr. Jeffrey, it is related, refused to be made a Lord of Justiciary, lest in passing the last sentence of the law he might be
associated with that friend of capital punishment, the infamous
Judge Jeffreys.   A similar sensitiveness led to his retaining
his own name as a Lord of Session, instead of assuming a
designation from his estate of Craigcrook.   "A Lord Craigcrook," said he, "would alarm everybody." †

Jeffrey was unconscious of personal celebrity, but delighted to
celebrate his contemporary Henry Cockburn.   The appreciation
was reciprocated by the other great barrister, who spoke of
him with affection.   Cockburn likewise discommended ap-
peals to the law courts.   "If," he said, "any one claimed my
coat, and showed that he really wanted it, I would give him
both my coat and vest, sooner than defend my right to them
in the Court of Session."

Cockburn and my father often met.   At a consultation in a
church case, my father asked him whether his reasons of dissent
and appeal to the General Assembly were well drawn.   "They're
much too good," said Cockburn ; "never show the enemy your
hand.   Always keep your best reasons till the entire case comes
up, so as to take your opponent by surprise.   Never blow the
trumpet and warn the opposition."

"Moral gladiatorship," said my father, "was presented in
the Assembly when Jeffrey and Cockburn were opposing
counsel.   Cockburn spoke more naturally, using the native
Doric, and his plain, candid manner might have induced the
belief that he was no hired pleader, but an honest countryman.
When he spoke pathetically, a hush was heard.   His drollery

* Children.
† To crook a craig is in Scottish parlance to hang some one.

excited shouts of laughter. In the Assembly, Jeffrey always spoke seriously, and with marked respect for the House—but he never failed, even in the most hopeless cause, to produce some impression favourable to his client."

Jeffrey and Cockburn were counsel together in a case in which it was sought to prove that the heir of an estate was of low capacity, and therefore incapable of administering his affairs. Jeffrey had vainly attempted to make a country witness understand his meaning, as he spoke of the mental imbecility and impaired intellect of the party. Cockburn rose to his relief, and was successful at once, " D'ye ken young Sandy —— ?" " Brawly," said the witness; "I've kent him sin' he was a laddie." " And is there onything in the cratur? Wad ye trust him in the market to sell a coo?" " 'Deed no," responded the witness, "there's naething in him ava; he wadna ken a coo frae a cauf!" A prosecution in the Justiciary Court was likely to break down, consequent on the counsel for the Crown being unable to elicit from a witness the particular position of the prisoner when she committed the offence. The witness had deponed that the prisoner was neither standing, nor sitting, nor lying, nor crouching. " Was she on her cutty hunkers," inquired Mr. Cockburn, coming to the relief of the Crown counsel. " Just so," smartly responded the witness.

When attending the General Assembly of 1806, my father had the satisfaction of sitting, as a member of that venerable court, with John Home, the author of " Douglas." After retiring from the ministry in 1757, Mr. Home obtained the sinecure office of Conservator of Scots Privileges at Campvere, and he was, by the ecclesiastical establishment of that place, elected annually as their representative elder to the Assembly. Mr. Home was now in his eighty-fourth year. My father was much struck by his reverend aspect: he seemed an impersonation of good-humour and gentleness. He died in September, 1808.

During the sitting of the General Assembly of 1806, my father first heard of Walter Scott. " The Lay of the Last Minstrel" had been published about a year, and its merits were still a subject of conversation in the capital. As all spoke highly of the poem, my father procured it from a circulating library, but with some difficulty, and at a high charge. He was so fascinated that he sat up at night and read the entire poem. His admiration of the author, which began on this occasion, gained strength; he obtained all Scott's works as they appeared, and always maintained that the author of the "Lay" was alone capable of producing "Waverley."

During one of his Edinburgh visits my father became acquainted with Archibald Constable. When they first met, Mr. Constable said, "I hope you'll be no stranger to me. Your parish I know as familiarly as our Edinburgh High Street. I was born at Carnbee ;* and many a day as a boy did I ride on the riggin' of Dunino Kirk." † Of Mr. Constable my father entertained a high opinion. He spoke of his fine commanding appearance and courtly unaffected manners. Mr. Constable, he said, delighted to serve all who came to Edinburgh from his birthplace ; while natives of the *East Neuk o' Fife* held responsible positions in his own establishment. His father was a farm-grieve, and his immediate progenitors were similarly employed. "But it was impossible," said my father, "to look at Archibald Constable, and entertain any doubt as to his having sprung from a gentle stock." In Fife the name of Constable is uncommon, but it abounds in the Carse of Gowrie or Eastern Perthshire, where those who bear the patronymic are substantial yeomen, and occupy good positions in society.

Not long before the period when my father became acquainted with Archibald Constable, the partnership between him and Alexander Gibson Hunter of Blackness had been dissolved. In Mr. J. G. Lockhart's "Life of Scott," that dissolution is attributed to Mr. Hunter's impracticable temper. This statement rests on no solid foundation. By the death of his father, in 1809, Mr. Hunter became owner of three fine estates in Forfarshire, and he proposed to leave Edinburgh to reside in the old family mansion of Blackness House, near Dundee. In these circumstances he retired from his connection with the publishing firm of Constable & Co., but in terms of perfect amity with the remaining partner. With reference to this subject I am privileged, through the kindness of Mr. Hunter's son, the present proprietor of Blackness, to subjoin a letter addressed

* In the memoirs of Archibald Constable he is represented as having been born on the 24th February, 1775. This is an error. The entry of his birth in the Baptismal Register of Carnbee parish is as follows :— "1773, Feb. 24, Thomas Constable and Elizabeth Myles had a child born, and baptized on the 27th, named Archibald."

† The old parish church of Dunino, which was taken down in 1826 to make room for the present handsome structure, was partially under ground, and the turf roof sloped so closely to the churchyard that goats grazed and children romped upon it.

to himself by Mr. Constable, in which, besides other interesting particulars, the uninterrupted intimacy which subsisted between Archibald Constable and the original partner of his publishing firm is emphatically set forth. The letter is as follows :—

" Edinburgh, 26th March, 1825.

" David Hunter, Esq., of Blackness.

" SIR,—I had the pleasure of sending you by carrier a set of the Novels, Tales, and Romances of the Author of ' Waverley,' in thirty-three volumes, and the Poetical Works of Sir Walter Scott, in eight volumes. They will aid the commencement of your library ; and I have to request you will receive them as a small memorial of my sincere regard for you, and as the representative of an early and most justly esteemed friend. Had your father been now alive, no man would have delighted more in the perusal of these works ; no one could better have appreciated their merits, or more fully rejoiced in their celebrity.

" You have, besides, other claims to the possession of these volumes from their publisher. One of these claims I cannot forget, and must now repeat to you, that I very often heard your father express a wish that the distinguished individual—since the author of ' Waverley '—would turn his mind to novel-writing ; and which, in the most warm terms, he used to predict, would place the great Unknown most prominently without a rival in literature. And this, I think, I can venture to assure you sometimes happened (in Mr. Hunter's own enthusiastic manner) in the author's own presence. This is a little historical notice which I cannot resist the gratification of now recording, and which, I am sure, cannot but be pleasing to you. I do not, however, pretend to say what effect, or any, these prophetic effusions may have had in producing the works originally, but the circumstance has very often occurred to me when thinking of former days.

" It will give me great pleasure to hear from you, and wit best wishes believe that I am always,

" My dear Sir,

" Your sincere Friend,

" ARCH. CONSTABLE."

" P.S.—I need not say that you will consider this letter, in so far as it relates to the works of the author of ' Waverley,' as *entirely* confidential and private ; I mean, in so far as regards the author."

With an esteemed associate of Robert Burns, my father enjoyed an agreeable intimacy. This was Allan Masterton, who, under his Christian name, has been celebrated by the Bard in the opening verse of one of his more popular songs,—

> " Willie brewed a peck o' maut,
>   An' Rob an' Allan cam' to pree."

Allan was, during Burns's visit to Edinburgh, a teacher of writing in the city, and possessing an excellent ear and much musical skill, he composed tunes to several of the poet's best songs. Among these are the " Braes of Ballochmyle," " Beware o' Bonny Ann," " Strathallan's Lament," and the song in which he is personally celebrated. In a letter to Captain Riddel, Burns describes him as " one of the worthiest men in the world, and a man of real genius." To my father Mr. Masterton related an incident which he said had produced on his mind a powerful and salutary impression. He was on a visit to London. Having proceeded to the metropolis in the Leith passenger boat, he proposed to return home by the same vessel. His luggage was being placed on board, when it occurred to him that, as he might not revisit England, it would be more interesting and profitable to return by coach. He acted on his resolution at once. When he reached Edinburgh he found that there was an alarm as to the non-arrival of the Leith passenger boat. It was never heard of. Mr. Masterton celebrated the birthday of the Ayrshire poet as the year came round. As he rose on one anniversary to propose the memory of his friend, his voice faltered, and he fell back and expired.*

I group together the names of three estimable persons with whom my father enjoyed an intimacy, of which he always spoke with satisfaction—the Rev. Sir Henry Moncreiff, Bart., minister of St. Cuthbert's, Edinburgh; Dr. John Jamieson, author of the Scottish Dictionary; and Dr. John Fleming, minister of Flisk. Sir Henry expressed himself in the Scottish dialect, a circumstance which did not mar the respect which attended his oratory in the General Assembly. He was a leader of the House. Possessed of a forensic turn of mind, had he chosen the legal profession, he would have acquired distinction, as did his son and grandson, who were raised to the bench. *Sir Harry*, as he was commonly named, was opposed to all innovations on the strict simplicity of Presbyterian worship.

---

* So my father related. I have been unable otherwise to obtain particulars of Mr. Masterton's latter years.

To show his distaste at the idea of sacredness being attached
to the church fabric, he always walked through the church
to the pulpit without removing his hat.   Dr. Jamieson was
jocular and full of anecdote; a hearty pleasant man, familiar
with the events of the "langsyne." The minister of Flisk, Dr.
John Fleming, was of a similar nature.   To sit between him
and Dr. Thomas Gillespie, minister of Cults,* at a synod
dinner, was an event which one fond of humour was not likely to
forget. " It was," said my father, "diamond cut diamond.
Each had his hit—at first gentle, then harder, till repartee
followed on repartee, with an intellectual gladiatorship difficult
to describe." Dr. Fleming became Professor of Natural Science
at Aberdeen.   In 1844 he was appointed to a professorial chair
in the New College, Edinburgh.   He died in 1857.

Dr. John Lee, latterly Principal of the University of Edinburgh, was a man of some singularities, and one of the most
remarkable scholars which his country has produced.   Born
of humble parents at Stow, in Mid-Lothian, he studied medicine, passed as M.D., and became surgeon-apothecary in a
military hospital.   Disgusted with the practice of physic, he
qualified himself for the ministry, and preached in London.
In 1808 he was presented to the church of Peebles, and four
years thereafter became Professor of Church History at St.
Andrews.   In 1820 he accepted the Professorship of Moral
Philosophy in King's College, Aberdeen, intending to lecture
one-half of the session at Aberdeen, and the other at St.
Andrews.   His intention was changed by an overturn of the
stage-coach, which nearly proved fatal to him.   From St.
Andrews he removed to Edinburgh, to become collegiate
minister of the Canongate.   In 1824 he was chosen a University
Commissioner, and was appointed minister of Lady Yester's
church.   In 1827 he was elected second clerk of the General
Assembly; in 1828 he delivered lectures as substitute Professor of Theology in the University of Edinburgh.   He was
appointed in 1830 one of the King's chaplains.   Still office fol
lowed upon office.   In 1835 he exchanged Lady Yester's for the
Old Church, Edinburgh; in 1837 he became Principal of
the United College, St. Andrews—in 1838 he was named
Secretary of the Bible Board.   The Deanery of the Chapel
Royal and Principalship of Edinburgh University came in
1840.   In 1843 the Professorship of Divinity was added

* Concerning Dr. Gillespie, see *postea*.

to the Principalship. In 1844 the Principal of Edinburgh College was both moderator and principal clerk of the General Assembly.

While so passing from office to office, and creditably performing the duties of each, Dr. Lee was ready to undertake any occasional work which might arise from the incapacity or infirmity of others. He was the most extraordinary book-collector in the kingdom, and knew the history of every book and pamphlet in British literature. On every volume of his library he made special annotations, describing its particular or relative value. More than once he was obliged to part with his books from want of space in which to contain them. At last he dispensed with shelving, and piled his books on the floors of his apartments. His memory was so retentive, that from his library heaps he could at once select any book which he desired to consult, and turn to the page where the information sought for was to be found. Of his health he constantly complained, but he was seldom laid aside by illness till his eightieth year, when he paid the debt of nature. Though he had obtained more offices than any of his contemporaries, and attained every honour which his country could bestow, including graduations in Law, Theology, and Medicine, he was not slow in expressing discontent that he had fared so poorly. He was impatient of contradiction, and sometimes fretful when no contradiction was offered. Though the best informed man of his time, he has produced no work in any degree worthy of his learning, or creditable to his industry. His public appearances were not striking. In the General Assembly he expressed himself in a monotonous undertone; and after he had spoken it was difficult to discover the purpose of his talk. His pulpit discourses were like his pastoral addresses, "beautiful and saintly," * but they lacked force.

With this strangely compounded and remarkable individual, my father maintained a cordial intimacy. When he was professor at St. Andrews they met frequently. In private life Dr. Lee was as facetious as he was in public stern and unyielding. His humour was sprightly and playful, and his laugh hearty and unconstrained. He delighted to relate witty anecdotes, always expressing himself with a *naïveté* which intensified the humour. "I have remarked, Dr. Lee, said a royal personage, "that the kitchens of Scottish monas-

* The latter were so characterized by Dr. Chalmers.

teries are very large."   " Scottish friars," responded the
doctor, with a shake of the head which was peculiar to him,
"did not object to the kitchen. They preferred it to the
library."

Principal Lee had a talent for mimicry, in which he indulged
to the last.   When on the verge of fourscore he made a visit
to his old friends at St. Andrews.   In the university library
he asked the late obliging librarian for a book, and during his
absence to procure it, took his place behind a large desk or
counter in thee ntrance-room. Principal Haldane, of St. Mary's,
then verging on fourscore, entered, and with eyes half closed,
as was his manner, requested the librarian to send him certain
books.   "You have not read what you have got," said a voice
from behind the counter.   "Eh !—eh !—Mr. M——," exclaimed the astounded Principal, "what—eh ?"   "I say, sir,"
persisted the voice, "you shall have no more books till you
return those you have got."   "Eh !—eh ! what, what !" said
Dr. Haldane, opening his eyes wide, and casting a glance
behind the counter, where the Principal of Edinburgh was
rubbing his hands and struggling with a laugh.   "Oh ! you
rogue, Doctor Lee, who would have supposed it ? But I'm
quite relieved, for I thought our friend Mr. M—— had lost
his reason."   There is an anecdote at Dr. Lee's own expense.
He was, as has been stated, inclined to complain of his health.
In the library of Edinburgh University he was met one
morning by the late Professor Robertson, who expressed a
hope that he was well.   "Far from well," said the Principal.
"I've had no sleep for a fortnight."   "Then, Principal," replied Dr. Robertson, "you're getting better, for when last we
met you had not slept for six weeks."

When my father was a lad of twelve, he received instructions
in the small-sword exercise from an humble veteran named
Stewart, who lived near his father's house at Coupar-Grange.
He took much to the old man, whose stories of " hair-breadth
'scapes" charmed his youthful fancy.   Years passed, and
Stewart's nephew entered, as a classical student, the University
of St. Andrews.   At my father's manse he found a warm
welcome.   His name was James Browne ; he was born in the
parish of Cargill in 1793.   At St. Andrews he distinguished
himself by his attention to the classics, but more so by a
persistent combativeness.   He was constantly getting into
scrapes—not by vicious indulgence, but by breaches of the
peace.   He challenged, boxed, whipped, and demolished all

from whom he differed ; and he inclined to differ with all
mankind. But for my father's good offices, he might, on
account of his propensity, have been compelled to exchange the
academic groves of St. Andrews for the pastures of Cargill.

As he grew older, Browne became somewhat less combative,
though in his thirtieth year he sought to vindicate his honour
by challenging to mortal combat the editor of the *Scotsman*
newspaper. After a short experience as a probationer of the
Church, he passed advocate, when he received the degree of
Doctor of Laws from his old professors at St. Andrews. But
his impetuous nature and a tendency for romancing unfitted
him for professional employment. He became a writer for the
press. As editor of the *Caledonian Mercury* he proved serviceable in discovering the West Port murders. He contributed
to the " Encyclopædia Britannica," and was sub-editor of the
seventh edition. His " History of the Highlands and the Highland Clans " is a respectable performance. He died in 1841.
Shortly before his death he became a pervert to the Romish
faith.

The office of parochial schoolmaster of Dunino became vacant
in 1813 by the death of Mr. George Cant, a man of eminent
accomplishments. My father sought to secure a suitable successor, and it afforded him peculiar satisfaction when the choice
of the electors fell upon one who had prosecuted learning under
difficulties, and was known as a poet. This was William
Tennant, author of " Anster Fair," a man destined to occupy
a high scholastic position, and to record his name among the
poets of his country. The poem of " Anster Fair " had in
1811 proceeded from the provincial press at Anstruther ; but
the author was now encouraged to issue an edition under the
auspices of an Edinburgh publisher. Among those who chiefly
countenanced the poet at this time was the minister of Dunino.
At his hospitable board he appeared once or twice a week,
and the shelves of his well-stored library were thrown open
to him.

For these acts of kindness the poet was not ungrateful. He
had formed a poetical society at Anstruther, styled the " Musomanik," and of this institution my father was constituted
chaplain. The following communication, addressed to the reverend chaplain by the leading members of the fraternity, is in
Mr. Tennant's handwriting :—

"*Ambrose's Tavern, Edinburgh, 25th March,* 1815.
"REV. AND VERY DEAR SIR,
   " Being assembled, as we now are, over a tavern glass, and
enjoying, as we now do, the pleasure of our poetical existences,
we cannot refrain from communicating to you somewhat of our
Musomanik raptures, and wafting over to the parsonage of
Dunino and its hospitable landord, by means of the conductor
of this sheet of paper, a little flash of that burning electricity
which animates our bosoms. We hope you are well-and happy,
and in possession of all those pleasures which hospitality and
open-heartedness never fail to pour upon the heads of their
fortunate votaries. We feel strongly inclined to expatiate and
expand ourselves in the luxuriance of epistolary gaiety ; but
we must clap a bit upon the foaming mouths of our fiery
Pegasuses. We, indeed, have nothing to say of importance—
it is all fume and folly and inanity ; but foolish and full of
smoke and fume as are our thoughts, our affections are real and
sincere, and we rejoice to take the opportunity, even though it
cost you ninepence, to signify to you our affectionate and
unanimous regard.
   " We must, therefore, close our card with wishing you all
good things. 'May you be blessed with the blessings of
heaven above, and the blessings of the deep that lieth under.'
   " We are, very dear Sir, with much esteem and regard,
      " Yours very sincerely,
      (Signed)   " WILLIAM TENNANT, *Laureate.*
                   " CHARLES GRAY, *Recorder,*
                   " W. MACDONALD FOWLER, *V.P.*
                   " MATTHEW F. CONOLLY, *Sec. Soc. Muso.*"

   The absence of the chaplain from the autumnal symposium
in 1814 is lamented by the laureate in these terms :—
   " We are all extremely sorry that you found it inconvenient
to attend our Musomanik Club on Friday. I assure you, that
rich and inexhaustible as is our own unparalleled wit and
humour, we were anticipating a large increase and additament
to our hilarity from your presence and conversation. Indeed,
this has been our only vexation and disappointment—first,
to flatter ourselves with the hopes of your company, and then
to be defrauded of it by I know not what unlucky and unto-
ward star."
   The chaplain, on subsequent occasions, did not disappoint
his poetical brethren by his absence. Next spring he assisted

D

in conferring honorary membership on Sir Walter Scott ; and as a compliment to himself, his friend Mr. Dempster of Dunnichen was, at the autumn meeting, honoured with a diploma. From these new members communications were received.   Sir Walter Scott wrote thus : —

" *To the Presidents of the Musomanik Society of Anstruther.*

" GENTLEMEN,

"I am, upon my return from the country, honoured with your letter and diploma, couched in very flattering terms, creating me a member of the Musomanik Society of Anstruther. I beg you will assure the society of my grateful sense of the favour they have conferred upon me, and my sincere wishes that they may long enjoy the various pleasures attendant upon the hours of relaxation which they may dedicate in their corporate or individual capacity to ' weel-timed daffing.'

"I remain, Gentlemen,

"Your much obliged humble servant,

"WALTER SCOTT.

"*Edinburgh, 27th March, 1815.*"

The laird of Dunnichen addressed his reply to the reverend chaplain :—

"*Dunnichen, 29th Oct.,* 1815.

"MY DEAR AND REV. SIR,

"The carriers of St. Andrews and Forfar brought me last night the favour of your letter and packet.   The compliment contained therein is one of those pieces of good fortune commonly preceded by some supernatural intimation or presage. Such was not wanting on this occasion, for, beside passing the day in uncommonly good health and high spirits, in the morning dream of that night I was honoured with an unexpected visit from Apollo.   Though my windows were shut, he opened my door, presented me with a sprig of laurel, and most benignly said, in the words of his favourite child,—

' Accede ! O magnos, aderit jam tempus honores,
Care Deum.'

I had hardly time to reply *Agnosco Deum,* when he vanished, and I awoke to the reception of my diploma, before sleeping again ; for which be pleased to return my thanks to all my worthy Maniacs. Assure them I am twice as mad as any of them, though not half so ingenious, and that I shall not fail to attend the next anniversary.

> "I remain,
> "Rev. and dear Sir,
> "Most respectfully yours,
> "GEORGE DEMPSTER."

The Musomanik Club, on the departure of the founders to other localities, suspended its sittings, not, however, before the publication of a volume in memorial of their fellowship. This volume, a thin octavo, is entitled "Bouts-Rimés, or Poetical Pastimes of a few Hobblers round the base of Parnassus." It contains many specimens of impromptu versification most creditable to the brotherhood.* The laureate rose step by step, till in 1835 he was, on the recommendation of Lord Jeffrey, appointed to the Chair of Oriental Languages at St. Andrews. He died in 1848, in his sixty-fifth year. As a linguist, he has left some evidences of his skill in a "Synopsis of Syriac and Chaldaic Grammar." Of his poetical compositions, a few only obtained praise. His fame rests on "Anster Fair," a poem in which elegant versification renders classic a narrative otherwise puerile. As a writer of prose, Professor Tennant did not excel; his style was always inflated, and occasionally turgid. In conversation he indulged a learned phraseology, which was rendered quaint and singular by a peculiar intonation. The recollection of early difficulties left an impression; for though his expenditure on books and book-printing was unrestrained, he was in household matters inclined to penury. It was the custom of the St. Andrews professors to invite their students to breakfast once a year. Mr. Tennant conformed to the practice, but not until eggs had fallen in the market to a price not exceeding one halfpenny per egg. A single egg for each student, with toast and butter, constituted the *déjeûner*. Shortly before his death, he received the degree of LL.D. from Marischal College, Aberdeen. He was lame in both his limbs, but he bore his infirmity with patience, and was not indisposed to join in any little jest concerning his restrained locomotion. "The tax assessor last year charged me for arms," he remarked

---

* For a full account of the Musomanik Society of Anstruther, see *Chambers's Edinburgh Journal* of the 25th July, 1840; "Lays and Lyrics," by Charles Gray, Edinburgh, 1841, 12mo., pp. 242—255; and Conolly's "Life of Professor Tennant," London, 1861, pp. 209—223.

to the late witty university librarian. "To charge you for the use of your arms is indeed exquisite cruelty," said the humorist. The professor laughed heartily.

Another member of the Musomanik Club is entitled to a passing notice—Charles Gray, then a-lieutenant, latterly a captain in the Royal Marines. This estimable gentleman delighted in cherishing the society of all who cultivated the gift of rhyming. In his two volumes of poems he has produced several songs of superior merit.* Captain Gray was a welcome guest at the manse of Dunino. He sung his own songs, and related his naval experiences with a good-natured egotism. He died in 1851 at an advanced age.

* See "The Modern Scottish Minstrel," Edinburgh, 1870, pp. 206,207.

· MEN I HAVE KNOWN.

FROM the last and best work of my late obliging correspondent, Mr. William Jerdan, of the *Literary Gazette*, I borrow the title of the present chapter. No other will so accurately describe the character of reminiscences which are chiefly biographical. During the last thirty years I have associated with many literary and other distinguished Scotsmen. Concerning those of the number who have left the scene, I desire to put on record my impressions and recollections.

The late Professor Gillespie of St. Andrews was my father's friend, and my own. He was an enthusiastic angler, and frequently prosecuted his favourite pastime in the Kenly stream. Dunino Manse was near, and when the Professor was weary of his sport, he would put up his rod and have a chat with my father. A literary man he essentially was, and with no inconsiderable share of genius. Born in 1778 at Closeburn, Dumfriesshire, the birthplace of the celebrated Dr. John Hunter of St. Andrews, to whom he was related, he was educated in the free school of Wallaceball, and at the University of Edinburgh. In 1813 he was presented to the church living of Cults, Fifeshire ; he afterwards was appointed assistant to Dr. Hunter in the St. Andrews Humanity Chair. When Dr. Hunter was promoted to the Principalship of his college in 1836, he became his successor. As Professor of the Roman language he inspired his students with a literary ardour ; he rejoiced to advance the interests of the deserving. His speculations on grammar, delivered in the form of " Saturday Conversations " to his class were abundantly ingenious. As a periodical writer he excelled. To *Blackwood's Magazine* he contributed interesting " Sketches of Village Character," and in Constable's *Edinburgh Magazine* delighted the facetious by his adventures of " Ill Tam," and " The Feelings and Fortunes of a Scottish Tutor."

In conversation, Dr. Gillespie was most diverting and jocund. His anecdotes were exhaustless, and every story received a charm from his peculiar relation of it. The most dejected were enlivened and cheered even by a short interview with the

facetious Professor. He related with inimitable effect how he
punished old Francy Robertson, the churlish hind, and terror
of the schoolboys. Francy took delight in thrashing every
youth who chanced to cross his path, and was detested accordingly. When found fault with for his cruelty and rashness, he
said that if the boys did not deserve castigation at the time
when he administered it, they were sure to deserve it before
they passed into manhood. Along with some schoolmates the
future Professor conspired to punish the old clodhopper. As
he was one day seated on a mud wall near the farmyard, two
of the conspirators walked up and engaged him in conversation.
Gillespie, as the most adventurous, crept cautiously behind the
wall, and got unseen to Francy's back. He now, by a small
fish-hook, adroitly attached to the churl's voluminous bonnet
the cord of a *dragon* or kite, which he forthwith let loose. By
a rapid sidelong sweep, kite and bonnet rose into the empyrean.
Missing his head-gear, and unsuspecting the cause of its flight,
Francy entreated the youths beside him to give pursuit. They
did, and likewise the maid-servants and others at the farm.
But just as the bonnet was again and again within grasp, off
it scampered into the air with ludicrous reluctance to be caught.
At length it was arrested by a cow's horns, the animal kicking
and running all the while with admirable precipitation. When
Francy at length got back his bonnet, it was found considerably
worse for its aërial and bovine experiences.

The Professor was on a visit to two maiden aunts. He had
the credit of being studious, and, to maintain his reputation,
he sat much by the fireside reading his favourite chap-books.
Suddenly the crook began to move, and the kail-pot which it
suspended over the fireplace moved too, till it hung right over
the hearth. "That will be some of Elspit Macgrowther's
tricks," said one of the sisters, referring to a suspected witch
who lived near. The other assented and rearranged the cook-
ing vessel. In a few minutes crook and pot moved again, and
turned right upon the hearth. "Preserve us a'," exclaimed
the sisters simultaneously. "The deil's i' the pat." Tom
feigned proportionate alarm, but after a time resumed his
stool by the ingle-side. Again the pot became erratic. The
sisters shrieked, and Tom fell over the stool in an affected
swoon. Amidst the confusion that followed, he contrived to
remove from the crook the little cord by means of which he had
produced the alarm.

The Professor's first teacher was like some others of his

class, a hero only in the absence of peril. During a thunderstorm he was utterly prostrate, and when a dark cloud passed across the sky, be began to look from the school windows in tremulous apprehension of approaching danger. The boys were familiar, with his weakness, but young Gillespie turned it into account. When a holiday was wanted, he caused some idle herd to gyrate a *thunder-spale* outside, while he and others raised the cries, "There's thunder!" "Did you see that flash?" "That's awfu'—the hale sky's in a bleeze!" "Go home, boys, go home quickly," the paralyzed dominic would exclaim; we are on the eve of a thunderstorm, and the rain will descend immediately."

When minister of Cults, Professor Gillespie experienced his first and worst attack of toothache. One Sunday the twinges were horrible, and shutting himself up in his library, he resolved to spend the afternoon in giving vent to his agony. At the entreaty of his wife he at length consented to try a plate of broth, the usual Sunday dish of the Scottish ecclesiastic. He had taken a few spoonfuls only when he declined to proceed further, and at once despatched his "man" John to the neighbouring town of Cupar to fetch the doctor. When the physician arrived he proceeded to assure him that an attack of toothache had assumed a very aggravated form. "I am spitting teeth," he said. "I found two in a plate of broth, and no doubt all will soon go." "Did you retain the teeth found in the plate?" inquired the physician. "I did," said the patient, "and hope you can restore them to my jaw; I slipped them quietly into my pocket not to alarm my wife, and there they are," presenting them.—"These are sheep's teeth," replied the physician. "Oh! I remember, I was supping sheep's-head broth," replied the pastor, "and I'm so thankful that my teeth are safe." The relation of this story by the facetious professor never failed to excite roars of laughter.

Dr. Gillespie was conversing with Mr. Espline, schoolmaster of Monimail, a leading person in his profession. "How do you schoolmasters employ yourselves on Saturday, which you keep, I believe, as a weekly holiday?" inquired the professor. "Why," replied Mr. Espline, "we often visit each other's houses; and after having a glass together, we occasionally read an essay to one another." "And I suppose," added the querist, "*Esse* has the same case after it as it has before it," quoting a well-known rule in Latin syntax.

In a field fronting his manse Gillespie erected a handsome

sun-dial. His cows, by rubbing against it, having menaced
its overthrow, he instructed the village joiner to enclose it with
a timber fence. The order was executed, and a note of the
cost handed in. It ran thus :—"For railing in the deil, 5s."
"Wonderfully cheap," said the professor. ˜ "I'm paid considerably more for railing him in, but have not succeeded yet."

When his fame as a writer had spread abroad, Dr. Gillespie
was invited to lecture in one of the Fife towns on a subject to
be selected by himself. To the Secretary of the lecture-room
he intimated that he would lecture on Burke. What was his
surprise, he said, when he came to fulfil his pledge, to find that
he was placarded over the place as having consented to lecture
"on Burke and Hare and the West Port murders !"

Dr. Gillespie talked seriously when he spoke of his recollections of Robert Burns. He remembered him distinctly. As
a youth he had waited at Dumfries to see him pass by, and had
regarded him with a veneration akin to idolatry. "But," he
added, "we boys well knew and deeply regretted that he was
allowing his splendid genius to be obscured by social indul-
gences."

Professor Gillespie cherished a deep interest in the Scottish
martyrs. Chiefly through his exertions, a handsome obelisk,
commemorative of those who suffered at St. Andrews, was
reared in that city. Adjacent to this monument a pile of
handsome buildings has lately been constructed, and named
Gillespie Terrace, in honour of his memory. He died at
Dunino on the 11th September, 1844. His second wife was a
sister of John, first Lord Campbell, and Lord Chancellor.

Dr. George Cook was another of my early friends. A man
of active habits and deeply imbued with common sense, he was
a judicious counsellor and effective administrator. He succeeded Dr. Chalmers as Professor of Moral Philosophy at St.
Andrews, and a better appointment might not easily have
been made. Originality of sentiment he did not claim, and
his style was unadorned. But he had mastered the science of
ethics by a course of pertinacious study, and he supplied to his
students the views of philosophers, both ancient and modern,
on every department of his subject. His lectures were delivered with an impassioned manner, which was intensified
by the deeply sonorous character of his voice. As a leader in
the General Assembly, he retained the confidence of his party,
and after his death a strong testimony to his eminent services
was entered on the public records of the Church.

Dr. Cook was a keen observer of human affairs, and rejoiced in relating his experiences of the whims and follies of mankind. When minister of Laurencekirk he was invited by the chief magistrate of Brechin to become a candidate for the office of first minister of that place. Having consented to preach in the parish church, he was on the previous evening entertained at dinner by the Provost, along with some leading members of the Town Council and congregation. At that period toasts were common, and the reverend candidate was warned by the host to select one which would not offend the convictions or prejudices of any one present. Intending to act upon the counsel, he proposed as his toast, "Honest men and bonnie lasses!" "I thought," said the Doctor, "that I had been abundantly happy in my selection, but I afterwards learned that a bailie came to the conclusion that a minister who was thinking about the fair sex on the Saturday evening would not be a suitable minister for Brechin. "So," he added, "I lost the parish."

Immediately after the event of the Disruption, Dr. Cook was met on the North Bridge, Edinburgh, by Mr. Walter Dunlop, of the Secession Church, Dumfries, a celebrated humorist. After some conversation on the extent and character of the secession, Mr. Dunlop exclaimed, "Well, Doctor, you cooked them lang, but you've dished them at last!"

Dr. Cook was son of Mr. John Cook, Professor of Moral Philosophy at St. Andrews, and a nephew of Principal Hill. He was born in 1773, licensed to preach in April, 1795, and settled at Laurencekirk in September of the same year. In 1825 he was chosen Moderator of the General Assembly, and in the following year was appointed a member of the Royal Commission for Visiting the Scottish Universities. He became Professor of Moral Philosophy at St. Andrews in 1828, an office which he held till his death, which took place in May, 1845. Of his several publications, his "History of the Reformation" is the most interesting; it has been commended for the candour which pervades it. A memoir of Dr. Cook would find readers, and it is to be regretted that it has not been written.

In 1838 the Principalship of the United College of St. Andrews was conferred on Sir David Brewster, a man of European fame, but who, though in his fifty-seventh year, and the reverse of wealthy, had not yet held any academical or other public appointment. It was alleged that he had an acrimonious temper, and that this unhappy peculiarity had

interfered with his earlier promotion. But in his mature years
and with his enlarged experience, it was hoped that he would,
in the position he had at length attained, bear himself
meekly. That hope was speedily overthrown, for however
genial in private life, Principal Brewster was, within a few
months after his appointment at St. Andrews, in a state of
hostility with half his colleagues. Nor was the strife of an
evanescent character. As the older professors stepped off and
were succeeded by others, previously apart from the scene of
conflict, it was found that academical contention did not cease,
but was rather on the increase. That there were some abuses
in university management may be conceded, but there were
certainly none which would have resisted the obvious appliance
of a firm and judicious administration. Sir David Brewster
proceeded differently, and sought to carry his measures *vi et
armis.*

It is unpleasant to refer to bygone feuds, but there is a
cause for the allusion. In a well-written and interesting work*
it has been alleged that Sir David Brewster was "*par excellence
the suffering elder of the Free Church,*" and that he was
specially selected for persecution by the adherents of the Established Church subsequent to the Disruption. His accomplished
daughter alludes to the attempt made by the Presbytery of St.
Andrews to deprive him of his Principalship for an alleged
violation of the Act of Union, by his retaining office in a
University while he had severed his connection with the Established Church. That he was the only member of a Scottish
University subjected to prosecution under the Test Act is
correct, but it must be remembered that he was the *only*
professor who had violated the provisions of the statute. And
Sir David was not subjected to prosecution from any ecclesiastical considerations, but solely on account of his having
rendered himself, by his temper, so obnoxious in office that the
fact of his having contravened an old Act of Parliament was
seized upon as an excuse to get rid of his presence at the university table. That this course was adopted, none can more
heartily regret than I now personally do, but I will here publish the confession that his prosecution arose from my own
individual suggestions. I discovered and made known the
provisions of the Union Act, and in the public journals urged

* "Home Life of Sir David Brewster," by his daughter, Mrs. Gordon.
Edinburgh, 1870.

the prosecution. With a speech founded on materials which I had collected, my father moved in the Presbytery of St. Andrews, that Sir David should be indicted at their bar. The proceedings which followed were, with entire unanimity, approved by the members of the University, but were abruptly terminated by a resolution of the General Assembly.

In urging the prosecution of Sir David Brewster by the Presbytery of St. Andrews, I had to gratify no feeling of personal dislike. I was in my nineteenth year, and in the impetuosity of hot youth sought to indulge what I then deemed a wise, but now perceive to have been a most mistaken patriotism. I heartily rejoice that the effects of my juvenile rashness proved scathless to the illustrious though irate philosopher, and that my injudicious procedure accelerated the abolition of Scottish University Tests. From St. Andrews Sir David Brewster was transferred to the Principalship of Edinburgh University in 1859. He was now bordering on fourscore, and was not unaware that rumours had reached the capital as to his dissensions at St. Andrews. From whatever cause, the latter years of his life were comparatively serene. His last hours were worthy of a philosopher and a Christian. He died at Allerly, near Melrose, on the 11th February, 1869, at the age of eighty-eight. With Sir David I had latterly some pleasant correspondence. He accompanied Lord Elgin to the public meeting at Stirling for inaugurating the national monument to Wallace, and readily subscribed to the Ettrick Shepherd's monument which I had originated. During the Nonintrusion controversy he often expressed himself with much bitterness, but he latterly was disposed to extend an abundant charity towards the religious convictions, and even the prejudices of others. By the gentler sex he was beloved. When he was bordering on eighty, Miss Phœbe Lyon, a charming young lady, begged that he would contribute some lines to her album. In vain did the philosopher protest that versemaking was not his *forte*. The lady would admit of no excuse; so Sir David snatched a pen and wrote thus :—

> " Phœbe,
> Y' be
> Hebe.
> D. B."

He delighted to recall the memory of those who had encouraged his early studies. One of these was the eccentric David

Stuart, eleventh Earl of Buchan. Sir David used to relate that
as he was becoming known by his contributions to the scientific
journals, Lord Buchan remarked to a friend, " David writes
good papers ; he cleverly expresses the ideas which I give him
from time to time !"

The late Dr. Robert Haldane, Principal of St. Mary's College, St. Andrews, is entitled to honourable remembrance. In
his twofold capacity of *Primarius* Professor of Theology and
first minister of St. Andrews, he discharged his duties with
remarkable industry, and no ordinary acceptance. His discourses were forcible expositions of Divine truth, and were
delivered with a manner singularly earnest and impressive.
As a university lecturer he did not excel, but his examinations
on his theological text-books were judicious and searching.
He delighted to reward the meritorious, and spared no efforts
in procuring posts of honour for those students who were conspicuous by their diligence. He exercised a boundless hospitality.

Principal Haldane was born in January, 1772, in the parish
of Lecropt, Perthshire, where his father rented a small portion
of land. By his father he was intended for agricultural pursuits,
but his mother, discovering his aptitude for learning, resolved,
on the proceeds of her personal industry, to send him to the
Grammar School. As a private tutor he acquired the means
of prosecuting his studies at Glasgow College, and in December,
1797, was ·licensed to preach by the Presbytery of Auchterarder. In 1807 he was ordained to the ministerial charge of
Drummelzier, in the county of Peebles, and after two years was
preferred to the Professorship of Mathematics at St. Andrews.
In 1820 he was promoted to the office of first minister of St.
Andrews, and to the Principalship of St. Mary's College. In
1827 he was elected Moderator of the General Assembly. He
died at St. Andrews on the 9th March, 1854, at the advanced
age of eighty-three.

Among the earliest of my literary friends was Dr. David
Irving, of Edinburgh, author of the " Lives of the Scottish
Poets." With this venerable gentleman I became acquainted
in 1843. He was then in his sixty-fifth year ; he looked considerably older. He dressed in a suit of superfine black cloth
—dress coat and vest, with breeches and silk stockings ; and
as he was tall and well formed, with a fine massive head, soft
features, and white flaxen hair, he presented a most commanding presence. His manners were mild and courteous, but he

was not free from prejudices, and both in speaking and writing would express himself keenly on whatever savoured of insincerity or assumption. With the majority of literary Scotsmen, for nearly half a century, he had enjoyed some acquaintance, and his reminiscences of them were especially pleasing. Those who were familiar with classic literature possessed his chief regard, while all pretenders to learning received no common measure of disapprobation and censure. With Thomas Campbell and his contemporaries he had been intimate, and it gave him pleasure to recount amusing incidents in their lives. Dabblers in verse were so obnoxious to him that few would venture to name in his presence a minor or provincial poet. In his advanced years he did not leave Edinburgh, yet he possessed correct information as to the condition and peculiarities of men of letters in every portion of the country. His love of books was a ruling passion. He obtained the best editions of the classic writers, and every valuable work illustrative of the national history. His books were well bound, and arranged on the shelves with the most business-like precision. Obliging and generous in other matters, he only permitted his books to be consulted in his presence, and rigidly adhered to a rule which he had early laid down, of permitting no friend to borrow from his shelves. His hand-writing was singularly beautiful—every letter was exhibited in its relative proportions, and his punctuation was balanced by the nicest rules of composition. For indifferent penmanship he would admit no excuse, maintaining that haste in writing might not justify an illegible MS. His private communications were conceived in the same measured style which was exhibited in his public writings, unless when he censured a printer for a typographical blunder, or *charged* against some literary charlatan.

David Irving was born at Langholm, Dumfriesshire, on the 5th December, 1778. From both parents he inherited a yeoman descent; but his father was a trader. The youngest of five sons, he was educated with a view to the ministry. In 1796 he entered the University of Edinburgh, and in 1801 graduated in arts. Before the latter date he published his "Life of Robert Fergusson, with a Critique on his Works." This literary performance he dedicated to Dr. Robert Anderson, editor of the "British Poets." At the age of twenty-three he produced his "Elements of English Composition," a work which, being adopted as a school-book, has passed into many editions. The intention of entering the ministry was abandoned, and under the encouragement of Dr. Robert Anderson, whose daughter he afterwards married, he commenced the career of a man of letters. In 1804 appeared his "Lives of the Scottish Poets," in two octavo volumes. Concerning this work, he writes in a letter to myself in October, 1843, "The Lives of the Scottish Poets were written 'yore agone in mine undaunted youth,' and exhibit too many marks of a premature publication." The self-criticism is unjust; for the "Lives" evince an extent of research, a maturity of reflection, and a power of composition altogether marvellous, when it is remembered that the author had not passed his twenty-sixth birthday. The work is held as an authority, and is a principal basis of the author's fame. During 1805 he published his "Memoirs of George Buchanan," which attracted the attention and praise of Principal Brown, Dr. John Hunter, and other Scottish scholars. In 1808 he received the degree of LL.D. from Marischal College.

For some years Dr. Irving received into his house in Edinburgh young gentlemen as boarders, and gave instructions in the Civil Law. In 1820 he was elected Principal Keeper of the Advocates' Library—an office of high responsibility and respectable emolument. He continued to devote his leisure to the illustration of Scottish literary history, editing various works for the Bannatyne and Maitland Clubs, and contributing many important articles in Scottish biography to the seventh edition of the "Encyclopædia Britannica." In 1837 he published his "Introduction to the Study of the Civil Law." From his duties as librarian he retired in 1848; his latter years were dedicated to classical studies, and to the society of his friends. He died, after a short illness, on the 10th May, 1860, in his eighty-second year. His "History of Scottish Poetry," on which he had been engaged upwards of thirty years, was published posthumously.

An anecdote connected with Dr. Irving's prevailing peculiarity—a love of literary order—may be related. Within a few hours of his decease, his eye rested on a lately acquired copy of Josephus, which stood on one of the bookshelves of the apartment. He requested that the volume might be handed to him; he tried to read, but the book fell from his grasp. He then desired that it might be returned to its place. When this was done, he expressed himself impatiently, and it was observed that it had been pushed in too far. The position was corrected, and he was satisfied.

With Dr. Thomas Dick, author of "The Christian Philosopher," and other esteemed works, chiefly astronomical, I became acquainted at an early age. By a relative I was introduced to him in his Observatory at Broughty Ferry, in my seventeenth year; I retained a pleasant recollection of his amenity, and when, twelve years afterwards, I observed in a newspaper that his circumstances were reduced, I considered how I might relieve him. Communicating with the venerable gentleman, he favoured me with a statement of his affairs, together with a narrative of the sums he had received from publishers for the copyrights of his works. This interesting document I have unhappily mislaid; but, if my memory does not betray me, it supplied the information, that he had received less than a thousand pounds for works which would have yielded him, had he retained the copyrights, twenty times that amount. From no British publisher had he obtained any pecuniary acknowledgment beyond the amount of payment originally stipulated. American publishers had been more generous, and he had received from Transatlantic admirers many substantial tokens of regard.

Dr. Dick was now (1855) in his eighty-first year. For nearly half a century he had subsisted on his copyrights, gifts from America, occasional grants from the Royal Literary Fund, and the profits of leasing his marine villa to sea-bathers during the months of summer. But he had been unable to make provision for old age, though his principal meal daily for forty years was bread and milk. Efforts had been repeatedly made to secure him a pension on the Civil List, but hitherto unsuccessfully. Another effort might prove fortunate, and, at his advanced age, no time was to be lost. On his behalf I prepared a memorial to the Prime Minister: it was subscribed by men of science throughout the kingdom. By Sir Thomas Makdougal Brisbane, President of the Royal Society of Edinburgh, it was forwarded to Lord Panmure for presentation. The prayer was supported by Lord Duncan, Scottish Lord of the Treasury, the Hon. Arthur Kinnaird, Sir John Ogilvy, Mr. Charles Cowan, and other members of the House of Commons. At first Dr. Dick was offered £10 a year from the Compassionate Fund, which, on my recommendation, he declined. Soon after Lord Palmerston granted him £50 a year on the Civil List—a boon which was most gratefully acknowledged. But the aged philosopher did not long enjoy the royal bounty; he died on the 29th July, 1857, at the age of eighty-three. I had made a

promise that, should I survive him, I would spare no effort to
secure a pension to his widow.   It was my privilege to accomplish what I had undertaken; and for the valuable aid which
I experienced on this occasion from Mr. Cowan, M.P., and
from my relative, Sir John Ogilvy, I desire now to record
a becoming acknowledgment.   The career of Dr. Dick may be
described as a life-long sacrifice.   The son of a linen manufacturer at Dundee, he was born in that town on the 24th
November, 1774.   Educated for the ministry of the Secession
Church, he was at an early age called to the pastorate of a
congregation at Stirling.   His ministerial services were most
acceptable; but, not long after his settlement, he invited
deprivation by acknowledging himself chargeable with an
unclerical offence.   He now devoted himself to teaching—first
at Methven in Perthshire, afterwards at Perth.   In 1827 he
built a cottage at Broughty Ferry, near Dundee, in which he
resided during the remainder of his life.   At the top of
the building an apartment was fitted up as an Observatory,
and provided with valuable telescopes and other astronomical
instruments.

With Dr. Dick I maintained a correspondence during the
two years which preceded his death, and he paid me a visit at
Stirling.   He was an unpretending, amiable, and friendly man,
most willing to communicate information, and most desirous
of encouraging those who evinced scientific and literary tastes.
He had a strong feeling of independence, and had long refused
to sanction the efforts of his friends in procuring a public recognition of his services.   His conversation partook of the
character of his works—he rejoiced in simple words to express
his deep sense of the divine goodness.   His letters abounded
in pious sentiment.   On the 19th November, 1856, he thus
wrote to me, in reference to the *Scottish Literary Institute*,
which I had lately established, and of which he was a member:—
"As it is enjoined upon us by the highest authority that we
should acknowledge God in all our ways, I shall consider it as
highly expedient that all the meetings should be opened with
prayer to God for direction and guidance.   This is not customary
in literary associations, but it cannot on that account be im-
proper.   We are too apt to consider secular and religious objects
as essentially distinct, whereas they are only parts of one system,
and every action we perform, if performed aright and from
proper motives, should be considered as a part of religion."
To Dr. Dick's writings, Dr. Livingstone, the celebrated

traveller, was indebted for his conversion. And many others who now occupy useful positions in the Christian Church have ascribed their spiritual awakening to a perusal of one or other of his publications. In the United States his works exercised a wide and most beneficial influence ; nor has that influence materially diminished. Dr. Dick finished his career as became one who had so long borne his cross and brought the message of peace and resignation to others. "I have been much troubled," he said to a clerical friend ; without were fightings, and within fears, but now I can say all is well." These were his last words.

Dr. John Reid, of St. Andrews, the eminent physiologist, was another of my early friends. In my eighteenth year I called to consult him as to the state of my health. I described my symptoms very minutely, making use of some medical phrases. Having examined my pulse, and applied the stethoscope, he inquired what medical book I had been reading ? I named the book. "Throw it into the fire," he said, "and in a week come back." I returned to report that my health was improved. "Beware of medical books," he said smilingly, "and you'll get quite strong." Thus commenced my acquaintance with one of the most genial and upright men I ever knew.

John Reid was a native of Bathgate, a town which produced another eminent physician, afterwards to be named. He was born on the 9th April, 1809. His father, who was a cattle dealer in good circumstances, gave him the best elementary education which the locality could afford, and sent him as a student to the University of Edinburgh. In 1825 he entered on his medical studies ; he became surgeon in 1829, and Doctor of Medicine in the year following. He subsequently attended anatomical lectures and demonstrations in the medical schools of Paris. In 1833 he accepted an invitation to become partner in the Edinburgh Anatomical School, along with Dr. Knox and Mr. William Fergusson. His duties were those of demonstrator, which implied his continual attendance in the dissecting-room. From this irksome situation he was relieved in 1836, when he was appointed physiological lecturer in the Edinburgh Extra-Academical School. In 1838 he became Pathologist to the Edinburgh Royal Infirmary, and in 1841 was preferred to the chair of Anatomy at St. Andrews. This latter appointment afforded him an opportunity for deliberate study, such as, without abridging his hours of rest, he had not hitherto enjoyed.

Under his predecessor, Dr. Briggs. the Anatomical chair at

E

St. Andrews was a sinecure, but Dr. Reid not only prepared a course of anatomical lectures for those who might enrol themselves in his class, but delivered a popular course on physiology, to which, free of charge, he invited both students and citizens. In connection with these public lectures Dr. Reid obtained golden opinions; while he promoted a taste for physiological inquiry at St. Andrews, which was altogether new. It was expected that he would attain the highest honours of his profession.

But a cloud was looming. In the month of November, 1847, a small blister appeared on his tongue, which ere long betrayed symptoms of cancer. In the following autumn he submitted to a surgical operation, himself assisting his friend Professor Fergusson in the excruciating process. I met him on his return to St. Andrews, and we had some conversation on his malady, and the attempted cure. He articulated with difficulty, but his utterances indicated cheerful resignation. It was evident he entertained little hope of ultimate recovery. To a period of the severest suffering, patiently borne, death came as a merciful deliverer on the 30th July, 1849. During the latter years of his life he had been closely preparing for the eternal world. A sincere and devout believer, he accepted his affliction as a salutary chastisement. He had inflicted pain on the inferior animals that he might discover the functions of the "Eighth Pair of Nerves," and he regarded the pain which he personally endured as a heaven-sent message, warning him that such cruelties were obnoxious to the Supreme. When he knew that his days were hastening rapidly to a close, and while he was obliged to have recourse to opiates to relieve the gnawing severity of his malady, he prepared for the press his "Physiological, Anatomical, and Pathological Researches," a work which was published posthumously. Of a tall, well-knit figure, with a fresh ruddy countenance, and broad massive forehead, Dr. Reid, till his last illness, bore the aspects of physical and intellectual strength. His manner was gentle and pleasing; in general conversation he did not much join, but he was in private abundantly sociable.

A memoir of Dr. Reid was prepared by Dr. George Wilson, of Edinburgh. This work, which is to be procured at a moderate price, is a most instructive Christian biography.* With

* "Life of Dr. John Reid," by George Wilson, M.D. Edinburgh, 1852. 12mo.

Dr. Wilson, the author of the memoir, I enjoyed a short but most pleasant intercourse. I can recall his genial demeanour, as seated in his laboratory he was ready to discuss any subject which might be brought to his notice. Like his friend Dr. Reid, Dr. Wilson was long a silent worker till he emerged suddenly into reputation and eminence. I do not recollect any one whose career was more meteoric. Till within one or two years of his appointment as Professor of Technology at Edinburgh, the lay world knew of George Wilson only as a skilful chemist, whose opinion in matters of analysis was entitled to respect. But at length the truth dawned that the analyst of Surgeons' Hall was capable of illustrating the arts, both industrial and recondite, with a power and precision and eloquence seldom surpassed. In 1855 he was appointed first keeper of the Edinburgh Industrial Museum, as the one man in Scotland pre-eminently fitted to occupy and adorn so responsible an office, while a University Professorship was created for his use. Besides, it was found that if an orator was needed to arouse the citizens to ardour, industrious, or social, or patriotic, none was so effective as that quiet, thoughtful chemist, who had so unexpectedly stepped from his laboratory into fame.

On the 22nd November, 1859, George Wilson, the ingenious philosopher and pleasing poet, sank into his rest. He was only forty-one,—just a year older than John Reid, whom in all respects, save in a robust frame, he strikingly resembled. Both were industrious workers, loving work for its own sake, and indifferent to its rewards. Both were generous and open-hearted. Both were great physical sufferers—for Wilson was a prey to acute sickness, and had suffered, without an anæsthetic, the amputation of his foot. Both were men of piety,—Reid during his latter years, Wilson during his whole life. Both, it may be added, have found appropriate biographers,—Reid in his friend Wilson, and Wilson in an accomplished and loving sister.

From Professor George Wilson, it is no violent transition to name another Professor of Edinburgh College, who was likewise cut off in the midst of a most useful and important career. I refer to Dr. James Robertson, Professor of Church History, but better known as Convener of the Endowment Scheme of the Established Church. With this admirable man I was well acquainted during his last years. The personal aspects of Dr. Robertson were not prepossessing. In person short and stout, his countenance had a thoughtful cast, but was withal stern and even austere. His voice was harsh, and his *brogue* the worst sort of that worst of all dialects—the Buchan. His talk on any theme which interested him was protracted, and his sermons and orations were most lengthy. He was prone to take offence, and when offended, was not slow in the expression of his resentment.

This is one side of the picture. Concerning the Doctor in other respects it is difficult to keep within the bounds of ordinary laudation. A man of powerful intellect, his perseverance was enormous. No individual minister of the Established Church since the days of Knox, did more " to lengthen her cords and strengthen her stakes." If he did not plant churches, he rendered secure and permanent those which had been designated. Under his advocacy, thousands of pounds were secured for the endowment of chapels in localities where religious ordinances were greatly needed, but where there were no means of supporting either ministers or missionaries.

Dr. Robertson possessed the art of procuring money for his " scheme" in a degree altogether unparalleled. He did not make successful raids only on the pockets of the liberal and open-hearted. These were of course approached in the first instance. But the penurious and the miserly also opened their treasures and placed them at the feet of the Scottish apostle. Twenty-three years ago I was visiting a friend in a rural parish about the centre of Fifeshire. In the neighbourhood lived an opulent miserly landowner, who had not presented himself in the house of prayer for many years, who never saw company, and lived in his old mansion with few attendants, and apparently actuated by aspirations no higher than those of adding house to house and field to field. Dr. Robertson, it was asserted, had boldly approached the citadel and been admitted. How he succeeded in effecting an entrance no one knew. But this was not all, for he likewise found admission into the laird's old miserly heart. In a short time it was announced in the public journals that —— ——, Esq., had contributed several hundreds to the Endowment Scheme.

Somewhere in the vale of Lochleven dwelt a narrow, rich old squire, whose premises were walled in as if to bid defiance to the cravings of the outer world, and of whom it was said that he never performed a deed of charity or inclined an ear to the tale of distress. Dr. Robertson came to the neighbourhood in prosecution of his mission. " Will he attack laird —— ? " was a jocular observation, as a proceeding totally beyond the bounds of reasonable belief. But what was the surprise of the neighbourhood when it was related that Dr. Robertson had actually been seen along with the hard-hearted laird, looking from the interior wall of his enclosures, while both were smiling together as in chiefest amity and most cordial friendship. The sequel may be guessed. There was a handsome addition to the Endowment Fund. An elderly miser had been induced by Dr. Robertson to make promise that he would endow a chapel ; but on the appointment of a clergyman the capital was not forthcoming. On approaching the miser the managers of the chapel received only fair promises, along with a variety of excuses for non-payment. At length Dr. Robertson was appealed to. He intimated his intention of visiting the neighbourhood, and was invited by the miserly gentleman to take up quarters at his house. Within a week the endowment was completed.

A landowner of surly temper, and most unapproachable, had resisted all attempts on his finance in connection with the Endowment Scheme. Several gentlemen of the locality accompanied Dr. Robertson to the vicinity of his residence, where they halted in ambush, while the champion of endowment marched up to the front door of the mansion-house. The man-servant appeared—there was a parley—a little delay—and Dr. Robertson was admitted. "He has got in," exclaimed the friends. And he remained within for some hours. At length the door opened, and the laird bid his guest a frank and friendly adieu. "Well, Doctor ! good news, I hope," said one and all. "I have got," said Robertson, "five hundred pounds." No other man in Scotland would have extracted a crown.

Dr. Robertson attended meetings of Presbyteries and Synods, and by stirring addresses aroused, on behalf of his cause, the energies of the clergy. An interesting speaker he was not ; but there was a moral and an intellectual force about him which was resistless. To his addresses one could listen for hours without a feeling that the speaker had been tedious, or had on his subject said more than was needful. Anecdotes he had none. He used no figures of speech ; he seldom indulged in illustrations ; he did not, more than naturally arose from his line of argument, refer to the higher motives for sustaining the cause of the Gospel. But he was strictly logical and profoundly practical. From his subject he might depart for a time, and those who knew him not might have concluded that

the thread of his discourse was lost ; but he was sure to return,
bringing to his argument new and redoubled force. His
speeches were like the mountain stream which arises in a
crevice of the topmost rock, and is constantly augmented by
the contributions of other hill-streams, till it becomes a vast
torrent, sweeping all before it into the river channel, and
thence into the estuary or the ocean.

James Robertson was son of a farmer at Ardlaw, in the
parish of Pitsligo and county of Aberdeen. He was born on
the 2nd of January, 1803, and at the age of twelve was enrolled as a student of Marischal College, Aberdeen. In 1825
he was elected schoolmaster of his native parish, and in other
three years was preferred to the head mastership of Gordon's
Hospital, Aberdeen. To the church of Ellon he was appointed
in 1832. From the first he preached without notes, and with
that power and energy which characterized all his public appearances, whether in the pulpit or on the platform. In the
non-intrusion controversy he took part with the Conservative
section of the Church, and became the chief auxiliary of Dr.
George Cook in withstanding in the General Assembly the
formidable logic of Dr. Chalmers and Dr. Cunningham. By
Dr. Chalmers he was regarded as one of the ablest of his ecclesiastical opponents, and one of the best intellects in the
Church. After the Disruption of 1843, he was promoted to
the Chair of Church History at Edinburgh, as successor to
Dr. Welsh, and was appointed Secretary to the Bible Board.
These offices afforded him the leisure needful for the prosecution of his great "scheme." How he conducted the duties of
that "scheme" has been partially related. But I may not
attempt in this passing manner to set forth his abundant
labours. These were prosecuted incessantly and often with
the lack of proper rest, till they silently undermined a constitution naturally robust. Dr. Robertson was attacked with
symptoms of illness which clearly proceeded from excess of
work. The best medical aid proved unavailing, and on the
2nd December, 1860, in his fifty-eighth year, he entered into
his rest. His premature decease was a cause of mourning in
all the churches. Though he did not survive to complete his
great scheme, he enjoyed a fair earnest of its accomplishment.
By his labours many desolate localities were blessed with a
provision for the supply of ordinances, and a nucleus was
formed, since, in many instances, filled up, for an endowment
of all the chapels.

A vigorous and untiring worker, Dr. James Robertson was likewise a man of prayer. When he entered on his ministry, he solemnly consecrated himself to God, and resolved by daily prayer to entreat the divine help. He kept his resolution. I met him on two occasions when we were both itinerating on behalf of public objects. He was holding public meetings and canvassing the opulent in support of his great "scheme." I was awakening public interest in the work of commemorating by public memorials, those who had contended in the national defence and struggled in the cause of letters. On these occasions I could hardly conceal my emotion, for I felt deeply that the cause of my illustrious friend was so much better than my own.

Hugh Miller was, like Dr. James Robertson, a native of the north. They somewhat resembled personally. Each had a rugged countenance, with a decided intellectual expression ; each was careless about the graces of utterance, and had a harsh and numusical intonation. Each, it may be added, executed heartily whatever he undertook. With Hugh Miller I had only a single interview : it was in the office of the *Witness* newspaper, when he subscribed the memorial for a civil list pension to Dr. Dick. His conversation impressed me favourably as to his kindly nature. He was very plainly attired in his favourite shepherd tartan dress, in which, with a plaid of the same stuff, and the geologist's hammer in the right side pocket, he was often to be seen on the streets of Edinburgh.

Hugh Miller might not in any garb disguise his intellectual superiority. He had a large head, with a brow square and massive, surmounted by a profusion of thick sand-coloured hair. His eyes were bright and penetrating. I sat beside him in the Edinburgh Royal Society when a paper was read by the Duke of Argyll : he was profoundly attentive. He latterly consented to deliver lectures to the public institutions ; but his manner was unsuited for the lecture-desk. His utterance was constrained ; he spoke in the Cromarty dialect, and his pronunciation was most faulty.

A native of Cromarty, Hugh Miller was born on the 10th October, 1802. His father, who was master of a small trading vessel, perished at sea during his childhood. He was educated at the grammar school by two maternal uncles, who urged him to adopt a learned profession ; but he selected the humble craft of a stonemason. As an operative stone-hewer in the old red sandstone quarries of Cromarty, he achieved those

discoveries in that formation which fixed a new epoch in
geological science. By composing verses at his evening hours
he relieved the toils of labour, and varied the routine of
geological inquiry. He obtained employment in cutting and
lettering gravestones; and in the prosecution of this branch
of his craft, he, in 1828, proceeded to Inverness. In that
place his literary aspirations were encouraged by Mr. Robert
Carruthers, of the *Inverness Courier*, in whose journal he first
appeared as a writer. His literary talents became known, and
he ventured to produce a work chiefly founded on local traditions. The volume appeared in 1835, under the title of
" Scenes and Legends of the North of Scotland." About the
same time he was appointed accountant in a bank at Cromarty,
and improved his domestic condition by marrying a lady of
literary tastes, who had, while he was practising his trade, discovered his genius and frequented his society.

In the veto controversy which agitated the Established
Church, the bank accountant at Cromarty took a deep interest. He warmly supported the cause of the evangelical
party, and in 1839, on the adverse decision of the House of
Lords in the Auchterarder case, produced a pamphlet on the
popular side in the form of a " Letter to Lord Brougham."
This production excited immediate attention, and the author
was invited to undertake the editorship of the newly projected
Witness newspaper. On his editorial duties Mr. Miller entered
in 1840, and his power was at once felt. Had his services
been retained sooner, it might, for the interests of his party,
have been better. As a controversialist he excelled, combining
force of argument with keen and crushing satire. But he will
be remembered chiefly as a geologist. His " Old Red
Sandstone," a book of charming English, and embodying
important scientific discoveries, appeared in 1841. Next
followed his " First Impressions of England and its People."
His " Footprints of the Creator," in reply to the " Vestiges of
the Natural History of the Creation," was published in 1849.
In 1855 he issued his " Schools and Schoolmasters," a work
descriptive of events in the history of his career as a craftsman.
" The Testimony of the Rocks," the most original and exhaustive of all his scientific works, appeared posthumously.
A martyr to brain disease, he died by a pistol-shot inflicted by
his own hand, on the 24th December, 1856. His premature
decease was regarded as a national calamity. The newspaper
which he conducted did not long survive him; it was for its

vitality mainly indebted to his terse and vigorous writing. As a man of science, Hugh Miller was an honour to his country.

Another distinguished Scotsman was my late noble friend James, eighth Earl of Elgin. With this distinguished nobleman I became acquainted in 1856, when I had the honour of inviting him to preside at an open-air meeting for the public inauguration of a movement for raising a national monument to Wallace on the Abbey Craig. His lordship consented to undertake the duty which I had ventured to assign to him; and from what immediately followed I was led to form that high estimate of his honour which I have now the pleasure to record. No sooner was the announcement made that he had consented to preside at the proposed demonstration, than representations were made to him that the undertaking to which he had lent his support must inevitably result in fruitless effort or disgraceful failure. Those who so communicated were influential; their statements were emphatic and precise; and living at Stirling and its neighbourhood, they had the best opportunities of being informed. To his lordship I was a stranger, and, under the circumstances, most persons in his position would have devised some ingenious excuse, and thereupon retired. But his lordship, anxious, if possible, to fulfil his pledge, was frank and open with me. It had been represented, he said, that no speakers from a distance would take part in the proceedings. It was difficult to assure his lordship to the contrary, for while our opponents stated to him on the one hand that no notable speaker would be present, they, on the other, communicated with the speakers as they were successively announced, assuring them that Lord Elgin had changed his mind. Nearly all the speakers credited these assurances, and sent letters of excuse. Lord Elgin remained firm. He was attended by Sir David Brewster, Cluny Macpherson, and some other notables. The meeting was held in the King's Park, Stirling, on the 24th of June, 1856, when twenty thousand persons were present. Lord Elgin made a noble oration, which essentially promoted the national enthusiasm. The success of the movement was no longer doubtful.

Lord Elgin was son of James Bruce, seventh Earl of Elgin, by his second wife, the youngest daughter of James T. Oswald, Esq., of Dunnikier. He was born in Park Lane, London, in 1811, and was educated at Eton and Christ Church. He was distinguished as a classical scholar, and completed his academical career as Fellow of Merton College. In 1841 he married the only daughter of Charles Lennox Cumming Bruce, Esq., whose grandfather, on the mother's side, was the Abyssinian traveller. As Lord Bruce, he was returned to Parliament for Southampton; but having, in 1842, on the death of his father, succeeded to the family honours as Earl of Elgin and Kincardine, he had to resign his seat as a commoner without being entitled, as a Scottish peer, to sit in the House of Lords. In this anomalous position he sought colonial employment, and was offered by Sir Robert Peel and Lord Stanley the office of Governor of Jamaica. In 1846 he was appointed, by the Whig Government, Governor of Canada. During the eight years that he presided in that colony he distinguished himself by a conciliatory policy, and by actively developing the resources of the country. In acknowledgment of his services he was in 1849 honoured with a British peerage.

During the year 1856, Lord Elgin remained at Broom Hall, his Scottish seat. In 1857 he was appointed ambassador to China. On his way thither he received information of the Indian mutiny, and at once gave instructions that the troops ordered to China should be despatched to Calcutta. The decision which he manifested on this occasion, new in the annals of diplomacy, imparted the highest indication yet afforded of his capability in meeting an emergency. His mission to China proved eminently successful. After the taking of Canton, he negotiated the treaty of Tien-tsin, which forms the basis of our present relations with the Celestial Empire. Returning to England, he was in 1859 appointed Postmaster-General in the Government of Lord Palmerston. The Chinese having proved unfaithful to their engagements, he proceeded on a second mission to China, which was attended by the humiliation of the Chinese, and the entrance in state into Pekin of the British representative. Soon after this triumph, Lord Elgin was appointed Governor-General of India. To the duties of this high office he devoted himself with his wonted ardour and intelligence. But a life of active usefulness was hastening to a close. He was assailed by a complication of disorders, culminating in disease of the heart. On the 6th November, 1863, he was informed by his medical attendant that his complaint was mortal. He received the intimation with composure, only expressing some regret that he had not been spared to the accomplishment of certain duties. During his illness, which was often acute and prostrating, he bore himself meekly, and affirmed his entire confidence in the work of a Saviour. Some days before his death he partook of the Holy Communion, and thereafter desired Lady Elgin to select a spot for his grave in the cemetery at Dhurasala. He sent a message to the Queen, expressing his devotion to her service, and desired that his best blessing might be conveyed to the secretaries of the Indian Government. He died on the 30th November. One of the best representatives of the house of Bruce, and a most faithful and enlightened public servant, he had only reached his fifty-second year. The first Lady Elgin died in 1841, and his lordship married secondly, in 1846, the fourth daughter of the first Earl of Durham, by whom he is survived.

In the death of Lord Elgin I felt that I had lost an honourable and true-hearted friend. Without show, without pretext, and seemingly unconscious of any superiority of rank, he delighted to serve all who seemed worthy of his regard. To the friends of his youth, irrespective of their worldly status, he attached himself with a cordial friendship. At Broom Hall, his family seat, he was beloved by old and young. Before he proceeded to India he was presented with his portrait at a public entertainment in Dunfermline, when the leading citizens took part in the demonstration. On his return from his first Chinese expedition I had the honour, at Stirling, of bidding him welcome to Scotland. I shall not soon forget the cordiality of my reception.

In person, Lord Elgin was above the middle height, and was strong, muscular, and well-built. His face was large, with a finely-arched forehead. His manner was frank and unrestrained.

Lord Elgin had returned to Scotland when the administrators of the Wallace Monument Fund were prepared to lay the foundation stone. Of course his lordship was requested to undertake the duty, but he suggested that some noted Scotsman, who had taken an active part in raising the funds, should share in the honours of the enterprise. Sir Archibald Alison was selected, and, in approval of the nomination, and of the proceedings of the day, Lord Elgin sent from Broom Hall the sword of King Robert the Bruce to be carried in the procession.

Sir Archibald Alison was younger son of the Rev. Archibald Alison, author of "Essays on the Nature and Principles of Taste." At the period of his birth his father was incumbent

of Kenley, Shropshire. In the parsonage-house of that parish
he was born, on the 29th December, 1792. His mother was
the youngest daughter of Dr. John Gregory of Edinburgh,
and sister of the more celebrated Dr. James Gregory. His
progenitors on the father's side belonged to the parish of
Kettins, in Forfarshire. In 1800 his father removed to Edinburgh, of which he was a native, and became senior incumbent
of St. Paul's Chapel, Cowgate. The future historian studied
at the University of Edinburgh, and in 1814 was called to the
bar. He did not at once devote himself to forensic practice,
but entered on Continental travel, which he prosecuted at
intervals for eight years. In 1823 he was, under the Conservative Government, appointed an advocate-depute, and he retained office till the close of the Wellington administration in
1830. On the return of the Conservatives to power in 1834
he was promoted as Sheriff of Lanarkshire.

In 1832 Mr. Alison published his "Principles of the
Criminal Law of Scotland," and not long after, his "Practice
of the Criminal Law." But he had chiefly occupied his leisure ·
in accumulating materials for his "History of Europe," a work
which he had projected in his twenty-second year. When, in
1833, the first volume of this work appeared, critics generally
predicted that, notwithstanding certain inequalities of style, it
would, on completion, secure the celebrity of the author. So
it has proved, for Alison's Europe, in twenty volumes, is, with
its literary blemishes and minor errors, the most valuable
history of the French Revolution, and of Continental events
since that period, which has been published. It was continued
by the writer to the period of the Crimean war.

The laborious industry which produced the "History of
Europe" was duly acknowledged. In 1845 the author was
elected Lord Rector of Marischal College, Aberdeen. By the
students of Glasgow he was afterwards honoured with the
rectorship of that university. In 1852 he was created a
baronet; and the University of Oxford conferred on him the
degree of Doctor of Civil Law.

While sedulously devoting himself to literary research—a
constant contributor to *Blackwood's Magazine*, and producing
other works beside his History—Sir Archibald was most
attentive to his duties as a magistrate. From eleven till four
o'clock daily he was to be found in his Court, either seated on
the bench, or discharging the other duties of his office. In his
chambers I frequently visited him to obtain his friendly

counsel or active help in resisting the annoyances to which, as secretary of the Wallace Monument Committee, I was so constantly subjected. Mainly through his assistance the appropriate design of the monument, now executed, was rendered possible.

Sir Archibald was influenced by no personal ambition; his patriotism was untainted by any grain of selfishness. When I invited him to preside at the laying of the Wallace Monument foundation-stone, he informed me that should any one of higher rank be found to undertake the duties, he would willingly retire. This statement he renewed in the following letter, with which he favoured me some ten days before the monumental celebration :—

Glasgow, June 13, 1861.

MY DEAR DOCTOR,

"I learn from Sir J. Maxwell Wallace that he is to be present at the Wallace Monument Demonstration, and the subsequent banquet. He is, I believe, lineally descended from the family of Sir William Wallace, and he is to give £100 to the monument, and his sister, Lady Fairlie, the same. Being a *Lieut.-General*, he will probably be the officer of the highest rank present, and he will therefore answer for the army. Of course you will assign him a suitable position in the proceedings at the laying of the foundation-stone. To the toast 'Lord Clyde, Sir Hope Grant, and their companions in arms,' my son Archy will, as you wish, make a reply. He is singularly enough nineteenth in direct descent from Robert Bruce. It will be curious to have two officers, descendants of Wallace and Bruce, brought forward on this occasion.*

"I will not shrink from the arduous and honourable duties which the committee design for me, if it is deemed in the interest of the meeting that I should do so. But I still think it is an honour much above my social position, and I would gladly yield to any popular nobleman who can speak, and resume my place as croupier. But I place myself entirely in your hands.

"I am, my dear Doctor, yours faithfully,

"A. ALISON."

* General Sir J. Maxwell Wallace was constituted Grand Marshal of the procession, the duties of which he discharged with military precision.

Sir Archibald was a zealous Freemason, and held the Provincial Grand Mastership. I was associated with him as a speaker, when a public building in Lanarkshire was inaugurated under Masonic auspices. He was not particularly happy, yet I felt, in mounting the rostrum as his successor, that my words were as icicles compared with those with which he had just electrified the assembly. He was, indeed, not essentially an orator. He lacked grace of delivery ; his utterances were painfully monotonous, and he failed even in his most impassioned bursts to raise his voice to a pitch befitting the character of his sentiments. At times he was lengthy and painfully minute, especially when he dealt with figures and statistics, for which he retained an unhappy partiality. Yet his public speaking possessed a charm peculiarly its own. Patriotic ardour, and a generous, gushing philanthropy pervaded and permeated his utterances. He delighted to set forth the intellectual and martial glory of old Scotland, and as he celebrated the poetic triumphs and heroic achievements of her sons, neither an expressive intonation nor muscular action were needed to arouse his auditory. After a short illness, he died on the 23rd of May, 1867. No citizen of Glasgow was ever more sincerely lamented. In his decease every patriotic movement in the city lost an advocate, every benevolent institution an effective pleader. Few men in a public office, and of strong political sentiments, gave less offence or were more conciliatory. Though he had possessed no eminence as an historical and controversial writer, or in any other public capacity, he would have been remembered as a generous citizen.

Of equal geniality with the historian of Europe, and an illustrious orator, was my late friend John Thomson Gordon, Sheriff of Midlothian. This accomplished man, whose star set much too soon, was son of John Gordon, M.D., a physician of some standing ; he was born about the year 1812. Called to the bar in 1835, he at once, from his brilliant and captivating address, gave promise of eminence. In 1848 he was, by his uncle, Mr. Andrew Rutherford, subsequently Lord Advocate, recommended to the office of Sheriff of Midlothian, and the appointment was bestowed upon him. Though Sheriff Gordon did not lay claim to extensive attainments as a lawyer, he discharged, so long as his health permitted, his magisterial duties with fidelity and intelligence.

I became acquainted with Mr. Gordon in 1852, when I was guest at a dinner of the Architectural Institute, of which, at that time, he was president. The Sheriff was then in his prime. Tall and well-formed, his appearance was elegant and commanding, and his manners, though abundantly hearty, were not deficient in dignity. As a chairman he might not have been excelled. On every topic he spoke fluently and in appropriate words, while his fine sonorous voice especially recommended him to his auditory. I met the sheriff frequently, both on public occasions and in private society. In the qualities of social companionship he was unrivalled. From a fund of unfailing jocundity he electrified every company. His exuberant joyousness never forsook him ; and at the close of a long meeting, when others were weary, he was still vigorous and eloquent.

On the platform, the sheriff was one of the most powerful orators of his time; among his Scottish contemporaries he had no equal. When he appeared as president of a meeting, he cast into the shade all who spoke after him. Were his speeches recovered and collected, they would hold a place among the best specimens of modern eloquence. But he lacked the concentrativeness necessary to the production of a great work. For social fellowship, it was often said, he sacrificed powers which might have been more usefully employed. This may have been ; yet who will forget an evening spent in the companionship of John Thomson Gordon ! Personal celebrity he sought not ; he was content to be recollected by his friends. After the publication of the memoirs of her father, Professor Wilson, by Mrs. Gordon, I remarked to the sheriff that I liked the work both from its substance and style. He said, "Mrs. Gordon had no assistance from me ; she would not have accepted any. I am charmed with the book, and desire only to be remembered as her husband." He said this with deep feeling.

By the late Prince Consort Mr. Gordon was honoured with a cordial friendship. I met him not long after the Prince's death, and took occasion to refer to the event. "Don't speak of it," he said, feelingly. "I have lamented him as a brother. No man knew I more intimately or understood better. I shall never cease to lament him."

The sheriff was for some years unable fully to discharge his magisterial duties. He afterwards rallied, but his constitution was permanently impaired. In the autumn of 1865 he proceeded to Caen, in Normandy, in the hope of benefiting by the change. He died suddenly at Thury Harcourt, near Caen, on the 22nd September, 1865, about the age of fifty-three.

Sheriff Gordon was one of the three sons-in-law of Professor Wilson, the *Christopher North* of *Blackwood*. Just six weeks before the sheriff's death, another of the sons-in-law passed away. I refer to my late friend, Professor William Edmonstone Aytoun. He was of Norman lineage, and was a cadet of the Aytouns of Inchdairnie. He was born in Abercromby Place, Edinburgh, on the 21st June, 1813. His father, Mr. Roger Aytoun, was a Writer to the Signet, and through his grandmother he represented the old family of Edmonstone of Corehouse. From his mother, a daughter of Keir of Kinmouth, Perthshire, he inherited a taste for Scottish ballad and an attachment to the memory of the cavaliers. He was educated at the University of Edinburgh, and became a Writer to the Signet; he subsequently passed advocate. At the bar he obtained a good practice, but his tastes partook more of a literary than a legal character. He contributed to *Tait's Magazine*, in which, with his early friend, Mr. Theodore Martin, he published the "Bon Gaultier Ballads." His connection with *Blackwood's Magazine* began in 1836, when in that periodical appeared his translations from Uhland. In 1843 he published his "Lays of the Scottish Cavaliers," which at once established his poetical reputation. He was in 1845 elected Professor of Rhetoric and Belles-Lettres in Edinburgh University, an appointment attended with small emolument, but otherwise suited to his tastes. In 1852 he was appointed Sheriff of Orkney, a lucrative office, and of which the duties did not imply a removal from Edinburgh, or an abdication of his professorial functions.

Possessed of an abundant leisure, Professor Aytoun now contributed to nearly every number of *Blackwood's Magazine*, and produced several separate publications. His poem of "Bothwell," which appeared in 1856, did not fulfil the expectations of his admirers, but his "Firmilian, or the Student of Badajoz," a poetical satire on the poets of the spasmodic school, regained his poetical laurels. In 1849 he married Jane Emily, youngest daughter of Professor Wilson; she died on the 15th April, 1859. In 1863 he contracted a second marriage with Fearne Jemima, second daughter of James Kinnear, Esq., Writer to the Signet. After an illness of about a year he died at Blackhills, near Elgin, on the 4th August, 1865, in his fifty-second year.

With Professor Aytoun I became acquainted in 1852. He was then a leading supporter of a short-lived and ill-omened association for the "Vindication of Scottish Rights." The administration of the Society's affairs got into the hands of an individual who, possessing patriotic ardour, unbalanced by common sense, set forth asa chief national wrong, that on a public building in the west of Scotland the Scottish lion was improperly quartered in the national shield. So the Society was laughed down, and the Professor, who had hoped from the movement better things, could never hear of it afterwards but with distaste. Like his friend, the historian of Europe, Professor Aytoun was a zealous Freemason. As Master of the "Canongate Kilwinning" lodge, which is associated with Burns, Hogg, and other celebrities, he increased the popularity of the craft, bringing with him to the interesting lodge-chapel in St. John Street, both as members and visitors, many eminent citizens and men of letters. He was fond of drollery, and could resist no opportunity of practising his facetiousness. During the summer of 1860, I chanced to meet him at dinner, at a fashionable watering-place. The guests were strangers to each other, the Professor being known only to the family of the host and to myself. He talked chiefly with an elderly gentleman, who sat near him, and who had at the commencement of the conversation referred to his holding office as a county magistrate. Conceiving that his new acquaintance valued himself on his magisterial status, he resolved to have some diversion at his expense. Brigandage in Italy was then occupying public attention, and on this theme being introduced the magistrate stated his belief that tranquillity would only be restored by an entire extirpation of the brigands. "Won't do, sir," said the Professor. Brigandage is not an unmitigated evil. Brigands are brave; they take their lives in their hands, and they earn their livelihood by their heroic deeds. Suppose," he continued, "you and I should to-morrow morning go up to the railway station, each provided with a brace of pistols in our vest pockets. Just as a train is starting, we might dart our heads into compartments of first-class carriages, and presenting our pistols at well-to-do solitary travellers, demand an instant surrender. We might, sir, do a good turn of business, and though discovered, we would no doubt be excused for our heroism." "I abhor your proposal," said the indignant J. P., "and will have nothing to do with it." "I could not accomplish it alone," said the Professor. After an interval the magistrate spoke of some of his own decisions in the administration of the Poor Law. The Professor said that he was himself a sheriff, and that he decided

F

quite differently. "Then I cannot commend your law," said the magistrate, who was evidently both puzzled and disgusted with the strange individual into whose society he had been thrown.

We adjourned to the drawing-room, where the Professor and I conversed. The magistrate embraced a convenient opportunity to take me aside, and to inquire whether I knew privately the gentleman with whom I had been talking, remarking at the same time that both his law and his principles were strangely unsound. "Not at all." I replied, "he is a capital lawyer, and is sound every way. He is the sheriff and vice-admiral of the Orkneys, a doctor of the civil law, professor of Rhetoric at Edinburgh, and the principal contributor to *Blackwood*." "Oh! I see, Professor Aytoun, of course. What a facetious dog he is," said the magistrate. "Pray introduce me to him!"

Of Aytoun the following anecdote is related in his memoirs by Mr. Theodore Martin. I give the anecdote in his biographer's words. "Being asked to get up an impromptu amusement at a friend's house in 1844, for some English visitors, who were enthusiastic about Highlanders and the Highlands, he fished out from his wardrobe the kilt with which he had electrified the men of Thurso in his boyish days. Arraying himself in this and a blue cloth jacket with white metal buttons, which he had got years before to act a charity boy in a charade, he completed his costume by a scarf across his shoulders, short hose, and brogues! The brevity of the kilt produced a most ludicrous effect, and not being eked out with the usual 'sporan,' left him very much in the condition of the 'cutty sark' of Burns's poem. With hair like Katterfelto's, on end in wild disorder, Aytoun was ushered into the drawing-room. He bore himself with more than Celtic dignity, and saluted the Southrons with stately courtesy, being introduced to them as the famous Laird of McNab. The ladies were delighted with the chieftain, who related many highly-exciting traits of Highland manners. Among other things, when his neighbours, as he told them, made a foray, which they often did, upon his cattle, he thought nothing of 'sticking a tirk into their powels,' when the ladies exclaimed in horror, 'O laird, you don't say so!' 'Say so!' he replied, 'on my saul, laties, and to pe surely, I to it.' A picture of Prince Charles, which hung in the room, was made the object of profound veneration. At supper he was asked to sing a song. 'I am fery sorry, laties,' he replied, 'that I have no voice; but I will speak to

you a translation of a ferry ancient Gaelic poem,' and proceeded
to chant 'The Massacre of ta Phairshon,' which came upon all
present as if it were the invention of the moment, and was
greeted with roars of laughter. 'The joke was carried on until
the party broke up, and the strangers were not undeceived
for some days as to the true character of the great Celtic
chief."

Though his humour inclined to sarcasm, Professor Aytoun
was radically genial. I remember that at our first interview
he referred to the illness of his gifted father-in-law, Professor
Wilson, in terms which left no doubt as to the intensity of his
affections. He spoke of the Ettrick Shepherd, and others he
had known in early life, with expressions of generous kindli-
ness. In his conversation I could not detect the least self-
assertion. On one occasion he expressed to me his dislike of
memoirs, and his feeling that a man's reputation should rest
solely on his works. I chanced to visit him when he was
preparing notes to his poem of "Bothwell," which was to
appear in a few weeks. I told him how anxiously the public
waited for the poem. He said, " I intend my reputation to
rest upon it." It was to prove otherwise. Though exposing
to ridicule the style of the spasmodic poets, he was most
friendly with several of them, who on their part duly appreciated his kindly nature. With his students he was a universal
favourite ; the attendance at the Rhetoric class rose after his
appointment from thirty to one hundred and fifty.

The third son-in-law of Professor Wilson, my late gifted
friend, Professor James Frederick Ferrier, died at St. Andrews
on the 11th June, 1864, in his fifty-sixth year. He was born
at Edinburgh in November, 1808. His father, John Ferrier,
Writer to the Signet, was son of James Ferrier, who represented an old Norman house, and held the office of a clerk of
Session. His mother, Margaret Wilson, was sister of the
gifted Professor, who became his father-in-law. His aunt,
Susan Edmonstone Ferrier, was the authoress of " Marriage,"
and other celebrated novels. He studied at Edinburgh University, and afterwards proceeded to Oxford, where he graduated. He subsequently travelled and studied in Germany. In
1832 he was called to the Scottish Bar, but it is doubtful
whether he ever sought employment as a lawyer. He was
elected to the Professorship of Universal History in the University of Edinburgh, and became a contributor to *Blackwood's
Magazine* and other serials. In 1845 he was preferred to the

chair of Moral Philosophy at St. Andrews. In 1852 he was candidate for the Moral Philosophy chair at Edinburgh, vacant by the retirement of Professor Wilson, but the Town Council of the city being generally adherents of the Free Church, elected a gentleman who belonged to that communion. The proceedings of the Edinburgh Town Council at this and a subsequent election, led to the patronage of the University being transferred from them to a body of trustees.

As an expounder of ethical science, Professor Ferrier maintained a growing popularity. As a philosophic thinker he was assigned a first rank on the publication of his "Institutes of Metaphysics" in 1854, and when Sir William Hamilton died, soon after, it was held by all save the sectarian traders of the corporation—that no living metaphysician was better fitted for the vacant chair.

Professor Ferrier studied with an incessant perseverance. He almost lived in his library. He entered it after breakfast, and continued in it, with a short respite for an early dinner, till a late hour of the evening. While his colleagues were enjoying their holidays, he sat at home wedded to his books. "You are always here," I said to him one day. "I am not so comfortable elsewhere," was the reply. "My books are around me, and my world is books." "You take an occasional excursion, I hope?" I have not done so for some years. I have no taste for running about." "But you must doubtless enjoy fine scenery? I have just been among the Grampians, seeing waterfalls, and lochs, and moors, and romantic dells, and have greatly enjoyed myself." "I like to read about what you describe, but for some years I have been unable to change my habit of keeping at home." "A great mistake," I persisted; "you will die; you will wear yourself out." "Perhaps," he said, "but I cannot help it." My prediction was unhappily realized. Only a year or two after our conversation, Professor Ferrier was seized with a complication of disorders. For some time he struggled against his ailments; at length he was obliged to delegate to others the duty of conducting his classes. After three years of bad health, he gently sunk into his rest. Apart from his eminence as a metaphysician he was an accomplished general scholar. He was abundantly hospitable, and of conciliatory manners. None who knew him will utter a word in his disprise.

As another contributor to *Blackwood's Magazine*, though he survived some others yet to be named, I would next refer to my late friend Professor George Moir. He was a native of Aberdeen, where he was brought up and educated. With a view to becoming an advocate, he proceeded to Edinburgh, and prosecuted the study of the law. He was called to the Bar in 1825, and amidst a host of brilliant competitors gradually found his way both as a pleader and chamber counsel. In his 25th year he contributed an article on "Spanish Literature" to the *Edinburgh Review*, which he followed by another on the "Lyric Poetry of Spain." In 1831 he began to write for *Blackwood's Magazine*, to which he contributed at intervals for twenty years afterwards. In 1838 he was elected Professor of Rhetoric in the University of Edinburgh, an office which he resigned in 1840, when he was appointed Sheriff of Ross-shire. He was in 1858 preferred to the Sheriffship of Stirling, and in 1864 elected Professor of Scots Law in Edinburgh University. The last appointment he was obliged to relinquish in 1866, from failing health. He died suddenly on the 19th October, 1870, aged seventy-one years.

Professor Moir was short in stature, and in his facial aspects afforded considerable indication of intellectual power. His manner was dry and distant, and his conversation seldom warmed into fervency. But he was withal a kind-hearted man, ready to do a good turn, and to promote any cause worthy of support. He was a keen lover of art, and took an intelligent interest in landscape-gardening. In order to complete the public grounds on the Castle Hill of Stirling, the laying out of which I had devised some years before, I asked Sheriff Moir to contribute to the cost. He replied, that he took a deep interest in improvements of the sort, and would inform me whether he would subscribe after his next visit to Stirling. Some weeks after, he took a solitary walk on the Castle Hill, and was observed to inspect the ornamental grounds from the different prominences. He afterwards wrote me, expressing his admiration of the improvement, and tendering a contribution.

Another Edinburgh professor, entitled to a place in these reminiscences, is my late excellent friend, Sir George Ballingal. This most estimable gentleman was born in the manse of Forglen, Banffshire, on the 2nd May, 1780, his father being the parochial clergyman. He received his school education at Falkland, and afterwards prosecuted medical studies at the universities of St. Andrews and Edinburgh. In 1806 he entered the army as assistant-surgeon in the First Royals, and accompanied his regiment to Madras. He was present at the capture of Java, August 1811, and was surgeon to the 33rd regiment during the occupation of Paris in 1815. Having retired on half-pay, he commenced private practice in Edinburgh. In 1823 he was appointed to the Chair of Military Surgery in Edinburgh University. In 1831 he received the honour of knighthood. He was elected a Fellow of the Royal Society, and of the principal medical societies of Europe. Sir George died at Edinburgh in 1855, aged seventy-five. In the branch of surgery to which his attention was especially directed, he was an enthusiast, and he delighted to communicate his knowledge without professional reserve. He had travelled much, and he related what he had seen in an interesting manner. He rejoiced to yield a helping hand to all who required his aid. An accomplished gentleman, his intercourse was at all times enjoyable.

Professor Pillans I knew only in his old age. He had an exact and most retentive memory, and took pleasure in repeating long passages from his favourite poets. He was an agreeable companion, told capital stories, and could portray the manners of those long departed. Of a generous nature, he was yet careful of his coin ; and had the art of living comfortably without profusion. It is pleasant to recall the venerable form of this professorial veteran of fourscore, and pleasant to think of our last meeting in Yarrow, when he descanted on his recollections of the Ettrick Shepherd, Thomas Campbell, and a host of others. He died at Edinburgh on the 27th March, 1864, in his eighty-sixth year.

Similarly entertaining in recollections of old times was my late gifted friend, Dr. John Strang, City Chamberlain of Glasgow. The son of a Glasgow wine-merchant, and his successor in trade, he early renounced the practice of business, and devoted himself to literary pursuits. In opening manhood he visited France and Italy, and prosecuted philosophical studies in Germany. His first publication was entitled " Tales of Humour and Romance, from the German of Hoffman and others." Having visited some of the chief art galleries of Europe he obtained celebrity as a fine art critic. In 1830 he published, under the pseudonym of Jeoffrey Crayon, jun., " A Glance at the Exhibitions of the Works of Living Artists, under the patronage of the Glasgow Dilettanti Society." During the following year he produced a small volume, entitled " Necropolis Glasguensis," advocating the conversion of the

Fir Park, which adjoined the Cathedral, into a place of public sepulture. This effort resulted in the construction of the Glasgow Necropolis, one of the most picturesque cemeteries in Britain.

In 1832 Dr. Strang edited, during its existence of six months, *The Day*, a Glasgow daily journal, to which he contributed many original compositions, both in prose and verse. His "Travels in Germany," in two octavo volumes, appeared in 1836. Shortly before, he was elected City Chamberlain, an office of which he discharged the duties with most remarkable acceptance. His statistical reports were held in high esteem, and form a local record of no inconsiderable value. His most popular work, "Glasgow and its Clubs," was issued in 1855, as a thick octavo, and soon passed into a second edition. During his last illness he prepared "Travelling Notes of an Invalid," which was published within a few weeks of his decease. He died on the 8th December, 1863, in his sixty-eighth year. He was LL.D. of Glasgow University, and Associate of several of the learned societies. Abundantly hospitable, he rejoiced to see at his table the cultivators of literature and art. He remembered several old Glasgow notables in their everyday life, and could vividly depict their peculiar manners. He was a laborious student, but seldom referred to his literary labours. Of a conciliatory disposition, he disliked controversy, and rejoiced to unite in harmony those who were estranged. His peculiar profile did not at first impress strangers with a proper conception of his powers. In conversation he excelled.

I now pay a tribute to the memory of one whose progress to distinction I watched from boyhood, and whose premature decease I mourned in common with his contemporaries. I refer to the Reverend John Robertson, D.D., Minister of the Cathedral Church, and Vice-Chancellor of the University of Glasgow. This most accomplished and excellent man was born in the city of Perth on the 9th April, 1824. Having in childhood lost his father, his upbringing devolved on his mother, who supported herself by keeping a small shop. As a youth, he was singularly retiring ; avoiding all sports he was constantly with his books. In all his classes he gained the top, and kept it. Before leaving the Grammar School he had mastered and protessed the twenty-four books of the "Odyssey," twelve books of the "Iliad," the "Medea" of Euripides, and the "Œdipus" of Sophocles ; and in his sixteenth year he could read

French and German. He became a student at St. Andrews University in 1840. Thither his fame had preceded him. He was hailed as a prodigy. He excelled in every department of study, and so modestly did he repeat his tasks that he seemed to offer an apology for his excellence. With the exception of another, also a native of Perth, and now a useful clergyman at Edinburgh, I do not remember that any of my fellow-students were so revered for extent and variety of attainments. Mr. Robertson's moral qualities were on a par with his intellectual precocity. When at any meeting of the gownsmen, however stormy, he was known to be on his feet, there was a hush, and each prepared to listen reverently. He had no rival, and he chose as companions the best scholars, or those whom he had known at Perth. He lost his mother when sixteen, and having no other near relative he made St. Andrews his home. At the Divinity Hall his talents were at once recognised by the professors, who took every opportunity to denote their approbation. From the Presbytery of St. Andrews he received licence to preach in February, 1848. Before the close of that year he was, on the invitation of the people, ordained to the pastoral charge of the united parishes of Mains and Strathmartin, in the county of Forfar.

By his flock Mr. Robertson was beloved. He visited from house to house, and so acceptably that the humblest of his people regarded him as a friend. His discourses were conceived in plain words, and delivered with an earnestness which commended his teaching even to the careless. Though seldom absent from his own pulpit, his reputation extended rapidly. In 1852 he was offered the first charge of Stirling, and some time afterwards the office of collegiate minister of St. Andrews Church, Edinburgh. These appointments he declined; but in 1858 he accepted an invitation to become minister of the Cathedral Church, Glasgow. The position was most influential, but none doubted the fitness of the presentee. The University of St. Andrews conferred on him the degree of D.D., and he was appointed Vice-Chancellor of Glasgow College.

At Glasgow Dr. Robertson laboured indefatigably. Interesting himself in the parochial charities, these were, by his efforts, augmented and consolidated. Latterly he undertook extensive labours on behalf of the University. His constitution was never robust, and from early youth he had taxed it severely. He suffered from a languid circulation. Early in 1863 he was seriously ill; but after a period of rest from his public labours, he considerably recruited. But his ailment returned, and he was laid aside from duty of every sort. He had lately married a daughter of Professor John Cook of St. Andrews, and he retired to that city—the scene of his early triumphs—there to be tended by loving and anxious friends. He died at St. Andrews on the 9th January, 1865, and his remains were solemnly interred in the Cathedral burying-ground—the citizens closing their shops during the mournful ceremonial. His memoirs have been published, with some specimens of his pulpit discourses. Yet all who knew him must feel that neither his well-written sermons, nor the appropriate words of his accomplished biographer, bring out with sufficient force the power and energy of his nature. He survives in the hearts of his contemporaries, and of those who profited by his ministerial counsels.

Eminently cheerful, Dr. Robertson much enjoyed the tale of humour. He used to relate an anecdote of Walter Nicoll, the beadle of Mains. Walter paid him a visit at Glasgow, and on Sunday worshipped in the Cathedral. With its noble columns, lofty arches, and elegant, stained windows, it is the most stately place of worship in Scotland. "This is a much finer church than Mains, Walter," said Dr. Robertson, after service, to his visitor. "I'm no sae sure o' that," was the rejoinder. "Indeed," said Dr. Robertson ; "surely you have no fault to find with the Cathedral." After a pause, Walter replied, "She's useless big—she's got nae laft—and she's sair fashed wi' thae pillars ! "

Another distinguished graduate of St. Andrews was the late Dr. Robert Lee of Edinburgh. With this ingenious and learned person I was slightly acquainted. He was born at Tweedmouth, Berwickshire, in November 1804 ; and being of humble parentage was trained as a boat-builder. His father was precentor in the Presbyterian Church, and encouraged him to study for the ministry. After the hours of labour he constructed a boat, which he sold, and with the proceeds repaired to St. Andrews, where he enrolled himself as a university student. He had the usual struggles. Distinguishing himself in his classes he procured teaching, and so obtained the means of support. He entered college in 1824, and eight years afterwards became a licentiate. In 1833 he was elected minister of Inverbrothock Chapel, near Arbroath. He was translated to Campsie, Stirlingshire, in 1836, and in August, 1843, was appointed to Old Greyfriars' Church, Edinburgh.

In 1847 the Professorship of Biblical Criticism in Edinburgh
University, newly instituted, was conferred upon him.   He
was an accomplished scholar.   With the Christian Fathers he
had formed a critical acquaintance, and he was conversant with
ancient and modern literature.   As a preacher he was remarkable for a clear intonation and a distinct utterance.   His
Scriptural expositions were original and ingenious, and those
who doubted the soundness of his conclusions were ever ready
to commend his mode of expressing his convictions.   Many
who had long been strangers to the sanctuary were, by his
preaching, attracted to Old Greyfriars' Church.

  Dr. Robert Lee will be chiefly remembered for his persistent
and successful efforts to render the worship of the Presbyterian
Communion more in harmony with that of other Protestant
churches.   He introduced a modified liturgy in Old Greyfriars'
Church, got his people to stand at praise and kneel at prayer,
and terminated the struggles of liberal Presbyterians, carried
on for half a century, by using an organ.   These enlightened
ameliorations of the Presbyterian ritual were achieved amidst
a course of opposition, and perhaps no other Scotsman would
have mastered the difficulties which he had to surmount.   His
acknowledged learning, and the excellence of his devotional
services, considerably availed him, while his acquaintance with
ecclesiastical polity, and unrivalled powers of debate, proved
overwhelming to his opponents.   None who were present in
the General Assembly of 1859, when the debate on "innovations" was proceeded with, can forget the masterly manner in
which he overturned the arguments of his opponents.   While
an ordinary innovator would have been subjected to censure, ·
he left the bar without rebuke, and without interference with
his congregational arrangements.   Subsequent General Assem-
blies allowed him to take his own course, till more becoming
postures in prayer and praise were actually permitted.   Congregations, too, were allowed to conjoin instrumental music
with the psalmody.

  If his life had been prolonged Dr. Lee would probably have
succeeded in introducing a modified liturgy.   As it was, he
laid the foundation of reforms in the Genevan system, which, as
old prejudices disappear, will unquestionably be carried forward.   He was attacked by paralysis in May, 1867, and died
at Torquay on the 14th March, 1868.   He was a keen controversialist, and smote his antagonists with relentless and cutting sarcasm.   Latterly he forbore the use of offensive weapons.

In early life he was disposed to censure keenly the bigoted and ignorant ; latterly he was more disposed to excuse than to condemn. He was a kind husband, an affectionate father, and a confiding friend. He sought the best interests of the Church of Scotland.

In these "Recollections" I may not omit the name of the late Dr. John Aiton, minister of Dolphinton. This somewhat eccentric but most worthy clergyman was son of Mr. William Aiton, sheriff-substitute of Lanarkshire. Educated at the University of Edinburgh, he was, in 1819, licensed as a probationer. In 1825 he was ordained to the pastoral charge of Dolphinton, where he ministered till his decease. He died at Pyrgo Park, Essex, on the 15th May, 1865, at the age of sixty-five. He was a somewhat extensive writer ; his more esteemed publications being " Clerical Economics : " " Life and Times of Alexander Henderson ; " and " St. Paul and His Localities." An eager disputant, he was uncompromising in the exposure of wrong-doing. Through his unsparing denunciations of certain abuses in the financial concerns of the Church, a better system of administration was inaugurated. Zealous in the cause of missions he sought to establish a special mission to the Jews in Palestine. He was a vigorous advocate of temperance, and a warm upholder of benevolent institutions. An extensive traveller, he delighted to relate his experiences at gatherings of the young, with a view to their improvement. Of a large and ungainly form, with severe features, and generally apparelled in very plain attire, his aspect was repulsive rather than inviting. Nor was his personal ungainliness compensated by pleasing and conciliatory manners. But he was withal of a genial nature ; he was opposed to contention at the law, and rejoiced to reunite the bonds of a severed friendship. He was a warm friend, a faithful pastor, and a true Christian.

Another country minister of great worth was my late ingenious friend, Dr. Patrick Bell of Carmyllie. This most estimable individual, whose name, as the inventor of the reaping machine, is familiar throughout Britain and America, was born early in the century on the farm of Leach, parish of Auchterhouse, Forfarshire. Being a second son, he was destined for the ministry, but he was more inclined to mechanical than theological pursuits. While a college student he invented an instrument for extracting sugar from beet, and contrived an apparatus for producing gas. From boyhood he had fixed his attention on the invention of a machine to supersede female labour in the reaping of corn. After many failures he succeeded in realising his object, and in the autumn of 1826 first applied his machine to the harvest-field.

In 1828 Mr. Bell's reaper assumed the form in which it is used now. But the importance of the invention was not recognised till long afterwards, and the inventor, a licentiate of the Church, was obliged to accept employment as a tutor in Canada, nothing better having offered. In 1843 he returned to Scotland, when he obtained the church living of Carmyllie. In this retired parish he laboured with exemplary fidelity. No inventor was more unpretentious or less of a self-seeker. Many of his clerical brethren were, long after his appointment to Carmyllie, unaware that he had invented the reaper ; and when, at a reaping-machine exhibition at Stirling in 1853, I introduced him as the inventor to a member of the Highland Society, I was supposed to labour under a mistake. In 1867 he read to the British Association at Dundee a paper setting forth the history of his invention. At length public attention awakened to his claims. The Highland Society proposed a testimonial. He was presented with a thousand guineas and some valuable articles of plate. The University of St. Andrews offered him the degree of LL.D. He did not long survive his honours ; he died at Carmyllie on the 22nd April, 1869.

Sir James Young Simpson, Bart., I claim only as an occasional correspondent. The son of an operative baker at Bathgate he was intended for the same trade. He entered on the first stage of it, but his aspirations pointed to a higher destiny. Through the assistance of an elder brother he entered the University of Edinburgh. In 1832 he took his degree of M.D., while in his twenty-first year. He became assistant to John Thomson, Professor of Pathology, and began to deliver extra academic lectures on obstetric science. In 1840 he was preferred to the chair of Midwifery. Success attended him from the first, and ere long his eminence was recognised. In 1847 he applied chloroform as an anæsthetic, thereby conferring one of the greatest boons which has ever been bestowed upon mankind. At first he used the anæsthetic in obstetric practice only. Some objected, quoting the words of the primeval curse, "in sorrow shalt thou bring forth children." When every argument had failed to satisfy the objector's scruples, he mentioned that Adam was thrown into a deep sleep, when the rib which formed Eve was extracted from him. This last argument never failed him.

Another anecdote may be related. He sought to improve every moment of his time. He was in 1848 waiting for a ferry-boat, and a patient afterwards expressed regret that his valuable time should have been wasted. "Not at all," said the Professor, "I was all the time chloroforming the eels." In 1852 he was elected President of the Royal College of Physicians. Other honours followed. The University of Oxford conferred D.C.L., and the leading medical and scientific associations of Europe bestowed their honours. In 1866 he was created a baronet. In 1869 he was placed on the roll of the honorary burgesses of Edinburgh. He was an accomplished archæologist. His contributions to the Scottish Society of Antiquaries evince painstaking research, with no inconsiderable powers of concise and correct description. He was a true philanthropist. During the latter years of his life he sought the best means of improving the salubrity of hospitals and reformatories. A reformer of morals, he endeavoured to check the progress of disease by promoting the laws of social order. An exemplary Christian, he would frequently, in the evening of days spent in the sick room, address meetings of earnest persons assembled for the purposes of devotion. He died of heart-disease, after a short illness, on the 6th of May, 1870. His remains were followed to Warriston Cemetery by a procession greater than probably ever before assembled at a public funeral in the city of Edinburgh.

His appearance was striking. His head was large, and a profusion of long tangled hair rested on a countenance displaying a brent brow, soft piercing eyes, a somewhat coarse nose, with dilated nostrils, and a well-chiselled mouth. His look was thoughtful, and an activity of glance and motion showed that his time was not to be wasted. He was compactly built, and of short stature.

To indulge in panegyric on the memory of one whose recent premature departure was so universally deplored, were inappropriate. He had fulfilled his mission ; and the example of professional ardour, large-hearted benevolence, and earnest piety, which he left behind, cannot be unfruitful. Some verses, which he composed at Geneva a few years previous to his death, may not unsuitably sum up these brief allusions to his history :—

"Oft 'mid this world's ceaseless strife,
 When flesh and spirit fail me,
I stop and think of another life,
 Where ills can ne'er assail me.

When my wearied arm shall cease its fight,
    My heart shall cease its sorrow,
And this dark night change for the light
    Of everlasting morrow.

" On earth below there's nought but woe,
    E'en earth is gilded sadness ;
But in heaven above there's nought but love,
    ' With all its raptured gladness :
There—till I come—waits me a home,
    All human dreams excelling,
In which, at last, when life is past,
    I'll find a regal dwelling.

" Then shall be mine, through grace Divine,
    A rest that knows no ending,
Which my soul's eye would fain descry,
    Though still with clay 'tis blending,
And, Saviour dear, while I tarry here,
    Where a Father's love hath found me,
Oh ! let me feel—through woe or weal—
    Thy guardian arm around me ! "

My late distinguished friend, Dr. Henry Cooke of Belfast, was associated with some Scottish affairs, and I will therefore be pardoned for noticing him. He was born at Maghera, in the county of Derry, on the 11th May, 1788. At the University of Glasgow he obtained a respectable acquaintance with the classics, and studied theology. As a licentiate of the Irish Presbyterian Church, he preached acceptably ; but his first appearances did not foreshadow his future eminence. In 1808 he was ordained Presbyterian minister at Duneane, in the county of Antrim. In 1811 he was translated to Donegore, in the same county ; and in 1818 was preferred to the Presbyterian congregation at Killyleagh, in County Down. By an influential body of Presbyterians at Belfast he was, in 1820, invited to undertake the charge of a new congregation ; and on his acceptance of the call, a place of worship in May Street was erected for his use. Crowds flocked to his ministrations, and he was hailed as the most powerful preacher in the north of Ireland.

The Presbyterians in Ireland had, like their English brethren, deviated in numbers from a strict adherence to their Church standards, as set forth in the Books of Discipline and the Westminster Confession. When Dr. Cooke entered on his ministry, the doctrines of Arius were professed and preached by a considerable number of the clergy. Against this defection he zealously protested: At a public discussion with the most eloquent of the Arians, Dr. Henry Montgomery, he over-whelmed that champion of the heterodox creed. Montgomery retired from the Presbyterian connection, and with his adherents formed a new Synod.

Recognised as the greatest debater in the Presbyterian Church of Ireland, Dr. Cooke was challenged by the Voluntary advocate, Dr. John Ritchie of Edinburgh, to a public discussion on church establishments. It took place at Belfast. Dr. Cooke maintained the cause of Establishments with a splendour and force of eloquence which surprised even his admirers. In connection with the debate I may mention an incident. Dr. Ritchie had assailed the memory of Lord Castlereagh, by characterising his act of suicide as " his last and best." After a few words, deprecating the allusion, and exhorting to sentiments of charity, Dr. Cooke added, " Shall we not rather hope, in the words of Sterne, that the recording angel dropped a tear upon the act, and blotted it out for ever ?" The Scottish advocate of Voluntaryism never recovered the onslaught of the Belfast orator.

Having overcome two noted champions of debate, Dr. Cooke ventured to challenge Daniel O'Connell, who was then prosecuting his repeal agitation ; but the agitator declined to enter the lists with him. Informed that O'Connell had described him as the " Cock of the North," Dr. Cooke said, " I hope, like the cock which startled the erring apostle, " I may bring him to repentance." His power of humour was of a first order. A temporary place of worship—constructed of timber—had been erected near the Arian meeting-place of Dr. Montgomery, much to the annoyance of that gentleman's daughter, a smart girl of twenty, who described it " only fit for cows." " Yes," said Dr. Cooke, " and there will be milk there—not the milk Miss Montgomery thinks of, but the sincere milk of the Word."

He was appointed President of the Presbyterian Theological Institute at Belfast, and Professor of Sacred Rhetoric and Catechetics in the Institution. As a professor, he excelled less as a lecturer than as a painstaking instructor in the elements of Christian doctrine. His only published writings consist of some controversial papers and pulpit discourses, and notes to Browne's Self-Interpreting Bible. Public speaking, whether on the platform or in the pulpit, was his forte. His enunciation was clear and forcible, and he possessed a remarkable fluency. I have heard him preach. It was one of his last pulpit appearances, and when he was on the verge of four-score. The discourse was long, and a little rambling, but there were few commonplaces and some eloquent references to passing events.

Dr. Cooke was eminently benevolent. On one occasion he offered to part with his watch on behalf of a charity; and when his church in May Street was erected, he specially requested that a portion of the gallery should be reserved for the use of the poor. He delighted to aid the deserving and relieve the unfortunate. When a ministerial brother was in difficulty, he was sure to experience in Dr. Cooke a sympathizing friend and judicious counsellor. Though warm in debate, he was in private kind and conciliatory. One of his last public acts was to accompany to their last resting-place the remains of his former rival, Dr. Montgomery. Unconscious of intellectual superiority, he was entirely free from self-assertion. I had ventured to compliment him on his powers of debate. " My discussion with Ritchie," he said, "you probably refer to. I overcame him simply because I trusted to my memory; while he was occupied, when I was speaking, in taking notes, and so lost himself."

In personal appearance he was tall and spare. He had a fine open countenance, with a commanding forehead, prominent nose, and eagle eye. He excelled in conversation, and was a favourite alike in the hall of the opulent and in the sick-chamber of the poor. He died on the 13th December, 1868, at the age of eighty. He was sincerely lamented. His congregation hastened to rear to his memory an appropriate cenotaph in the vestibule of May Street Church, and the Belfast citizens have resolved to commemorate him by a monumental statue.

Dr. Robert Chambers, one of my earliest friends, died at St. Andrews on the 17th March, 1871. When I last saw him in August, 1869, he was in feeble health ; he believed, he said, that the end was near. He had been an indefatigable worker, especially at an early period, and had, to some extent, under-mined a constitution naturally robust. Of all my literary friends, he was the most benevolent and amiable ; I never heard him utter unkindly sentiments even of the erring ; he was disposed to excuse and compassionate, rather than con-demn. With a fine open countenance, which literally glowed with benignity, he won the affections of all who knew him ; he has probably not left an enemy. His services in connection with cheap literature will prove his more lasting memorial ; but few of his writings could be spared.

He was born on the 10th July, 1802, at Peebles, where his father, James Chambers, conducted business as a manufacturer. On account of reverses in trade his father removed to Edinburgh in 1813, with his family of six young children. Robert had already passed through a course of classical study at the Grammar School, and in his private reading had exhausted the stores of a circulating library. In his twelfth year he began to peruse the *Encyclopædia Britannica*, which supplied to him the want of university training. Thrown very much on his own resources, he became a dealer in old books; he afterwards joined his elder brother William as a bookseller and printer. In 1822-3 he produced his "Traditions of Edinburgh," a work which brought him prominently into notice, and has maintained its popularity. Then followed in succession his "Popular Rhymes of Scotland," his "Picture of Scotland," his "Histories of the Scottish Rebellions," three volumes of "Scottish Ballads and Songs," and his "Lives of Eminent Scotsmen." When his brother William started *Chambers's Edinburgh Journal* in February, 1832, he became a most efficient coadjutor. To the early volumes he contributed many admirable essays, which have latterly been reproduced. In 1851 he published "The Life and Works of Robert Burns," in four volumes ; and in 1858-61, in three octavo volumes, "The Domestic Annals of Scotland." In 1861 he produced "The Book of Days," one of the most laborious and interesting of his publications.

In the proceedings of scientific and other learned societies at Edinburgh, Robert Chambers for many years took a deep interest. He was an accurate antiquarian scholar, and his two acknowledged geological works, "Ancient Sea Margins of Scotland," and "Tracings of Ireland," are justly held in estimation. The authorship of the "Vestiges of the Natural History of Creation" is correctly assigned to him ; but this work, though abounding in ingenious and startling speculation, does not evince the philosophical acuteness which is to be remarked in his other writings. In January, 1863, he received from the University of St. Andrews the honorary degree of Doctor of Laws. From 1861 to 1863 Dr. Chambers resided in London; he subsequently removed to St. Andrews, where he enjoyed the invigorating game of golf, and in comparative retirement prosecuted his peculiar studies. In his death Scotland lost a powerful and effective illustrator, science an intelligent and earnest expositor, and the brotherhood of letters the most genial and generous of its members.

The last in this chapter to be named is Sir Roderick Impey Murchison, Bart. With this illustrious person I was privileged to enjoy a slight and brief acquaintance. He was one of the first who joined the Grampian Club, which I had the honour to originate, and I had occasion to wait on him about the business of the institution. His manners were most courteous, and he was abundantly communicative. He carefully attended to the affairs of business, and was punctual in his arrangements and correspondence. He rejoiced in his scientific and other honours; otherwise he seemed unconscious of superiority. He was cautious in joining new enterprises, but tenacious in upholding any undertaking to which he had attached himself. He was abundantly patriotic and judiciously generous. He retained his natural vivacity till his last illness, and so long as his physicians permitted, held intercourse with his friends. Any detailed sketch of his career would here be out of place. His name is inscribed in the scientific annals of his country. Geological science must extend greatly, and geographical discovery be prodigiously expanded, ere the name of Murchison is forgotten. Sir Roderick died at London on the 23rd October, 1871, in the seventy-ninth year of his age.

SCOTTISH MINSTRELS.

IN his personal character Robert Burns has been much mis-represented. He erred—grievously so—but he was not irre-ligious. From his father he inherited a respect for piety and a reverence for the Scriptures. Tent-preaching, with the irre-gularities which attended it, he denounced and ridiculed—wisely so. Several clergymen and others he assailed rashly; but while he censured some he should have spared, his satire in other instances subserved the cause of morals. In 1856, when on a visit to Ayrshire, I spent an afternoon with Mrs. Begg, the poet's sister. She was verging on eighty, but retained her faculties, including perfect hearing and memory. She spoke of the bard in terms of deep affection. She remembered him well; she was five-and-twenty when he died. Before his re-moval to Dumfriesshire she saw him constantly. Their father died when she was about twelve years old, and Robert became head of the house. He took their father's place in conducting household worship, and instructed his younger sister, my infor-mant, in the shorter catechism. "He was as a father to me," said Mrs. Begg, "and any knowledge of the Scriptures I had in my youth I derived from his teaching. His whole conduct in the family," she added, "was becoming and orderly." She did not remember that he ever deviated from the strictest sobriety.

Mrs. Begg spoke much of her brother's genius, and seemed to feel strongly that great as his fame was, his merits had not been duly recognised. I spoke of the approaching centenary of his birth, and ventured to predict that a demonstration would attend it, which would show her that the poet held a deep place in the national affections. She did not survive to witness the full realization of my augury, but she knew of the preparations.

The facial aspects of the bard, Mrs. Begg assured me, were striking. "His countenance," she said, "beamed with genius, and those meeting him on the highway turned round to have a second look at him." I remarked that I understood that his eye was penetrating. "He had dark eyes," she replied, "and a quick discerning glance, but every feature was kindled up with thought and feeling. Most of his engraved portraits are incorrect; some bear scarcely a resemblance. She regarded Beugo's engraving, and a lithograph by Schenck and Macfarlane, as the best likenesses. The poet's forehead, she said, was nigh, and the top of his head was flat. This latter peculiarity I afterwards observed in the cast of his skull.

Respecting Burns's general appearance I obtained some particulars in 1859, from an aged tradesman who lived at St. Ninians, Stirlingshire. This person, who was in his ninety-third year, informed me that during a visit to Ayr in 1786, he saw Burns in the course of a canvass for subscribers to the first edition of his poems. He retained a distinct recollection of his appearance; he was pointed out to him as a clever ploughman who had written capital verses. He wore a slouched cap, a striped vest, and a long overcoat. He was rather robust, and had a thoughtful quick look. Every one spoke of him with respect.

With the poet's eldest son, Robert, I was a little acquainted. When I knew him he was living in Dumfries. He was a considerable scholar, and was fond of speculations in etymology. His head was somewhat bald, and bore a striking resemblance to his father's cranium. There was little resemblance otherwise between the poet and his eldest son; for though the latter composed songs, these were under mediocrity. His reminiscences of the bard were interesting. He was ten years old when his father died, and he remembered him distinctly. In the family library were included the works of the principal English poets, and his father encouraged him to read them. But my informant did not know, during his father's lifetime, that he had himself composed verses, and at first could not comprehend what was meant when so many persons after his death spoke to his mother about *the poet*. Burns sought no celebrity in his household.

The poet's two younger sons, Colonels William Nicol and James Glencairn Burns, I long knew. The former died lately (21st February, 1872), in his 81st year. Colonel James Burns bore a little resemblance to his father, and he unhappily inherited from him a tendency to rheumatism. At the Glasgow City Hall Banquet of the centenary celebration, he supplied the information that his father expressed himself to his mother in these words, " Jean, an hundred years hence they'll think o' me mair than they do now."

As an officer of excise, Burns was most attentive to his duties. This was lately ascertained under peculiar circumstances. A chief officer of excise in London had conceived a strong prejudice against the bard, and, Mrs. Stow-like, had resolved to extinguish his claims to respect by examining his accounts and proving them inaccurate. The result of his inquiry removed his prejudices and established the poet's character for business. His entries in the excise books were found to be neatly and carefully made, and every account was correct. "A first-rate man of business," said the examiner, "could not have been more methodical or more accurate."

Respecting the bard's latter habits, I obtained from the late Rev. Thomas Tudor Duncan, M.D., minister of the New Church, Dumfries, some interesting particulars. His father, the Rev. George Duncan, minister of Lochrutton, a man of genial manners and enlightened character, extended to the poet, when he first came to Dumfries, a generous hospitality. Mr. Duncan taught his sons, Henry, afterwards minister of Ruthwell, and my informant, then youths under seventeen, to regard him as a literary prodigy. At Lochrutton manse, Burns met country gentlemen and other leading persons of the district, and on these occasions conducted himself respectably. Reports, however, arose that at Dumfries he chose low company, and indulged in social excesses. For some time the minister of Lochrutton discredited the rumours; but at length it was impossible wholly to disregard them. Most reluctantly he felt called on to discontinue his invitations; others who had hospitably entertained the poet also gave him the cold shoulder.

In a well written " History of Dumfries " by my ingenious friend, Mr. William M'Dowall, the fact that Burns was at this stage of his career abandoned by many of his old friends is minutely set forth. Mr. M'Dowall writes : " During an evening in the autumn of 1774, when High Street, Dumfries, was gay with fashionable groups of ladies and gentlemen passing down to attend a county ball in the Assembly Rooms, Burns was allowed to pass with hardly a recognition on the shady side of a street. Mr. David M'Culloch of Ardwell, noticing the circumstance, dismounted, accosted the poet, and proposed that he should cross the street. 'Nay, nay, my young friend,'

said the bard, 'that's all over now.' After a pause, he quoted
two verses of Lady Grizel Baillie's ballad:—

> 'His bonnet stood ance fu' fair on his brow,
> His auld ane look'd better than mony ane's new;
> But now he lets 't wear ony way it will hing,
> And casts himself dowie upon the corn-bing.
>
> 'O! were we young, as we aince ha'e been,
> We sud ha'e been galloping down on yon green,
> And linking it over the lily-white lee;
> And werena my heart light, I wad dee.'"

The gift of genius will not excuse the infraction of social
order and its laws; and Burns was not condemned rashly.
His poetical reputation was at its zenith. By many of the
most distinguished persons in North Britain he had been
hailed and feasted; from following the plough he had been
received into the best Edinburgh society; he maintained a
correspondence with eminent men, and intelligent women; and
though for the present a gauger, he knew there was a disposition to elevate him to a collectorship of excise. He had, therefore, many inducements to maintain a correct deportment,
while his religious upbringing and his own sense of what was
due both to God and man, likewise demanded carefulness of
conduct. Yet he fell into a snare. It was proper that he
should pay the penalty. He did so, and it was 'a severe and
terrible one. He had a tendency to heart disease, and it cannot be doubted that the agony which he endured in the with-
drawal of friendship accelerated the progress of the malady
which latterly fettered and crushed him. In the possession of
Mr. Gracie, of Dumfries, son of the poet's old friend, Mr.
James Gracie, banker, I have seen a volume of Dr. Blair's
Sermons, which, containing discourses on calumny and the
ingratitude of the world, presents on the margin pencil annotations by the poet confirming the preacher's words, and apply-
ing them to his own case. Local prejudices linger with a
powerful tenacity. When an English gentlewoman visited
Dumfries in 1814, she found, as she has related in a printed
tour, that Burns was chiefly talked of as a libertine; and
sentiments of a similar character have been expressed to myself in Dumfries within the last twenty years.

One virtue Burns possessed pre-eminently, and none of his
detractors have denied him the credit of it. I refer to his

independence. My father used to relate the following anecdote, which he probably received from Allan Masterton. The
poet was dining with his friend and patron, Lord Glencairn.
Opposite to him sat a young English nobleman, who, presuming
that the poet was a clown for whom the host had conceived an
ill-judged fancy, filliped some drops of wine from his wine-
glass into his face. The bard looked up and perceived the
insult. Taking up his wine-glass, he dashed the contents at
the aggressor, saying, " In our country, my lord, we do it
thus." The nobleman wiped his face, and offered an apology.

For some years I held in my possession the original MS. of
Burns's ode, " Scots Wha Ha'e." It was appended to a letter
addressed to Captain Miller of Dalswinton. The letter is in
these words :—

" DEAR SIR,—The following ode is on a subject which I
know you by no means regard with indifference :—

> " ' O liberty—
> Thou mak'st the gloomy face of nature gay,
> Giv'st beauty to the sun, and pleasure to the day.'

It does me so much good to meet with a man whose honest
bosom glows with the generous enthusiasm, the heroic daring
of liberty, that I could not forbear sending you a composition
of my own on the subject, which I really think is in my best
manner, &c.

" ROBERT BURNS."

By a son of Captain Miller the letter was presented to Mr.
Wallace, of Kelly, M.P. for Greenock, as the supposed head
of the Wallace family, and therefore its proper custodier. On
the death of Mr. Wallace, it passed to his brother, Lieut.-
General Sir James Maxwell Wallace. Sir James mounted the
letter in a mahogany frame, and with a view to its being
finally deposited in the Wallace Monument at Stirling, placed
it in my hands. When I left Scotland in 1863, I returned it
to Sir James. After his death in 1867, it was, at a public
auction, sold by his survivors, and purchased by a stranger.

Persons of genius, it is believed, inherit their powers chiefly
from their mothers. In the case of Robert Burns this opinion
is not verified. His sister, Mrs. Begg, assured me that their
mother's mental qualities were very ordinary. " But our

father," she added, "was possessed of decided intellectual
vigour, and would unquestionably have made a figure but for
the continual pressure of poverty. He foresaw the future
eminence of my brother Robert ; he said to my mother, when
the boy was only eight or ten, ' Rob is a genius, and some day
the world will know it.' He said so thoughtfully ; and my
mother, who had great faith in his sentiments, cherished his
words."

It is to be regretted, that amidst their enthusiasm for the
name of Burns, Scotsmen have not been very systematic in the
acknowledgment of his claims. Till her two sons in India
were enabled to support her, Jean Armour, the poet's widow,
and the heroine of his songs, was maintained chiefly through
the bounty of Lord Panmure. A nephew of the poet is at
present a lunatic patient in the poor-house of Govan, where,
too, her countrymen permitted the daughter of the compiler
of " Bibliotheca Britannica " to be supported by parochial
charity.

The triumphs which attended the lyric genius of Burns
brought forward a host of competitors for the poetic wreath.
Of these, the majority have passed away and are forgotten.
One eminently entitled to remembrance is Robert Tannahill.
This ingenious song-writer was born at Paisley on the 3rd June,
1774. With a limited education at school, he became a hand-
loom weaver in his native town. In 1807 he published a
volume, entitled " Poems and Songs," and several of the compositions which it contained at once passed into celebrity.
The Ayrshire Bard has produced no songs superior to " Jessie
the Flower o' Dunblane," " Bonnie Wood o' Craigie Lea,"
" Loudoun's Bonnie Woods and Braes," and " The Braes o'
Balquhither."

From Matthew Tannahill, a younger brother of the Paisley
Bard, I obtained some particulars of his history. He began to
compose verses in boyhood, while his schoolfellows were at
play. Free of vanity in its more degrading forms, he was
abundantly conscious of poetic skill ; and being disappointed
in obtaining recognition from George Thomson, the correspondent of Burns, or from Archibald Constable, the publisher,
he became melancholy and depressed. To relieve disappointed
hopes he had recourse to stimulants. To his brother, my
informant, he began to complain of a prickling sensation in
his head. " You should give up drinking," said Matthew,
" for I've heard that such a feeling often precedes insanity."

Robert promised, but the resolution came too late. During a visit to Glasgow he exhibited symptoms of lunacy. On his return home he complained of illness, and took to bed. His brother, who attended him, left him in the evening about ten, believing that he was better. On returning two hours afterwards, he found the bed empty, and perceived that he had gone out. With the neighbours he made a search, and at length discovered the poet's lifeless body in the river Cart. Tannahill terminated his own life on the 17th May, 1810, at the age of thirty-six. With a generosity eminently characteristic of them, the inhabitants of Paisley provided an annuity for Matthew Tannahill, the poet's brother, when, from old age, he was incapacitated for labour. In countenance he much resembled his brother Robert, and his portrait is made to represent the poet in several editions of his works.

In a solitary nook at Aberfoyle, resided, a few years ago, two solitary females, where they were discovered by a clerical friend, who, at my request, obligingly sought them out. These were the widow and daughter of William Glen, author of the song "Waes me for Prince Charlie." Glen died in 1826, in his thirty-seventh year, and, according to his wife's statement his MSS. soon after disappeared. One volume fell into the hands of Mr. Gabriel Neil, an ingenious antiquary at Glasgow, who kindly placed it at my disposal. From its pages I selected several good songs, and published them. Glen was unfortunate in business, and the depressed condition of his affairs led to the dispersion of his MSS., and nearly bereft him of posthumous fame.

Next to Burns in rank, as a national song-writer, is Carolina Oliphant, Baroness Nairne. This excellent gentlewoman was, according to papers in her family, born at Gask, Perthshire, on the 16th August, 1766 ; but if we are to credit the baptismal register of her parish, on the same day of the preceding month. She was third daughter of Laurence Oliphant, of Gask, the representative of a house claiming descent from Robert the Bruce, and a zealous adherent of the House of Stuart. She was named Carolina, in honour of Prince Charles Edward.

From her youth Carolina composed verses. She was a zealous admirer of Burns, and about the period that the Ayrshire Bard became a contributor to Johnson's *Museum*, she commenced to substitute songs of a pure and wholesome character for the unrefined words associated with certain popular

airs. In 1792 she produced her first song, a new version of
" The Ploughman." It was sung at a public dinner given by
her brother to the Gask tenantry, on his succeeding to the
paternal estates. The death of the first-born of a dear friend
led her to compose the " Land o' the Leal." The history of
this composition is interesting. Her school companion, Mary
Anne Erskine, daughter of the Episcopal clergyman at Muthill,
married, in 1796, Archibald Campbell Colquhoun, of Killermont, Sheriff of Perthshire. About a year after her marriage
Mrs. Colquhoun gave birth to a daughter. When about a
year old, the child sickened and died ; and to console the
afflicted mother, Carolina sent her the verses of the " Land o'
the Leal," which soon afterwards found a place in the collections. In 1806 she married her cousin, Major William Murray
Nairne, who by the reversal of an attainder afterwards became
Baron Nairne. After their marriage, Major and Mrs. Nairne
resided at Edinburgh, where the Major held office as Assistant-
Inspector of Barracks. After his death, which took place in
1830, Lady Nairne lived in England and Ireland, and afterwards at Brussels and Paris. At Brussels, in December, 1837,
she sustained heavy affliction, by the death, in his twenty-
ninth year, of her only son, the sixth Lord Nairne. In 1843
she returned from the Continent to her native Gask, where she
expired on the 26th October, 1845, at the advanced age of
seventy-nine. Her songs " Caller Herrin'," " The Laird o'
Cockpen," " The Lass o' Gowrie," " Wha'll be King but
Charlie," " The Hundred Pipers," and others, have obtained a
celebrity equal to the best songs of Burns.

Of a singularly retiring nature, Lady Nairne sought to avoid
distinction as an authoress. From the few friends to whom
she communicated the secret of her minstrelsy, she exacted a
promise that they would not reveal the origin of her songs.
While she lived her secret was preserved, but after her death
her relatives wisely resolved to do honour to her memory, by
publishing her best songs with music. More recently I have
presented her compositions in a compact little volume, accompanied with a memoir. In so doing I experienced some difficulty, for in the repositories of some of her correspondents
her MSS. had got mixed up with those of others. Even in
carefully preparing a second edition, I was led to include in
the volume three compositions which more recent information
has satisfied me were written by others.

Sir Walter Scott was descended from the Scotts of Harden,

the elder branch of the great Border sept of that name. There is a curious similarity in the aspects of these Scotts. An engraved portrait of the late Mr. William Scott, of Teviot Bank, might be accepted as that of the author of " Waverley." The facial lineaments of the poet are common to his clan. They are of the Saxon type—rugged, massive, heavy, almost stolid. Scott's *bonhommie* was derived from his maternal ancestors. The Rutherfords were genial, cultivated people—of mild and retiring manners. A cousin of Sir Walter, the late Mr. Robert Rutherford, Writer to the Signet, I have met. With others he joined in expressing admiration of his illustrious relative, but he shrunk from referring to his relationship. He was extremely diffident.

Scott, it is well known, was ambitious of founding a family. He more valued his descent from the Haliburtons than from the Scotts. From the former he inherited a right of sepulture in Dryburgh Abbey ; and he was at pains to print for his family use, " Memorials of the Haliburtons." Except in possessing a pedigree, they were undistinguished.

Sir Walter did not marry very fortunately. Lady Scott was not expert as a household manager, nor did she compensate by feminine graces for lack of housewifery. Her mother was a Frenchwoman, and having acquired French manners, she never abandoned them. English she spoke imperfectly, substituting *de* for *the*, and otherwise betraying ineptitude in mastering the British tongue. There is a history connected with her early life and marriage which has been very partially related.* In 1796, Williamina Stuart, daughter of Sir John Stuart of Fettercairn, gave Scott her final " No," after a suit which he had prosecuted with juvenile ardour and persistence. During the same year he experienced a second heartstroke in the unexpected marriage of his friend, William Erskine's sister, to Mr. Colquhoun of Killermont. Whatever were his intentions towards the latter, the young lady herself believed that her marriage would cause him some disquietude, for in the immediate prospect of it she wrote him an epistle (inserted by Mr. Lockhart in the " Memoir,") in which she endeavours to offer him some consolation. When in this letter she alludes to " a dark conference they had lately held together," I incline to think that she refers to the Williamina rejection being confided to her.

* " The note at pp. 40-42 of my friend Mr. Gilfillan's " Life of Sir Walter Scott," was communicated by me.

Stung by unsuccessful love-making in one, if not in two instances, Scott resolved to compensate himself for wounded feelings and disappointed hopes. With Miss Erskine, the daughter of a poor Episcopal clergyman, he would not have added to the family fortunes; it had been far otherwise if his suit had prospered with Williamina Stuart, who was an heiress. Scott was, however, drawn to Williamina from no worldly or mercenary considerations. Their mothers were early friends, and he loved her with his whole heart. But his love experiences had chilled him not a little ; and probably he now contemplated an alliance which might render him independent of his profession as an advocate, which had heretofore done little for his finances or his fame. On the rising of the Court of Session in July 1797, he accompanied his brother John, and their friend, Adam Fergusson, in a tour to the English Lakes. After visiting Carlisle, the vale of Eamont, Ulswater, and Windermere, they rested at the little spa of Gilsland. There Scott first met Charlotte Margaret Charpentier.

The circumstances of the meeting are not very circumstantially related by Mr. Lockhart. I have obtained some details which I think may be relied upon. Arthur, Earl of Hillsborough, afterwards second Marquess of Downshire, resolved, while in his twenty-second year, to make the Continental tour, and obtained from the Rev. Mr. Burd, an early friend, letters of introduction to M. Jean Charpentier of Paris, who held office as provider of post-horses to the royal family. This introduction was attended with unhappy consequences, for Charlotte Volere, the wife of M. Charpentier, flattered by the attentions of the young English nobleman, foolishly eloped with him. She had a son and daughter, the former named Charles, the latter Charlotte Margaret, the second name resembling that of Lord Hillsborough's mother. Charlotte Volere soon died, and Lord Hillsborough conceived himself entitled to provide for her children. He placed the daughter in a French convent for her education, while for the boy he secured a lucrative appointment in India, his name being changed to Carpenter, on his naturalisation. In receiving his appointment, Charles Carpenter bound himself to settle on his sister an annuity of £200. He became commercial resident at Salem, and proceeded to remit the promised pension.

Having completed her education, Miss Carpenter proceeded to London under the care of Miss Jane Nicolson, granddaughter of William Nicolson, Bishop of Carlisle, who became her companion, on being recommended by Mr. Burd, now residentiary canon at Carlisle. At London, a young lady of pleasing aspects, with an income of £200, was sure to attract suitors. Miss Carpenter gave preference to an admirer of whom Miss Nicolson disapproved. The disapproval was communicated to her guardian, now Marquess of Downshire. He proposed that the ladies should visit the English Lakes, and requested his friend, Mr. Burd, to secure them proper accommodation. As an early removal was desirable, Lord Downshire desired the ladies to immediately proceed to Carlisle, and there wait on Mr. Burd, who would further direct them. When they reached Carlisle, Mr. Burd and his family were on the eve of leaving for Gilsland as summer quarters; they invited their visitors to accompany them.

At Gilsland, Mr. Burd's party established themselves at the Spa Hotel, and, according to custom, were, as the latest guests, assigned seats at the bottom of the table. Scott had with his friends arrived only a little before; he chanced to sit beside Mrs. Burd, who, perceiving that he was a Scotsman, and ascertaining that he hailed from Edinburgh, inquired whether he knew her friend, Major Riddle, then stationed in Edinburgh Castle, and who with his regiment had lately been engaged in suppressing a popular outbreak at Tranent. Scott mentioned that the Major was one of his friends, and that he was in perfect health when he had seen him a few weeks before. A conversation so auspiciously begun, naturally led to renewed intercourse, and afterwards to intimacy. Scott was not indifferent to the charming *brunette* who formed one of the clergyman's party. He danced with her at the ball, handed her to the supper-room, and seating himself by her side, attempted to talk French with her. It was whispered that the brown-eyed beauty possessed an income sufficient to meet the wants of an ordinary household. After a few weeks, he made proposals to her, and was accepted subject to the approbation of her guardian. Scott now communicated with Lord Downshire, and received in reply a formal letter, in which the Irish nobleman showed every disposition to be speedily relieved from a charge which was burdensome to him. To his communication his Lordship desired an answer by return of post; and it is to be presumed that it was satisfactory, for, with the exception of writing another short note, the Marquess did not further concern himself in the daughter of Charlotte Volere or her husband. If the husband expected an invitation to the Marquess's seat, he was doomed to disappointment, for, though his lordship survived some years, he remained silent.

Scott's marriage took place in St. Mary's Church, Carlisle, on the 24th December, 1797. To her expectant lord, the bride elect, ten days before, wrote thus: "It is very unlucky you are such a bad housekeeper, as I am no better." This was true; and she did not improve. Her domestic administration was thriftless. At times she ventured, perhaps good-naturedly, to charge her own want of economy upon her husband. "Dis is de hotel with no pay," she said to my friend, Mrs. Hogg,* in her drawing-room at Abbotsford, in allusion to a party then assembled.

Of Sir Walter I received some pleasing reminiscences from Mrs. Hogg. She said to me, "Before I personally knew him, I regarded him with a veneration which I cannot express; and when he led me from the drawing-room to the dinner-table at Abbotsford, soon after my marriage, I felt ready to sink under the honour. But when I had sometime sat beside him, and listened to his stories, my veneration changed into respect—a respect which was increased on every subsequent interview. One of our children was born with a weak foot; and Sir Walter, when he heard of it, expressed much concern. He spoke of having suffered much from lameness, and attributed his misfortune to want of care and proper treatment. He never met me or my husband without tenderly asking for our little pet. "How's the footie?" he would say. The question, expressed in Sir Walter's own kind manner, went to my heart." †

Those whom he had long known and regarded with affection, Sir Walter addressed by familiar names. My late friend, William Banks, of Edinburgh, was principal clerk and draughtsman to William H. Lizars, the eminent engraver, in St. James's Square. He had recommended himself to Scott's notice by some successful drawings, and was ever after hailed with a "How are ye, Willie?" In like fashion did he address the two Ballantynes, William Laidlaw, William Erskine, and Allan Cunningham. Constable was his "fat friend;" James Hogg, "Shepherd;" and Sir Adam Fergusson was *Linton*—by that name he had been hailed by a Newhaven fisherman, who took him for a companion.

---

* Widow of the Ettrick Shepherd.

† This anecdote, and the others at p. 333 of Mr. Gilfillan's "Memoir," I supplied to that work.

Those who have read the little story of Pet Marjorie, have obtained an insight into the simple, loving nature of the author of "Waverley." The precocious child of six so delighted the warm-hearted poet, that he made himself a child again to join in her amusements. Writes Dr. John Brown in his inimitable sketch of this short-lived prodigy : " Having made the fire cheery, he set her down in his ample chair, and standing sheepishly before her, began to say his lesson, which happened to be—

> ' Ziccotty, diccotty dock,
> The mouse ran up the clock,
> The clock struck wan,
> Down the mouse ran ;
> Ziccotty, diccotty dock.'

" This done repeatedly till she was pleased, she gave him his new lesson, gravely and slowly timing it upon her small fingers—he saying it after her—

> ' Wonery, twoery, tickery seven ;
> Alibi, crackaby, ten, and eleven ;
> Pin, pan, musky, dan ;
> Tweedle-um, twodle-um,
> Twenty-wan ; eerie, orie, ourie ;
> You—are—out !' " *

Sir Walter was elected rector of St. Andrews University in March, 1825. The election of a rector unconnected with the ruling body was opposed to the then existing laws, and this fact was communicated to Sir Walter by Principal Nicoll. When a deputation of the students soon after waited upon him to request his acceptance of office, he gently counselled them to "respect the laws, and mind their studies."

My late friend, Professor Shank More of Edinburgh University, gave me the following illustration of Scott's delightful *bonhommie*. As my friend was in gown and wig walking one morning in the Parliament House, two gentlemen stepped up and politely asked him whether Sir Walter Scott was coming to court, and if so, when he would arrive ? They added that they were Americans, and being in London on business, had come to Scotland on purpose to see the author of "Waverley." At that moment Scott entered the room ; after pointing him out to the strangers, my friend walked up and hailed him.

* "Marjorie Fleming." By John Brown, M.D. Edinburgh, 1871, 12mo. p. 9.

Having stated to him what had taken place, Sir Walter said, "They pay me a great compliment by coming so far. I'll take your arm, and will walk up and down, that they may have a proper view." Professor More, in relating this anecdote, said that Scott was always considerate in his treatment of strangers, and that, though his patience was often sorely taxed, he constantly maintained his native geniality.

In regard to the Christian character of Sir Walter Scott, I have been favoured with the following from my valued friend, Dean Ramsay :—

. . . "You ask me of the impression left on my mind by my visit to Abbotsford on the occasion of Lady Scott's death. It is indeed a very easy and a very pleasing office to give you that impression. I could not but feel all the time I was there that our great Sir Walter was as much to be loved for the qualities of his heart as he had so long been admired for the high gifts of his intellect and his genius. He displayed throughout the whole time the subdued and calm spirit of a Christian mourner. There was manifest an entire acquiescence in the wisdom and goodness of his heavenly Father, who had bereaved him of the wife and companion of his early years. His kind, gentle manner to his domestics ; his devoted attention to his daughter, who was in deep distress ; his serious appearance during the funeral service ; his own proposal in the evening to have domestic worship, and his devotional manner at the time, have left a deep and pleasing impression on my mind—the impression that I had witnessed so much gentleness and so much right feeling, which I could not but perceive were the genuine emotions of his heart. Sir Walter Scott was one of the good and the great of his race and country."

Allan Cunningham has been named. For this worthy man and ingénious poet Scott cherished a sincere affection ; when he visited the metropolis he always saw him, and he procured for two of his sons cadetships in the Indian army. Allan Cunningham died in 1842. With his son, Peter Cunningham, author of "A Handbook to London," and other interesting works, I enjoyed an intimate acquaintance. He was a kind-hearted pleasant man, though perhaps rather too fond of society. About two years ago he died at St. Albans, where he sometime lived in retirement. A laborious, painstaking writer, the various works published under his care attest his strict editorial and critical accuracy. In this respect he was a contrast to his father, who while to be commended as an original writer, lacked the power of research essential to properly editing the works of others. His edition of Burns contains many errors, which a little care would have avoided.

The Cunninghams belonged to an old family, who were lords of that portion of Ayrshire which still bears their family name; they afterwards became tenant-farmers, and latterly land-stewards and artificers. Contrary to ordinary rule, they seemed to gather intellectual force as they fell in social importance. Allan Cunningham had three brothers, who, under unpromising circumstances, cultivated learning and became authors. His elder brother, Thomas Mounsey Cunningham, was an ingenious poet.

A nephew of Allan Cunningham—son of one of his sisters—was my late friend, William Pagan, of Clayton, Fifeshire, a man of considerable culture, and well known as author of a work on " Road Reform." Mr. Pagan became chief magistrate of Cupar-Fife, where he long conducted business as a solicitor and banker. He was remarkably facetious, and indulged a ready humour. He invented a method of keeping potatoes hot during dinner by means of a portable tin vessel which might be attached to the grate. " A capital contrivance," I remarked, " you should give it a name." " Yes," he responded, " I will call it Pagan's Patent Portable Potato Pan !" Mr. Pagan was born in Dumfriesshire on the 6th May, 1803, and died at Clayton on the 21st December, 1869.

Among Sir Walter Scott's literary friends the most remarkable was James Hogg, the Ettrick Shepherd. Not eccentric in the sense of Hugh Miller's persisting in wearing his mason's apron long after he had laid aside the workmen's tools, Hogg was nevertheless a strange compound of genius and waywardness. A genius he was, and of a very high order; but not content with the gifts which he had received so bountifully, he laid claim to others which he did not possess, and the assumption of which rendered him ridiculous. He possessed a brilliant fancy, and when he entered the realms of faery, or soared among the stars, he was among Scottish Bards without a rival. But when he dealt with the concerns of ordinary life, or detailed his own mundane experiences, he was prone to borrow too freely from his imagination. He alleged that he was born on the 25th of January, 1772, the day on which Burns saw the light thirteen years before, while a reference to the family Bible or the baptismal register, would have shown him that he was baptized in December, 1770. He was nearly self-educated,

H

but he had received from his parents a little further training
than he was willing to avow. His early mishaps in sheep-
farming were not entirely owing to diseased flocks, but were
partly due to his mismanagement. In the concerns of business
he was utterly helpless, and under no possible circumstances
could have succeeded.

He sprung from a race of shepherds, and of his descent he
was proud. In his writings, he constantly styled himself
" The Ettrick Shepherd." When introduced into the literary
society of the Scottish capital, he laid aside the rough vestments of the sheep-fold and apparelled himself in decent black.
In church none would appear more becomingly attired. From
his youth accustomed to the native Doric, he never attempted
any other dialect. But his conversation was not coarse, or in
the ordinary sense vulgar. His chief peculiarity was to talk
about himself, and to this weakness those who knew him easily
reconciled themselves. Though abundantly egotistical, his
conceit did not lead him to disparage others. He quarrelled
with Scott and Wordsworth for having, as he conceived, under-
valued him, but some kindly words made him friendly as
before. As a writer of prose fiction, he only reached mediocrity ; and some of his longer poems, such as " Mador of the
Moor," were hastily composed, and rashly printed. But he was
withal a great poet. His ballad of ". Kilmeny " in the " Queen's
Wake " is unrivalled as a pure and perfect ideal of fairy super-
stition. The " Witch of Fife " is startling in its wild unearth-
liness, and many passages in the " Pilgrims of the Sun " are
sublime and splendid. His ballads and songs are replete with
pathos and pastoral dignity. Though he had written only
" When the Kye come hame " and " Flora Macdonald's Lament," he would have been entitled to sterling reputation as
a song-writer.

Sir Walter, when he resided at Abbotsford, would occasionally take a ride into Ettrick to spend an hour or two with the
Shepherd at Altrive. On one of these occasions, as Mrs. Hogg
related to me, Sir Walter remarked in the Shepherd's library
a set of volumes bound in calf, and labelled " Scott's Novels."
He drew out a volume ; it was " Waverley." " Ah ! your
binder has introduced a *t* too many in the word Scots," said
Sir Walter. " Not at all," answered Hogg, " I wrote the copy
mysel'." The Novelist smiled, for he had not yet divulged his
secret.

A frequent and welcome visitor at the Shepherd's house was

John Gibson Lockhart, who, after his marriage with Sophia
Scott, resided at Chiefswood, a pleasant villa near Abbotsford.
In those days he had contracted few of those cynical asperities
which afterwards characterized him; and though his conversation was not free from its peculiar blemishes, the Shepherd
regarded him with a sincere affection,. and hoped that an
increased experience and the genial example of Sir Walter Scott
would cause him to abjure his acrimony. It was with these
expectations that, when he proceeded to London, in 1825, to
edit the *Quarterly Review,* the Shepherd approved of his
nephew, Robert Hogg, accompanying him as literary assistant.
Robert returned to Scotland after a few months, and the
Shepherd found that, as he became older, the Reviewer became
less amiable, and that he took delight in exposing the weak-
nesses, and injuring the fame, even of those who had befriended
him.

Before his departure for London, Lockhart returned the
hospitalities of his literary friends by inviting them to an
entertainment at Edinburgh. A considerable number assembled, and all were merrily disposed; but the host had fallen
into one of his worst moods, and would not speak. The only
word he uttered was a monosyllable. A friend, who sat near,
asked him to name the wine circulated during dinner. He
said " Hock!" For this anecdote I am indebted to my late
friend, Mr. William Tait, of Priorbank, the originator and first
publisher of the magazine which bore his name. Mr. Tait
mentioned the name of his informant—one of the party.

The Ettrick Shepherd married somewhat late in life. His
wife, Margaret Phillips, was daughter of a respectable farmer
in Annandale, and had, through her brother-in-law, Mr. James
Gray, of the High School, mixed in good society at Edinburgh.
Not a few years before she consented to share his lot, she had
been celebrated by the Shepherd in two of his best songs,
" When Maggie gangs away," and " Ah, Peggy since thou'rt
gane away." His choice of this excellent woman as his partner
in life was one of the most prudent steps of his career. It was
so characterized by Sir Walter Scott as he proposed the toast
of the newly married pair at Abbotsford; but who, when he
had got the length of saying " I did not think our friend had
so much good sense," was interrupted by the Shepherd with
" I dinna thank ye for that, Sir Walter !"

With Mrs. Hogg I became acquainted in 1853, when she
was spending a season at Bridge of Allan. I was surprised

to learn that though eighteen years a widow, she had received
from the State no recognition of her husband's genius.   Finding that she declined personally to represent her claims, I
invited public attention to the subject in the *Times* newspaper,
and drew up a memorial in her favour, addressed to the
premier, Lord Aberdeen.   Subscribed by upwards of forty
eminent persons, including the late patriotic Earl of Eglinton,
Alfred Tennyson, and Sir Archibald Alison, the memorial was
forwarded to the Premier, while its prayer was supported by
the Marquess of Breadalbane, Lord Panmure, and several
Scottish Members of Parliament.   Lord Aberdeen granted a
pension of £50, and soon afterwards I had the pleasure of
handing to Mrs. Hogg a cheque for £100, subscribed on her
behalf at Cincinnati.

On the occasion of obtaining his signature to the memorial
for Mrs. Hogg's pension, I had a short interview with Scott's
attached friend, Sir Adam Fergusson, then beyond fourscore.
He was very feeble, and his vision was so imperfect, that I had
to guide his hand in subscribing the memorial.   He spoke
about old times ; and after mentioning his last interview with
the Shepherd, he burst into tears, saying, " Poor Hogg ! Poor
Hogg !"

Mrs. Hogg and her family I knew intimately.   Of her four
daughters, one was married in London, and died young ; she
is interred in the Highgate cemetery.   Two others are comfortably married in Scotland.   The eldest daughter, a spinster,
enjoys a civil-list pension, which she received from Lord
Palmerston.   James Hogg, the poet's only son, engaged in
banking concerns at Ceylon, and afterwards at Sydney.   He
now resides at Linlithgow.   Mrs. Hogg died at Linlithgow on
the 15th November, 1870, about the age of eighty.   She was
an admirable woman.   Judicious in household administration,
she devoted herself to her husband's comfort and to the proper
upbringing of her children.   The Shepherd's profuse hospitality had subjected her to some inconvenience, and his
personal habits were not quite conformable with her tastes.
But she never uttered a complaint.   Only on one subject she
felt keenly : she conceived that her husband's reputation was
endangered by the words and acts attributed to him in the
Noctes of *Blackwood's Magazine,* and she insisted that those
papers should be stopped.   With her husband's poetical designation she had no sympathy ; she always spoke of him as Mr.
Hogg.   After his death she courted retirement ; and though

she resided in Edinburgh for nearly eighteen years, few literary persons in the city knew that she was amongst them. She was a zealous adherent of the Free Church, and was much respected for her piety and unostentatious benevolence. She latterly resided at Linlithgow, where I used to visit her frequently. Irrespective of her pleasing reminiscences, I always experienced in her society pleasure and edification. She was a kindly hostess, an intelligent companion, and a generous friend.

Sometime before his death the Ettrick Shepherd edited a new edition of Burns, conjointly with William Motherwell. This poet merits more than a passing notice. Born at Glasgow in 1797, he was educated at the High School of Edinburgh and the University of Glasgow. He became sheriff-clerk depute of Renfrewshire, and editor of a local periodical. In 1818 he edited the "Harp of Renfrewshire," a collection of modern songs; and in 1827 published a collection of ancient and modern ballads. In 1832 he appeared as author of a volume of original poems, some of which attracted wide attention. His ballad of "Jeanie Morrison" is in graceful simplicity and feeling, altogether unsurpassed. Motherwell was in 1830 appointed editor of the *Glasgow Courier*, a conservative organ. He died 1st November, 1835, at the age of thirty-eight. It was said that he fell a victim to social excesses, and I fear the belief was not unfounded. Respecting him, a correspondent has communicated to me the following anecdote : "In the session 1818-19, Motherwell and I sat on the same bench in Professor Young's junior Greek class in Glasgow University. On one occasion Motherwell was not present in time to answer to his name when the roll was called, and he was fined a penny. On the plea that he had entered before the whole of the names were called over, he refused to pay, and was ordered to remain after the dismissal of the class to give reasons for his recusancy. I lingered to hear the anticipated wrangle. The professor asked him why he refused to pay. 'Because,' said Motherwell, 'the rule is that the roll should not be *commenced* till the bell has ceased ringing, and I was in the class-room before it had done so.' 'Why make so much work about a penny ?' said the professor. Motherwell answered, ' Yes sir ! I *will* dispute about a penny, and I would dispute about a straw if I knew I was in the right !' The fine was remitted."

With Thomas Lyle, a contemporary of Motherwell, I became

acquainted in his latter years. He had edited a respectable volume of " Ancient Ballads ; " but his fame mainly rested on his having written the song of " Kelvin Grove." Poor Lyle was one of those sons of genius who are born to mischance. As a surgeon, he long practised at Airth in Stirlingshire, but being regarded as more devoted to gathering rare plants than to the art of healing, he was not successful in his practice. Latterly he removed to Glasgow, but his circumstances amended but slightly. He was subjected to much annoyance on account of the song on which his poetical reputation rested being some time assigned to another. He proved his title, and never forgot the little conflict he had in sustaining it. Lyle was born at Paisley in 1792, and died at Glasgow in April, 1859. My friend, Dr. John Robertson, of the High Church, visited him on his death-bed, and had suitable conversations with him. As he had latterly lived in obscurity, his departure was scarcely noticed in the newspapers. Kelvin Grove, which he has celebrated, is nearly as forgotten as the poet himself. A part of the city of Glasgow is now built upon its banks.

Not more familiar with the public than the name of Thomas Lyle is that of Alexander Carlile. Yet a song from his pen maintains a popularity even exceeding that of " Kelvin Grove." " Oh, wha's at the window ? wha, wha ? " founded on Wedderburn's " Quho is at my windo' ? quho, quho ? " is familiar to every lover of Scottish melody, and is sung with equal zest in the cottage shieling and in the fashionable boudoir. Mr. Carlile was a respectable manufacturer at Paisley. During his latter years, when I knew him, he was a grave and reverend-looking old man. He was much in his library, which was stored with the best works. He had studied at Glasgow University, and he was an occasional contributor to the periodicals. Some years before his death he published a volume of poems, but the work did not find acceptance. He composed his one popular song early in life.

Mr. Carlile was eminently patriotic. When, in 1856, the movement for a monument to Wallace was publicly inaugurated, he wrote to me in these terms : " I am glad to see a stir made about a monument to Wallace. I have long wondered that our great hero should have so long remained without such an honour being conferred on his memory. The Abbey Craig is just the spot for such a purpose. Not merely capitalists, but the public at large should be appealed to. Enthusiasm could easily be awakened, and a large sum might be raised.

Bruce, too, should have his monument at the stone which, during the battle, bore his banner." Mr. Carlile saw the Wallace Monument enterprise launched, and in progress. He died in August, 1860, at an advanced age.

Also the author of a popular song, another native of the West of Scotland, is entitled to remembrance. When a student at the University of Aberdeen in 1826, John Park, afterwards minister of St. Andrews, composed " Where Gadie rins," which has ever since maintained its popularity. He was a native of Greenock, where his father kept the "White Hart" hotel. Having studied for the ministry, he was in 1831 elected pastor of Rodney Street Presbyterian church, Liverpool. In 1843 he was presented to the church living of Glencairn, and in 1854 was translated to the first charge at St. Andrews. He was an eloquent preacher and an accomplished musician. He composed many tunes, some of which have been published. In regard to his song " Gadie rins," Dr. Park thus communicated with me in 1855 :

" The air is old. I heard it whistled by a fellow-student at Aberdeen, and tried these words for it. The only words he could give me as old ones were—

'O an I were where Gadie rins,
   Where Gadie rins, where Gadie rins,
 O an I were where Gadie rins,
   At the back o' Benochie.'

But he told me that a Scottish officer in Egypt had been much affected and surprised on hearing a soldier's wife crooning the song to herself, and this I believe was the hint upon which I tried the verses. The air is undoubtedly old, from its resemblance to several Gaelic and Irish airs. I have been surprised—though it would be affectation not to say agreeably surprised—by the interest which has been felt in connection with this trifle." –

Dr. Park died on the 8th April, 1865. He was an amiable, kind-hearted man ; and had his vigorous intellectual powers been more concentrated, he would have secured a wider fame.

Andrew Park, another west-country bard, composed twelve volumes of poems. "Silent Love," his best poem, passed into several editions. Park was born at Renfrew, in March, 1807, and was trained to business. He was first a dealer in hats, and afterwards a bookseller ; but his restless sociable nature disqualified him for the duties of the counter. When I became acquainted with him in 1856, he was a gentleman at large, subsisting by his wits, and courted for his society. Of an agreeable demeanour, and always appareled in becoming vestments, he was presentable at any table, and he dined out almost daily. His home, if he had one, must have been stored sparingly, for his works sold slowly, and he would not have recourse to a subscription. He died at Glasgow, in December, 1863. His admirers have, in the cemetery at Paisley, reared a monument to his memory.

With Hugh Macdonald, the Glasgow poet, I formed a slight acquaintance in 1857. I was struck with his unpretentious frankness. He was then editing the *Glasgow Times*. To that newspaper he contributed "Days at the Coast," a series of papers descriptive of scenery on the Clyde, which he afterwards published in a collected form. He had previously been subeditor of the *Glasgow Citizen*, and he afterward joined the literary staff of the *Morning Journal*. He died in March, 1860, at the age of forty-three. Macdonald's poetic writings were published posthumously, accompanied with a memoir. They evince elegant fancy, and an enthusiastic love of nature. His volume of prose sketches, entitled "Rambles round Glasgow," abounds in historical information, combined with pleasing descriptions of natural scenery. Macdonald was born in humble circumstances, and persisted in using the native Doric. By a considerable circle of literary friends, his genius was much appreciated. After his decease a thousand pounds were subscribed as a provision for his family.

The greatest poetical genius of the west country for at least half a century was James Macfarlan. This strangely constituted individual may not be easily described. The Ettrick Shepherd used to say when a limner failed to produce a satisfactory portrait of him, that his "face was out of all rule of drawing." He was right, for his cheek-bones did not match, one being longer than the other. In the character of James Macfarlan there was a like want of symmetry. He was a poet born, yet rags, meanness, leasing, and drink were also in a manner native to him. Viewing him on one side, we discover a lofty poetical genius of noble aspirations; observing him on the other, we remark a spectacle at which the moralist would stare and the compassionate might weep.

Having read some of Macfarlan's verses I desired to form his acquaintance, and I met him by appointment at the office of the *Glasgow Bulletin*, some time in 1856. Our interview was short, and had I chanced to meet him prior to reading his verses, it would have been shorter still. Appearance of genius he had none. Of slender form, tattered garments, and commonplace features, he seemed every inch the *gaberlunzie*. Nor did his manner of conversation tend to modify the impression. Low society he loved, and his best verses were written amidst the fumes of tobacco and drink. His muse was always ready; and on the margins of old newspapers, amidst the distractions of a taproom, he would inscribe admirable verses. With equal promptitude he could invent a tale of distress, or feign a family bereavement, to obtain sixpences. He was born in the Calton, Glasgow, in April, 1832. His education consisted in desultory attendances at schools in Glasgow, Kilmarnock, and Greenock. His father, a native of Ireland, was a pedlar, and for the same precarious occupation destined the young poet. But he would not take to the pack; he preferred to contribute verses to the Glasgow newspapers. At length he procured the secretaryship of the Glasgow *Athenæum*. This appointment was soon forfeited to reckless inebriety and neglect of duty. He now reported to the newspapers, but his irregular habits again threw him out of employment. In 1854 a London bookseller undertook to publish a volume of " Poems " from his pen : but as he did not pay the printer, as had been stipulated, the sheets were " wasted." He published his "City Songs" in 1855 ; some profit which this work brought him was dissipated by his excesses. He afterwards printed some poetical opuscules, which, bleared and dingy, he sold for what he could procure. What he realised by hawking his verses he consumed in the pothouse.

I corresponded with Macfarlan for some time, and tried to help him ; but at first to little purpose. In 1861 he sent me a poem on " Wallace," which I printed and distributed, receiving a few pounds for the writer. I afterwards engaged him as contributor to a periodical, on the condition that he would keep sober ; he became an abstainer, but I suspect violated his pledge, for he soon after begged me for money under the menace that if it did not reach him by an early post he would destroy himself. Of a sudden his letters ceased, and I conceived that he had again plunged into dissipation. But he was ill. Lack of proper food and clothing, together with his unfortunate habits, had seriously impaired a constitution at no time robust. He was confined to his sick chamber, if a cold wretched attic without furniture, and nearly without bed-

clothes, might be so named.   Some kind neighbours showed
an abundant compassion, and supplied him with food, medicine, and warm clothing.   A physician gratuitously attended
him, and my late friend, Dr. John Robertson, of the High
Church, conversed with him on his spiritual concerns.   The
dying poet expressed a deep regret for his follies, and avowed
his confidence in the Saviour.   He died at Glasgow on the 5th
November, 1862, at the age of thirty-one.   No poet more ingenious had sprung from the ranks of the people since the days
of Burns.   He did not compose songs, though several of his
compositions might be set to music and sung.   His muse celebrated the nobler instincts and aspirations of humanity.   His
language is chaste, exact, and terse ; in the graceful flow of
numbers he strikingly excels.   The dignity of the industrial
calling has never been celebrated more powerfully than in his
ode to " The Lords of Labour," which I subjoin :—

" They come, they come,'in a glorious march,
    You can hear their steam-steeds neigh,
As they dash through Skill's triumphal arch,
    Or plunge 'mid the dancing spray.
Their bale-fires blaze in the mighty forge,
    Their life-pulse throbs in the mill,
Their lightnings shiver the gaping gorge,
    And their thunders shake the hill.
Ho ! these are the Titans of toil and trade,
    The heroes who wield no sabre ;
But mightier conquests reapeth the blade
    That is borne by the Lords of Labour.

" Brave hearts like jewels light the sod,
    Through the mists of commerce shine,
And souls flash out like stars of God,
    From the midnight of the mine.
No palace is theirs, no castle great,
    No princely pillared hall,
But they well may laugh at the roofs of state
    'Neath the heaven which is over all.
Ho ! these are the Titans of toil and trade,
    The heroes who wield no sabre ;
But mightier conquests reapeth the blade
    Which is borne by the Lords of Labour.

" Each bares his arm for the ringing strife,
    That marshals the sons of the soil,
And the sweat-drops shed in their battle of life
    Are gems in the crown of toil.
And better their well-won wreaths, I trow,
    Than laurels with life-blood wet ;
And nobler the arch of a bare, bold brow,
    Than the clasp of a coronet.

Then hurrah for each hero, although his deed
  Be unknown by the trump or tabor;
For holier, happier far is the meed
  That crowneth the Lords of Labour !"

I hope some enterprising publisher may be induced, under suitable editorship, to collect and publish Macfarlan's writings. The undertaking commended itself to Charles Dickens, but he too has passed away.

Alexander Smith, author of the "Life Drama," and otherwise celebrated as a poet and miscellaneous writer, was born at Kilmarnock, on the 31st December, 1829. By his father he was trained as a pattern-drawer, but he did not relish the vocation. To the columns of the *Glasgow Citizen* he contributed verses in early manhood, but these seem to have passed without notice. In 1851 he sent a selection of his more matured compositions to the Rev. George Gilfillan, soliciting his opinion and advice. Mr. Gilfillan commended the poetry, and introduced the writer to the columns of *The Critic*, a London serial. In that periodical the "Life Drama" first appeared. In 1852 it was published in a volume by Mr. Bogue, who paid the author one hundred pounds. Mr. Smith suddenly found himself famous ; he proceeded to London, where he became the *lion* of literary circles. On his return to the north he was entertained by the Duke of Argyll at Inverary.

In 1854 the Secretaryship of Edinburgh University became vacant, and Mr. Smith was encouraged to become a candidate. The Town Council were patrons, and a personal canvass was necessary. The poet called at the house of a magistrate, but only found the bailie's sister, who endeavoured to persuade him from wasting time in a hopeless candidature. "Poor gentleman," she said, "you have not a shadow of chance ; my brother is pledged to another." But Mr. Smith persevered, and was chosen. After his election, a friend who had accompanied him in his canvass sent him a telegram announcing the event. The poet answered in these words, "Poor Miss D—k !" He had not been known as a humorist before.

Not long after Alexander Smith entered on his duties in Edinburgh College, I asked him to subscribe the memorial to the Prime Minister on behalf of Mrs. Hogg. He did so, remarking that, unlike those who had previously signed, he could add no literary honours to his name. "No matter," I replied ; "Lord Aberdeen will know that one Alexander Smith only would be invited to subscribe a petition like the present." "If I live," said the poet, "I will make the name known throughout the world." I was gratified by the aspiration. The poet afterwards consented to write an essay on Scottish Ballads, for the third volume of my "Scottish Minstrel;" he changed his mind and contributed it to the *Edinburgh University Essays*. In the same year he published his "City Poems," and soon afterwards married. He planted his household tree at Wardie, near Granton. As secretary to the University he received at first a salary of £150; latterly £200. He employed his spare time in writing for the booksellers, and in contributing to public journals. His prose compositions were not less esteemed than his poems. In 1863, he published "Dreamthorpe," a volume of essays. His "Summer Life in Skye," a work of entertaining reading, was issued in 1865. During the following year, he published in *Good Words*, and afterwards separately, his well-written romance, "Alfred Hagart's Household." He worked hard and constantly, till his health became unsettled. On the 20th November, 1866, he was prostrated by typhoid fever; he died on the 5th of January. All who knew him lamented his premature departure. His manners were genial, and he was, when health allowed, always at the post of duty. Of middle stature, he was well built; he had a massive forehead, but an unpleasant squint impaired the general expression of his countenance. As a poet, he will be remembered more for striking passages in the "Life Drama," than for any sustained effort.

John Younger, the St. Boswells shoemaker, and author of the "Prize Essay on the Sabbath," was sufficiently conscious of intellectual superiority, but was withal a man of fine taste, some poetical fancy, and great conversational talent. Had he received substantial scholastic training, he would unquestionably have attained eminence. An hour's talk with Younger was a positive enjoyment. In conversing he did not abandon his work, and was never more diligent with the awl than when engaged in a keen argument or in relating some literary experience. In 1849 he gained, among 1045 competitors, the second of three prizes offered for an Essay on the Sabbath. On this occasion he was conveyed to London, introduced to the Prince Consort, and celebrated in Exeter Hall. Latterly he became postmaster at St. Boswells; he also added to his revenues by hook-dressing. He died in 1860, leaving several volumes of compositions carefully written out and ready for publication.

With Elliot Aitchison, the Hawick weaver-poet, I got acquainted in 1854 ; he was a little mean-looking man, with no appearance of genius. But he composed verses full of sentiment and music, and it is to be regretted that a morbid diffidence kept him in the shade. I tried to befriend him by drawing attention to his merits, and thereby incurred his resentment. A newspaper writer represented after his decease that I had embittered his last years. Aitchison died in 1858 at an advanced age. A plain tombstone in Wilton churchyard marks his grave.

James Telfer, the Liddesdale poet, I never met ; but we some time corresponded. He had been a shepherd, and became a schoolmaster ; better he had continued at his original occupation, for his school-fees never exceeded thirty pounds a year, and his school-house was a ruin. He published a volume of well-written " Tales and Sketches " and composed ballads in the Scottish manner. He died in 1863 aged sixty-two. Since his death his merits have become more generally known, chiefly through the good offices of Mr. Robert White, of Newcastle, who early recognised his genius. Telfer unhappily indulged in sarcasm against those who had offended him. He loved seclusion, and was taciturn, but in the presence of familiar friends he evinced considerable powers of criticism.

With Henry Scott Riddell, author of " Scotland Yet," and other popular songs, I enjoyed a long and pleasant intimacy. Riddell had, like Telfer, originally been a shepherd, and though he subsequently became a licentiate of the Church, and mixed in society, he retained the simple manners of the pastoral life. Through illness he was unable to follow the ministerial profession, and for many years occupied a cottage at Teviothead, which he held from the Duke of Buccleuch, with an annuity and small portion of land. His poetical merits, I conceived, were worthy of State recognition ; but I failed, after repeated efforts, to procure him a pension on the Civil List. I got him, however, some treasury grants and one or two donations from the Royal Literary Fund.

Under more favourable circumstances Henry Scott Riddell would have obtained a wider fame. Unlike Burns, and Hogg, and Tannahill, his songs were not always set to music by competent composers ; and an unhappy inactivity of nature prevented his seeking a proper publicity. His prose writings were unhappily verbose, but with a little pruning would have sustained a literary reputation. He was an expert correspondent, a kind friend, and an agreeable companion. His countenance presented a capacious forehead, firm-set lips, and a penetrating eye. He celebrated the simple joys of rural life. He died at Teviothead on the 28th July, 1870, at the age of seventy-two.

During a Border sojourn I became acquainted with Andrew Leyden, a younger brother of Dr. John Leyden, the celebrated poet. He was on the border of fourscore, and was poor and unprovided for. He had been a shepherd, and was latterly employed in work about a farm. I tried to befriend him, but whether my efforts were attended with any real benefit to him I could never discover. He was a well-informed man, much superior to the ordinary hind ; and there was an air of gentility about him. He remembered his distinguished brother, but imperfectly so. To the poet a handsome monument has been raised on " the green " at Denholm, his native village.

Connected by marriage with the Scottish Border was my late friend the Rev. Thomas Gordon Torry Anderson, incumbent of St. Paul's Episcopal Church, Dundee. Mr. Torry Anderson wrote good verses, and was an esteemed musical composer. I subjoin the " Araby Maid " from his pen ; it is, I conceive, much too little known :—

> " Away on the wings of the wind she flies,
>   Like a thing of life and light—
> And she bounds beneath the eastern skies,
>   And the beauty of eastern night.

> " Why so fast flies the bark through the ocean's foam,—
>   Why wings it so speedy a flight ?
> 'Tis an Araby maid who hath left her home,
>   To fly with her Christian knight.

> " She hath left her sire and her native land,
>   The land which from childhood she trode,
> And hath sworn, by the pledge of her beautiful hand,
>   To worship the Christian's God.

> " Then away, away, oh ! swift be thy flight,
>   It were death one moment's delay ;
> For behind there is many a blade glancing bright—
>   Then away—away—away !

> " They are safe in the land where love is divine,
>   In the land of the free and the brave—
> They have knelt at the foot of the holy shrine.
>   Nought can sever them now but the grave."

Mr. Torry Anderson died in June, 1856, in his fifty-first year. A kind, genial man, he exercised a generous hospitality.

My late revered friend, Alexander Bald, of Craigward Cottage, Alloa, rejoiced to extend his kindly countenance to the sons of genius and song. He visited the Ettrick Shepherd when following his flocks, and was one of the first to acknowledge him as a poet. At Alloa he established a Shakespeare Club, which, under his auspices, was yearly attended by some poetical stars. To old age he continued his poetical ardour, constantly befriending the votaries of the muse. He died in October, 1859, at the age of seventy-six. Alexander Bald was singularly benevolent; I cherish his memory with affection. His brother Robert, distinguished as a mining engineer, was also possessed of many Christian excellences.

The last to be named among Lowland Bards is my late friend John Hunter, LL.D., of Craigcrook Castle. This excellent man was son of Dr. James Hunter, and grandson of Dr. John Hunter, both of St. Andrews. He was born in the manse of Dunino, in 1801; he studied at St. Andrews and became a Writer to the Signet. In 1848 he was appointed Auditor of the Court of Session, a lucrative and honourable office, which he held till within a short period of his death. He died in December, 1869. John Hunter added elegant accomplishments to rare natural gifts. Each Saturday afternoon he received at Craigcrook, poets, artists, and men of genius, to whom he dispensed an abundant hospitality. On many themes he could have written effectively, but he never sought distinction as an author. He printed anonymously, in 1843, a thin volume of poetical "Miscellanies."

THE CLERGY AND PARISH OFFICERS.

THE Rev. Ebenezer Erskine, of Stirling, one of the founders of the Secession Church, was assisting at a communion in a neighbouring parish. A lady belonging to the congregation was much impressed, and, expecting similar benefit, went to hear Mr. Erskine in his own church the following Sunday. After service, on this occasion, she waited on Mr. Erskine, and told him that she had not been so much edified as when she heard him in her parish church. "I fear," she added, "that I have not been hearing to-day with a proper spirit." "Yes," said Mr. Erskine, "last Sunday you went to hear the Gospel, and to-day you came to hear Ebenezer Erskine."

There is the well-known story of the celebrated John Howe, who when asked by a nobleman what he could do for him, replied, "Allow me, my Lord, to swear the next oath." Apropos of this anecdote, one much less known is related of the Rev. Robert Innes, minister of Huntly. A company of soldiers were being inspected by their officer, who at the time used oaths. Mr. Innes stepped behind him, and taking off his hat, proceeded after every oath to say, "Amen!" The officer turned round, and asked him what he meant. "I am joining in prayer," said Mr. Innes. "Thank you," said the officer; "but I have no further need of a clerk. Soldiers! to the right about—march!"

The Rev. Dr. Lawson, of Selkirk, had frequently sought a favourable opportunity of inducing his medical attendant to forbear the use of profane oaths. He had sent for the physician to consult him upon the state of his health, when, after hearing a narrative of his complaints, the M.D. said sharply, "D—— it, sir, you are the slave of a vile habit, and you will not recover unless you give it up." "What is that habit?" inquired the patient. "It is your practice of smoking—it is injuring your constitution." "I find it is an expensive habit," said Dr. Lawson, "and if it is injuring me I will abandon it; but you, too, have a vile habit, and were you giving it up, it would be a great benefit to yourself, and a comfort to your friends." "What is that?" inquired the physician. "The habit of swearing," replied the divine "True," said Dr. ——, "but that is not an expensive habit, like yours." "Doctor!" rejoined Dr. Lawson, "you will discover it to be a very expensive habit indeed, when the account is handed to you."

A clergyman in the north of Scotland was reproving a parishioner for his habits of intemperance. He represented to him that whisky was his greatest enemy. "Are we not told in Scripture to love our enemies?" said the irreverent bacchanalian. "Yes, John," responded the minister; "but it is not said we are to swallow them."

The following anecdote has often been related, but seldom correctly. The Rev. George More, minister of the Original Secession Church, Edinburgh, was riding to the village of Howgate, in the vicinity of the city. The day was stormy, snow falling heavily. Mr. More was enveloped in a Spanish cloak, with a woman's shawl tied round his neck and shoulders. These loose garments, covered with snow, and waving in the blast, startled the horse of a commercial traveller who chanced to ride past. The alarmed steed plunged, and menaced to throw its rider, who exclaimed, "You would frighten the devil, sir!" "May be," said Mr. More, "for it's just my trade."

The Rev. Charles Roberts, the writer's great grandfather, was an Episcopal clergyman, and chaplain to the troops at Dundee. One Sabbath morning, on his way to the military chapel, he was accosted by two young officers from the barracks. One of them engaged Mr. Roberts in conversation, while the other, as had been previously concerted, snatched his sermon from his pocket. They expected that in the confusion of discovering his loss, he would be unable to proceed, and that the result would afford occasion for merriment with their companions. They were disappointed. Instead of evincing embarrassment, Mr. Roberts deliberately announced as his text Proverbs xiv. 9,—"Fools make a mock at sin." He preached powerfully and with effect. The military striplings waited upon him at the close of the service, returned his MS., and begged his forgiveness.

Trade was unusually brisk among the weavers of Kirkcaldy, and they consequently drunk hard on the Saturday evenings, occasionally sallying forth on the Sunday morning, to the

great annoyance of the sober. In prayer one morning the celebrated Mr. Shirra, in allusion to the custom, spoke thus :—
" O Lord, while we recommend to thy Fatherly care and protection all ranks and conditions of men, we, in a particular manner, pray for the check and ticking weavers of Kirkcaldy. In Thy wisdom and mercy be pleased to send them either mair sense or less siller."

Another minister of the Secession Church, Mr. Walter Dunlop, of Dumfries, was prone to publicly censure the peculiarities and errors of his flock. A member of his congregation had been presented with a gay, party-coloured vest by his son, a college student. It became part of his holiday attire, but was scarcely in keeping with his age or the gravity of his deportment. One Sunday, while at service in Mr. Dunlop's church, he fell asleep during the first prayer, and so remained in a standing posture when the rest of the congregation had, at the close of the exercise, resumed their seats. Mr. Dunlop looked at him attentively as he announced his text, and thereafter exclaimed, " Willie, my man, ye may sit doun—a' the folks, I think, hae noo seen your braw new waistcoat."

The celebrated Dr. John Erskine, of Greyfriars, Edinburgh, was remarkable for the evenness of his temper. His handkerchief had disappeared every Sunday during his descent from the pulpit, and suspicion fell on an elderly female, who sat on the pulpit stair. In order to discover the depredator, Mrs. Erskine sewed the corner of the handkerchief to the minister's pocket. Returning from the pulpit, he felt a gentle pull, when, turning round and tapping the old woman on the shoulder, he exclaimed, " No the day, honest woman : no the day."

The Rev. Dr. Smart, minister of the Secession Church, Stirling, thus accosted a clerical brother, detected of plagiarism:—
" I hear you have become a Sabbatarian." " Have I not always been so ?" responded the person addressed. " Oh, you have got beyond us all," was the reply ; " for I hear you neither think your own thoughts, nor speak your own words, on that holy day."

The Rev. James Wright, minister of Logie, had obtained his living through the influence of a relative, an heritor of the parish. The relatives quarrelled, probably owing to the keen oversight of the rights of office exercised by the incumbent. The heritor paid stipend ; and in the hope of affronting the minister, he despatched to the manse Johnnie Armstrong, the public executioner of Stirling, to settle the amount due.

Johnnie was enjoined to obtain a discharge; it was readily granted, and in the following terms :—" Received from John Wright, Esq., of Loss, &c., by the hands of his *doer*, the hangman of Stirling!"

Early one morning a person carrying a gun, and who was fond of saying smart things, accosted the Rev. Mr. Bull:— " I am going to shoot a greater fool than myself, if I can find him. Then responded Mr. Bull, " You had better take break- fast, for you have a long day's work before you."

Mr. Dunlop had occasion to pass through a hamlet in the parish of Caerlaverock. It was a long straggling village, with a farm-steading at each end. In passing the first farm he discovered that the fowls had got among the corn, and inti- mated the fact to a servant girl at the steading. As he passed on he heard the girl call out, " Deil chouk thae geese, they're aye in the corn." When he reached the opposite end of the village, he found the farmer's swine among his corn. A ser- vant in pursuit exclaimed, " Deil chouk thae swine !" " He canna wuh yet, my woman," said Mr. Dunlop ; " he's choukin' geese at the ither end o' the town."

There was an attempt to alarm Mr. Dunlop by the feigned appearance of an apparition. He was in the habit of walking on moonlight nights in a plantation near his house. A figure in spectral vestments suddenly stood before him. " Ay, ay," exclaimed Mr. Dunlop, altogether unmoved, " is this a general risin', or are ye just takin' a daunner by yersel ?" The mock apparition retired.

The late Rev. Dr. Dow, of Erroll, and the Rev. Dr. Duff, of Kilspindie, were both ministers in the Carse of Gowrie, and had maintained an uninterrupted intimacy. On a New Year's day Dr. Dow sent to his friend, who was a great snuffer, a snuff-box, inscribed,—

" Dr. Dow to Dr. Duff,
   Snuff! Snuff! Snuff!"

The minister of Kilspindie resolved not to be outdone either in generosity or in pungent humour. Though withal sober and exemplary, the pastor of Erroll was known to enjoy a glass of toddy with his friends. So his clerical brother sent him a hot-water jug, bearing on the lid this couplet :—

" Dr. Duff to Dr. Dow,
   Fou ! Fou ! Fou !"

A country minister preached on the Sabbath after his marriage from the text, "Oh, wretched man that I am!" At next meeting of Presbytery he was assailed by the waggery of his brethren. He implored silence, using these words of the apostle, "I wish that all men were not almost, but altogether such as I am,"—when an arch brother exclaimed, "Finish your quotation, 'except these bonds.'"

During a vacancy in the church of Linlithgow, two neighbouring ministers were candidates, and both were so well supported that Lord Melville, who had the disposal of Crown patronage in Scotland, appointed Mr. Dobie, minister of Mid-Calder, as a neutral. The disappointed candidates were Dr. Meiklejohn of Abercorn, and Mr. Wilson of Falkirk. Some time afterwards, at a Presbytery dinner, Mr. Dobie happened to sit between the unsuccessful candidates. "It is curious," remarked Dr. Meiklejohn, "that you have come again between us ; for it was between us, you know, that you got your church." "Ah yes," replied Mr. Dobie, dryly ; "it is wonderful by what feeble instruments Providence attains its ends."

The late Mr. Walker, of Muthil, was preaching in a neighbouring parish. Next day he was met by one of the resident landowners, who explained to the reverend gentleman that he had not been hearing him in the afternoon, as he could not *digest* more than one sermon. "I rather think," said Mr. Walker, "the appetite is more at fault than the digestion."

The Rev. Dr. Lawson, of Selkirk, was Professor in the Divinity Hall of the Associate Church. One morning he appeared in the Hall with his wig uncombed and on one side. A student whispered to his neighbour, "See, his wig is no redd the day." The Doctor heard the remark, and when it came to the turn of the utterer to deliver a discourse, he was invited to the pulpit with these words—"Come awa, Mr. ——, and we'll see wha's got the best redd wig."

The Rev. Dr. Gillan, formerly of St. John's Church, Glasgow, obtained the church living of Inchinnan on the resignation of Dr. Lockhart, who succeeded his brother as owner of Milton-Lockhart. Dr. Lockhart left a number of sermons and other MSS. in an attic room of the manse, intending to remove them on his return from a Continental tour. In a letter to Dr. Gillan, he expressed a hope that the MSS. were kept free of damp. Dr. Gillan replied that "the MSS. were all quite dry, especially the sermons."

Mr. Birnie, minister of Lanark. was possessed of a nature

alike conciliatory and facetious.   After the erection of a new
parish church, a conflict arose between the corporations of the
tailors and shoemakers respecting a right to sittings in the
gallery.   All attempts to promote tranquillity proved fruitless,
till Mr. Birnie pronounced a decision in the following couplet :—

> " It is weel ken'd through a' the toun
> We draw on our hose before our shoon."

After the Disruption in 1843, very hostile feelings were
entertained by a portion of the seceding party against those
who remained.   Several parishioners of Blackford, Perthshire,
called on the Rev. John Clark, the parochial incumbent, and
preferred the request that they might have the services of a
non-erastian sexton.   " Will you allow us, sir, to dig our own
graves ? " said one of the party.   " Certainly," said Mr. Clark,
" you are most welcome ; and the sooner the better ! "

The Rev. William M'Cubbin, minister of Douglas, was a
noted humorist.   In repartee he on one occasion overcame
the Hon. Henry Erskine.   They were seated at the dinner-
table of a common friend.   A dish of cress being presented,
Mr. M'Cubbin took a supply on his plate, which he proceeded
to eat, using his fingers.   Erskine remarked that he reminded
him of Nebuchadnezzar.   " Ay," retorted Mr. M'Cubbin,
" that'll be because I'm amang the brutes."

The Rev. William Campbell, minister of Lilliesleaf, remembered as " Roaring Willie," was celebrated for his humour.
Returning from the General Assembly one hot day of June,
he found himself, as inside passenger in the stage-coach, much
oppressed by the excessive warmth.   When his discomfort
had reached the utmost pitch of endurance, he began to utter
sounds like the barking of a dog.   He said, " My friends, I
think it fair to mention that I was lately bit by a mad dog,
and I am afraid the heat of this place is bringing on the
disease.   *Wow—wow—wow !*   I feel it coming on.   I hope I
shall not hurt any one.   *Wow—wow—wough—wough—wough !* "
Several of the passengers called out lustily to the driver to
stop the coach, and all precipitately rushed out.   Mr. Campbell
got abundant accommodation during the remainder of his
journey.

Mr. Campbell lived at a period when festivities at the farm-
houses were prolonged till morning hours.   Returning from a
convivial meeting somewhat late, he stumbled, and being somewhat stunned, he fell asleep on the roadside.   In the morning

he was awakened by a cottar wife, who exclaimed, on helping him up, "Eh! Maister Cammel, wae's me! wae's me!" Realizing the awkwardness of his plight, Mr. Campbell held up his hand, deprecating further censure—then said, "Whist, woman; it's a wager!" Having silenced suspicion, he leisurely returned to the manse.

The Rev. Mr. M'Ewen, minister of the Secession Church, Dundee, was both eccentric and humorous. He was assisting at Montrose on a sacramental occasion. Dr. Jamieson, the author of the "Scottish Dictionary," then Secession minister at Forfar, was his fellow-assistant, and both were to sleep in the same bed. To a male bed-fellow Mr. M'Ewen, though a married man, entertained a morbid aversion. He got into bed first, and had scarcely lain down when he began to relate that he had lately been in the Highlands, and feared he had contracted a disorder common there, suiting the while the action to the word. Dr. Jamieson was content to seek repose on the floor of the apartment.

A clergyman who was a hard labourer on his glebe, and when so occupied dressed in a very slovenly manner, was one day engaged in a potato field, when he was surprised by the rapid approach of his patron in an open carriage, with some ladies, whom he was to meet at dinner in the afternoon. Unable to escape in time, he drew his bonnet over his face, extended his arms, covered with his tattered jacket, and passed himself off as a potato bogle.

The Rev. Michael M'Culloch, D.D., minister of Bothwell, was a man of sterling independence and great self-decision. To his friend, Mr. Thomas Brisbane, minister of Dunlop, he said, "You must write my epitaph if you survive me." "I will," said Mr. Brisbane, "and you shall have it at once." Next morning Dr. M'Culloch received the following :—

"Here lies interred beneath this sod
That sycophantish man of God,
Who taught an easy way to heaven,
Which to the rich was always given;
If he get in, he'll look and stare
To find some out that he put there."

Scottish pulpit prelections were often of a homely character. Mr. James Oliphant, minister of Dumbarton, was in the pulpit especially quaint. When reading the Scriptures, he was in the habit of making comments in undertones, on which account seats near the pulpit were best filled. In reading the passage of the possessed swine running into the deep, and being there choked, he was heard to mutter, " Oh that the devil had been choked too !" Again, in the passage as to Peter exclaiming, " We have left all and followed thee !" the remark was, " Aye boasting, Peter, aye bragging; what had ye to leave but an auld crazy boat, and maybe twa or three rotten nets ?"

There was considerable ingenuity in the mode by which Mr. Oliphant sought to establish the absolute wickedness of the devil. " From the word *devil*," said Mr. Oliphant, " which means an *enemy*, take the *d*, and you have *evil ;* remove the *e*, and you have *vil* (vile); take away the *v*, and it is *ill ;* and the last letter sounds *hell*.

The Rev. Peter Glas, of Crail, used the broadest Scotch, and in the pulpit discoursed so familiarly as occasionally to invite a colloquy with members of his flock. Many of his parishioners being fishermen, he prayed specially for their welfare. One day, using the expressions, " May the boats be filled wi' herrin' up to the very tow-holes (spaces for the oars), a fisherman lustily called out, " Na, no that far, sir, or we wad a' be sunk." Describing the sufferings endured by the Christians during the persecution under Nero, Mr. Glas proceeded : — " The persecutors tore the flesh from the bones of their living victims with red-hot—red-hot "—" pinchers may be, sir," exclaimed James Kingo, convener of the trades, who sat in the Weavers' Gallery. " Thank you, Convener." said the minister, " you're quite right—red-hot pinchers."

The late Dr. Pringle, of Perth, had in the pulpit a habit of blundering. Having occasion to quote the words " from the crown of the head to the sole of the foot," he misquoted them thus—" from the crown of the foot to the sole of the head," and then correcting himself, fairly overcame the risible faculties of his audience by saying, " Toots ! from the sole of the head to the crown of the foot."

Mr. Thomas Mitchell, minister of Lamington, in praying for suitable harvest weather, expressed himself thus :—" O Lord, gie us nane o' your rantin', tantin', tearin', winds, but a thunnerin', dunnerin',' dryin' wind.

Expounding the 116th Psalm, Mr. Shirra, of Kirkcaldy, remarked on the words of the eleventh verse, " I said in my haste, all men are liars," Aye, aye, David, you would not have required to make any apology for the speech had you lived now ; you might have said it quite at your leisure.

Mr. Alexander Peden, the famous Covenanter, with some of his adherents, had been hotly pursued by the Government dragoons. Nearly exhausted by the rapidity of his flight, he ascended a small hill and thus prayed :—" O Lord, this is the hour and the power of Thine enemies. They may not be idle ; but hast Thou no other work for them than to send them after us ? Send them after them to whom Thou wilt gie strength to flee, for our strength is gane. Turn them about the hill, O Lord, and cast the lap o' thy cloak over puir Saunders, and thir puir things, and save us this ae time, and we will keep it in remembrance, and tell to the commendation of Thy guidness, Thy pity and compassion, what Thou didst for us at sic a time." A cloud of mist arose, which enabled Peden and his party to escape. Meanwhile orders arrived that the dragoons should proceed in quest of Renwick and another party.

The Rev. Neil M'Vicar was minister of St. Cuthbert's, Edinburgh, when the city was occupied by the troops of Prince Charles Edward, after the battle of Preston Pans. He had a large congregation, and a considerable portion of his hearers were known to have Jacobite predilections. Nothing daunted, Mr. M'Vicar prayed, as usual, for King George, and added, " In regard to the young man who has come among us in search of an earthly crown, may he soon obtain what is far better—a heavenly one." The Prince, to whom a report of Mr. Mc'Vicar's expressions was communicated, said, " Let him alone, I would rather have the heavenly crown, were it secure."

Familiar utterances from the pulpit never exceeded those used by the Rev. Nathaniel M'Kie, minister of Crossmichael. Expounding a passage in Exodus, Mr. Mc'Kie proceeded thus : " And the Lord said unto Moses—Sneck that door ! I'm thinking if ye had to sit beside the door yoursel', ye wadna be sae ready leaving it open ! It was just beside that door that Yedam Tamson, the bellman gat his death o' cauld ; and I'm sure, honest man, he didna let it stay muckle open. And the Lord said unto Moses—I see a man aneath that laft wi' his hat on. I'm sure ye're clear o' the soogh o' the door. Keep aff yer bannet, Tammas ; and if yer bare pow be cauld, ye maun just get a grey warsit wig, like mysel'. They're no sae dear—plenty o' them at Bob Gillespie's for tenpence,"

The Rev. John Ross, minister of Blairgowrie, indulged his

propensity for verse-making in his pulpit announcements.   One day he intimated as follows :—

"The Milton, the Hilton, Rochabie, and Tammamoon,
  Will a' be examined on Thursday afternoon."

One of the oddest of the old school was the Rev. William Leslie, laird of Balnageith, and minister of St. Andrews, Lhanbryde.   During the war with France he received his weekly newspaper one Sunday morning just as he was leaving the manse for his duties in church.   While the precentor was singing the first psalm, he was busy with his newspaper ; and when the precentor ceased, he said, " Just sing another verse, John, till I finish this paragraph." .During the discourse, he gave the news of a recent battle, so that his procedure at the commencement of the service was the more readily excused. On another occasion, Mr. Leslie remarked, during the discourse, " You must excuse me, brethren, not entering so fully into the subject to-day, since I have an appointment to dine at Ardivit."   He referred to the country seat of a hospitable landowner.   Mr. Leslie was celebrated for the eccentric phraseology of his certificates.   One of his maid-servants was competitor for a prize offered by the Duke of Gordon to the servant in Morayshire who had been longest in her situation. From Mr. Leslie she received the following certificate :—

"Lhanbryde, August 3, 1836.

" By this writing, I certify and testify that Kate Bell came into my family and service at the term of Whit Sunday, in the year eighteen hundred and fifteen, and, without change, has continued to the date hereof, being a useful, canny servant at all work about the cows, the dairy, the sick nurse, the harvest hay and corn, the service of the parlour and bed chambers, and, of late years, mainly the cook.   That in my regards *she merits* any boon that our club has to bestow, having, in 1815, in her *teens*, been a comely, tight lass, though now fallen into the sere, and but little seductive, though a little more self conceited now than she was then—as much perhaps a good quality, when not in excess, as a fault.   In respect whereof, etc.,

"WILL. LESLIE."

No applicant to the Bible Society ever received a more extraordinary certificate than the subjoined :—

"Elgin, 3rd August, 1825.

" DEAR SIR,—The bearer, Jane Taylor, met me accidentally walking out this forenoon. She said if I would write this note, certifying that she is a very poor woman, you would make her the gift of a Bible. I think her whole appearance may, without my certificate, bear the most satisfactory evidence of her extreme poverty; and as she has not so much common understanding to be sensible that she may save her soul by the public worship of our pure Presbyterian Church, as surely as by the public worship of any of the schismatic synagogues, she increases the weight of her poverty by misapplying the greater part of what she gets from the collections made by the Presbyterians, for the poor of the parish, in support of schisms which the apostle, classing among the deepest sins, has assured us ' shall not inherit the kingdom of heaven.' And I am not very well assured, therefore, that a Bible will be of much real advantage to her, but I think it may not be amiss that you put it in her power to try ; as I am satisfied on the other hand, that having the Bible will not be to her prejudice.

" With every kind and good wish, I am, dear sir, respectfully yours,

" WILL. LESLIE.

" Bailie John Russel,
  " Treasurer of the Bible Society."

Poverty and the parishioners of Lhanbryde were close companions. The pastor was frequently required to recommend urgent cases to the charity of his more opulent neighbours. Each certificate bore the impress of his peculiar idiosyncrasy. The following is sufficiently amusing :—

"Lhanbryde, March 12, 1829.

" To all whom this does not concern, it is certified that the bearer, Ann Forbes, is the widow of Jock Laing, of no small consideration in his day, for the gratification of the fair by his fiddle, and subduer of stots in the plough by his strong and harmonious whistle, that he left his wife in poverty, and that she has applied for this as a license to beg, by which it is trusted that she may have use and wont success in this occupation, 'and a begging she will go.' In respect,

" WILL. LESLIE."

In drollery it would be difficult to exceed the following :—
" To all those of His Majesty's loving subjects only who

can sympathise with a transgressor of His Majesty's laws, under the impression that, though it was illegal, it was honestly innocent, I hereby certify, that William Rainey, the bearer, a simple, honest, and laborious day labourer in the back settlements of the improved Moss of Braemuckity, was in the bygone harvest subjected to the fine of twenty sovereigns and twenty shillings for the illicit distillation of ten shillings worth of ill-made malt, under the corporal punishment of the jail for half a year ; which punishment, that the country might not be punished by the loss of his highly useful labour in securing the crop, the bench reprieved for three months, in which space, with the price of the cow—dear to him as the poor man's ewe lamb of old—which a better king than our most gracious sovereign roasted for his supper—the transgressor managed to pay a dozen of sovereigns, notwithstanding of which, he must still undergo the whole punishment of the half year's incarceration, unless he can now succeed in eliciting the balance by the last resource—*begging*. In this regard he is recommended to those who have feeling hearts and half a sovereign in their purse. For the least moiety thereof he will be thankful now, and grateful all his life.

"Given by the minister of St. Andrews, Lhanbryde, at my house in Elgin, the 24th of April, 1826.

"WILL. LESLIE."

William Jack would not probably make much progress in his canvass, with no better recommendation than the following :—

"To all His Majesty's loyal subjects who can feel for a fellow sinner in distress. I beg to certify that the bearer, William Jack, is a son of my old bellman, a man well-known in this neighbourhood for his honest poverty and his excessive indolence. The bearer, William Jack, has fallen heir to all his father's poverty, and a double share of his improvidence. I cannot say that the bearer, William Jack, has many active virtues to boast of, but he has not been altogether unmindful of Scriptural injunction, and has laboured, with no small success, to replenish the earth, although he has done but little to subdue the same. 'Twas his misfortune to lose a cow, by too little care and too much bere (chaff) ; likewise that walking skeleton, which he called his horse, having ceased to hear the oppressor's voice, or to dread the tyrant's rod, now the poor man has nothing to look to, but the skins of the defunct, and the generosity of a benevolent public, by whom he hopes to be stimulated, through these testimonials, with receipt.

"WILLIAM LESLIE.

"Lhanbryde Glebe, 1829."

From my friend, Sheriff Barclay, I have the following anecdote :—

One clergyman meeting another the conversation turned on swine feeding, no small concern in the economy of the country manse. The one startled the other with the apparently rude remark, "Speaking of swine, how's your wife ?" No insult was intended. The gentlewoman was widely famed for swine-culture.

When it was proposed by the Secession congregation at Haddington to give *a call* to the afterwards celebrated Mr. John Brown, one of the members expressed his dissent. Subsequent to his ordination, Mr. Brown waited on the dissentient, who was threatening to leave the meeting-house. "Why do you think of leaving us ?" mildly inquired Mr. Brown. "Because," said the sturdy oppositionist, "I don't think you a good preacher. "That is my own opinion," said Mr. Brown, "but the majority of the congregation think otherwise, and it would not do for you and me to set up our opinions against theirs. I have given in, and I would suggest that you might do so likewise. "Weel," said the grumbler, "I think I'll follow your example, sir."

The unadorned literature of the pulpit exercised its more immediate influence on the church officer and parochial sexton. A late octogenarian minister in Fifeshire was proceeding to give out his text, when he suddenly remembered that he had left his MS. in his study. Explaining his loss and taking up his hat, he added, "Just sing from the beginning of the 119th Psalm, and I'll be back immediately." His return being delayed, the beadle met him at the door with the exclamation, "Come awa, sir, come awa, for we're a' cheepin like mice."

"How is it, John," asked a Fifeshire incumbent of his church officer, "that you so readily fall asleep when I'm preaching ; and when a stranger is in the pulpit, that you keep awake ?" "I can soon explain that," replied the officer. "When you are in the poopit yersel, sir, I ken that a' is richt ; but when a stranger preaches, I like to watch his doctrine a wee."—"Well,

John, you were very attentive, I remarked ; I hope you were pleased with my preaching," said a young probationer to the beadle who was disrobing him. "It was a' soun'," said the beadle, emphatically ; a criticism which admitted of a two-fold interpretation.

One of the shrewdest of parish beadles was Saunders Grant, village tailor at M——. "How is it, Saunders," inquired the minister, "that those two young neighbours of mine have their churches quite full, while, though I preach the same sermons that I did twenty years ago, my people are falling off !" Weel, I'll tell ye, sir," said Saunders, "its just wi' you as wi' mysel'. I sew just as weel as ever I did, yet that puir elf —— has ta'en my business quite awa. Its no the sewing that'll do, sir, it's the new cut ; it's just the new cut."

The Rev. Mr. C——, of East K——, was officiating on the occasion of a funeral. As he was about to return thanks after the service of wine and cake, the beadle whispered in his ear, "Be as dreich* as ye can, sir, for the glasses are frae Glasgow, an' I hae to wash them a' before we lift."†

Alexander M'Lachlan, beadle of Blairgowrie, had contracted a habit of tippling, which, though it did not wholly unfit him for his duties, had become matter of scandal. The Rev. Mr. Johnstone, the incumbent, resolved to reprove him on the first suitable opportunity. A meeting of kirk-session was to be held on a week-day at noon. The minister and beadle were in the session-house together before any of the elders arrived. The beadle had evidently been tippling, and the minister deemed the occasion fitting to administer a reproof. "I much fear, Saunders," began Mr Johnstone, "that the bottle has become —— " "Ay, sir," interrupted the officer, "I was jist to observe that there was a smell o' drink amang 's !" "How is it, John," said Mr. Johnstone to Saunders, on another occasion, "that you never go a message for me, but you contrive to take too much drink ? People don't offer me spirits when I make visits in the parish." "Weel, sir," said Alexander, "I canna precisely explain it unless on the supposition that I'm a wee mair popular wi' the folks."

A Paisley gentleman asked one of the beadles in that place as to what remuneration he received from those of the congregation who had children baptized in the church. "Sixpence," replied the officer, "is the ordinar' thing, ithers gie a shilling ;

---

* Lengthy.   † "Lift" is the *lifting* or removal of the corpse.

and those wha hae a proper notion o' baptism, gie the length o' half-a-crown."

Rob Herrick, gravedigger at Falkirk, was preparing the grave of a person deceased whom he held in esteem. To a gentleman who happened to come up, he concluded a eulogy on the departed by saying, "He was sic a fine chiel, that I'm howkin' his grave wi' a new spade." Herrick was not always disposed to celebrate the departed. A gentleman walking in the churchyard observed that the sward on a particular grave was unusually fresh and green. "Ay," replied Rob, "it's a bonny turf, but it's a pity to see it laid upon sic a skemp." Dr. F——, physician in Dumfries, who was a member of the kirk-session, had severely admonished the parish sexton on account of his habits of intemperance, and threatened to expose him. "Ah! doctor," said the gravedigger, with a roguish smile, "I've happit mony o' your *fauts*, an' ye maun just hide some o' mine."

George Scott, a sexton in Perthshire, rejoiced that an epidemic was raging in the parish; "for," said he, "for the last six months I ha'ena buried a leevin' sowl, binna a scart o' a bairn."

The country minister usually employs a man servant to dress his garden, manage his glebe, and attend to the out-door concerns of the parsonage. This person enjoys the distinctive title of "the minister's man," and if long in office, he becomes abundantly familiar with his employer. He identifies himself with what he conceives to be the best interests of his master. A minister in Greenock was proceeding on a journey to London, and his man carried his luggage to the railway station. Hearing the minister make application for an insurance ticket, he whispered to him confidentially, "Ye had better leave the ticket wi' me, sir, for they're gie an ready takin' thae things aff a corpse."

The minister's man at Lintrathen, though sufficiently respectful, seldom indulges in the complimentary vein. On a recent occasion he handsomely acknowledged a compliment by returning another. The minister had got married, and was presented with a carriage, for which John was appointed to provide a horse. Driving out with his wife, the minister said to John, in starting, "You've got us a capital horse." " Weel, sir, "said John," "its just aboot as difficult to choose a gude minister's horse as a gude minister's wife, and we've been gie an' lucky wi' baith."

The "man" is sometimes humorous at the minister's expense. A late minister at Cardross was of penurious habits. His "man" complained that he grudged even the mare's corn. On proceeding to ride out one day, the minister remarked, "The beast 's a little skeich, John." "I am afraid," responded John, "that the caff* has ta'en its head."

William Wallace, a minister's man in the south of Scotland, had, in his youth, frequently obtained at the annual district ploughing-matches the premium awarded to the first ploughman. The minister, forgetful of his "man's" reputation, had ventured to criticise a portion of his tillage. "Weel, minister," rejoined Wallace, "if ye can preach as weel as I can plow, ye'll tak the prize o' a' Nithsdale."

Peter Drummond, minister's man at St. Monance, Fifeshire, was one of the most amusing and eccentric of his class. The minister, Mr. Gillies, had reproved Peter for giving a short day's work, as he "left off at sunset, while his neighbours were known to thrash their grain with candle light." "Weel, sir," said Peter, "gin ye want the corn flailed by cannil licht, I'll dae yer wull." Next day, at noon, Mr. Gillies was passing the barn, and hearing the sound of Peter's flail, he stepped in. A candle was burning on the top of a grain measure. "Why this folly and waste?" said Mr. Gillies, pointing to the candle. "Dinna ye mind, sir," said Peter, "that you wantit the corn thrashed wi' cannil licht!" The minister replied, angrily, "Peter, you shall have no more candles." Some days after, Mr. Gillies was to set out on horseback to visit a sick parishioner. He requested Peter to saddle the horse. It was evening, and Peter, after remaining some time in the stable, led out the cow saddled and bridled. "I wish I ha'eua made a mistak, sir," said Peter; "but since I've got nae cannil, it's no muckle wonder that I hae pit the saddle on the wrang beast." Fairly overcome by Peter's drollery, Mr. Gillies gave him back his candles.

Unmarried clergymen usually intrust the management of of their domestic affairs to an experienced servant—one who is well reputed for her carefulness and discretion. These housekeepers are especially noted for plain speaking. "I'll take a little gruel to-night," said a young clergyman one Sabbath evening to his housekeeper. "Ye'll be the better o't, sir," said Janet, "for I observed in the kirk that there was something soor on your stomach."

* Chaff.

The late Rev. Dr. Wallace, of Whitekirk, had long in his service a faithful servant, who was justly respected by visitors at the manse. Among these was a late Earl of Haddington, a good-humoured country nobleman. "That's a fine pig," said the Earl, as, accompanied by old Janet he was surveying the minister's farm-stock. "Ou ay, it's an uncommonly gude swine," said Janet, "an' we ca't Tam, after yer lordship."

The church psalmody is led by an official, usually in humble life, who is styled the precentor. In rural parishes the precentor frequently retained office, long after he had become inefficient for public service.

The late Rev. Dr. Murray of Auchterderran, conducted pulpit duties after he had become an octogenarian. The precentor had likewise been long in office, and the insufficiency of his vocal powers had frequently been complained of. The doctor was reluctant to supersede an official so many years associated with him in his duties ; but resolved to give a hint which might induce him to resign. During a week-day conversation with him, the doctor proceeded—"Some o' the folks, John, were saying that you are scarcely so able for your duties now, and were suggesting"——Not permitting the minister to conclude the sentence, John broke in—"Ay, ay, sir, that's just what some o' them hae been sayin' to me aboot yersel." "If that be so," said the minister, "they must put up with us both a little longer."

In some of the northern counties there is almost in every parish a body of persons who bear the pre-eminent designation of "the men ;" and who, in virtue of their claim to superior sanctity, are permitted to exercise a sort of general superintendence both over minister and kirk-session. In church they occupy a conspicuous position near the pulpit, and there appear with the distinctive badge of a dark handkerchief enveloping their temples A candidate for admission into their ranks is called upon for a certain period to sit in church with his head enclosed in a white handkerchief. Full admission into office is evidenced by an assumption of the dark-coloured badge. During divine service the *men* nod approval, or groan disapprobation with the utterances of the pulpit. At the communion season, they hold meetings in the churchyard to supplement the services of the church ; and they are afforded by the minister an opportunity, at the Monday's dinner, of criticising the services of his assistants. A distinguished clergyman from the south who had been assisting at a communion in Ross-shire, met on the following

Monday with several of the *men* at the manse.   He listened with attention to their homely criticisms of the various services on the occasion ; but waited in vain for any allusion to his own.   "You have not mentioned my name, gentlemen," said the reverend stranger; "I hope my services were not altogether unacceptable."   "Ah, sir," promptly replied one of the *men*, "ye had fine psalms."

MAGNATES AND MAGISTRATES.

SCOTTISH gentlewomen supported the cause of Prince Charles Edward with all the fervour of devotion. Cherishing her family traditions, the Baroness Nairne preserved a lock of the Prince's hair, which she received from her mother ; and latterly parted portions of it among her friends, as the best token of her regard. Miss Dunbar, of Thunderton, afterwards Mrs. Anderson, of Aradowal, and Miss Flora Macdonald, caused sheets in which the Prince had slept to be carried with them in their journeyings, that they might not lose the opportunity of being shrouded iu their folds.

The lady of John, twelfth Lord Gray, secretly favourable to the Prince, was opposed to her husband risking his neck and his estates on the doubtful chance of his success. Having been slighted by the Duke of Cumberland, Lord Gray resolved to identify himself with the insurrection by joining the forces of the Prince. Aware of his vehement temper, Lady Gray did not offer any ostensible opposition. His lordship was complaining of a slight illness, and Lady Gray recommended that at bedtime he should take a foot-bath. He consented to the mild prescription, and Lady Gray instructed the attendant'to bring into the apartment a pitcher of boiling water, while she personally charged herself with the duties of the bath. His lordship having uncovered his limbs, Lady Gray plunged the contents of the pitcher on his legs and feet. A frantic roar testified that she had triumphed. Lord Gray was so scalded that locomotion was impossible. Her ladyship screamed in affected horror ; and the family physician was summoned. When his lordship recovered the use of his limbs, it was too late to offer service in the rebel cause, which had already issued in defeat and ruin.

Some Scottish gentlewomen have made hard hits. When John Graham of Claverhouse was Sheriff of Wigtonshire, he was, in presence of the witty Viscountess Stair inveighing against Knox. "Why be so severe on him?" said her ladyship; "you are both reformers: he gained his point by *clavers* [talk], you maintain yours with *knocks*."

Sir J. R., who was of questionable reputation, was entertaining a party of friends. After dinner he intimated a toast; and looking in the face of Miss M., who was more distinguished for wit than beauty, said, "I'll give you ' Honest men and bonny lasses.'" "With all my heart," exclaimed Miss M., "I'll drink it, for it neither applies to you nor me."

Colonel M'Donald, who commanded the Perthshire cavalry, was, at an evening party, complaining of his officers, and alleging that all the duties of the regiment devolved upon himself. "I am," said he, "my own captain, my own lieutenant, my own cornet." "And trumpeter too!" added a lady.

The lady of a late M.P. for Fifeshire was soliciting a miner for his vote to her husband, then on his canvass. At a short distance was a group of juvenile miners, one of whom remarked to his neighbour, "Oh, man, she has awfu' red hair; she wad set a body a-lowe." "You are quite safe," said the lady, turning to the speaker; "you are too green to burn."

During a visit to Abbotsford, the late Miss Catherine Sinclair was a party to a discussion as to the chieftainship of clan Macdonald, when the rival claims of Lord Macdonald, Glengarry, and Clanranald were discussed. Sir Walter Scott, knowing that Miss Sinclair was descended, through her mother, from Alexander, first Lord Macdonald, began jocularly to disparage the claims of that family, the Macdonalds of Slate. Miss Sinclair interrupted him. "Say what you please, Sir Walter, you will always find the slates at the top of the house!" She added, "Do you know my uncle's reply when Glengarry wrote to say that he had discovered evidence to prove himself the chief of the Macdonalds? 'My dear Glengarry,—As soon as you can prove yourself to be my chief, I shall be ready to acknowledge you; in the meantime,—I am *yours*, MACDONALD.'" Miss Sinclair, conversing with the old Earl of Buchan, brother of Lord Chancellor Erskine, expressed astonishment at some instance of ingratitude. "Never be surprised at ingratitude," said the peer; "look at your Bible. The dove to which Noah thrice gave shelter in the ark, no sooner found a resting-place for the sole of her foot than she returned no more to her benefactor." "Very true," replied Miss Sinclair; "give a man a ladder to go up, and immediately he turns his back upon you.'"

A clever Edinburgh gentlewoman, fond of repartee, was overcome by David Hume. "If I am asked what age I am," she said to the philosopher, "what answer should I make?" "Say," said Hume, "that you are not come to the years of discretion."

A gentlewoman, who proposed to match her daughter with an opulent baronet in the same county, was overmatched by the intended suitor. Taking the baronet aside, she said to him, with affected concern, "The people say, Sir William, that you and Julia are to be married; what shall we do about it?" "Oh," quietly responded the baronet, "just say she refused me!"

Lord Nairne, long an exile in France, on account of his share in the Rebellion of 1745, had conceived an intense disgust at the sober habits of the Continent. One day, having several Scottish friends at his table, he exclaimed, "I cannot express, gentlemen, the satisfaction I feel in getting men of sense about me, after being so long plagued wi' a set o' fools, no better than brute beasts, that winna drink mair than what serves them."

An uncle of the Earl of Kelly, an eccentric Jacobite, hearing that one of his sons had accepted from Government the office of superintendent of the hulks, sarcastically remarked, "Had the lad said he wanted a place, I think I micht have got him made hangman o' Perth."

James, seventh Earl of Abercorn, was asked by his brother George, who was in orders, to use influence on his behalf for a living worth £1,000 a year. The Earl wrote in answer, "Dear George, I never ask favours. Enclosed is a deed of annuity of £1,000 a year. Your affectionate brother,—Abercorn."

Henry, second Duke of Buccleuch, precise in his personal arrangements, desired to procure everything he used of the best quality. Being on a visit to the west of Scotland, he chanced to injure a portion of his dress, and stopping at Glasgow sent from his hotel for "the principal tailor." The messenger, not knowing the Duke's purpose, conveyed the message to Principal Taylor, of the University. The Principal speedily attended the Duke at the *Black Bull.* As he entered the parlour, the Duke addressed him, " Sir, I have sent for you to take my measure for a pair of trousers; my own have met with a slight accident, and I hope you can furnish me with a new pair by to-morrow morning." "My name is Taylor," replied the Principal; "but I am not professionally a clothier, but Principal of the University, and one of the city clergy."

"How awkward!" exclaimed the Duke. "I sent for the *principal* tailor, and my blundering messenger has put you to the trouble of this visit. I hope, Principal, you will dine with me, and that you will allow me to compensate you for the loss of your valuable time." The Principal remarked that he was much concerned in the welfare of the City Infirmary, which was deeply in debt. "Would £500 be useful to the institution?" said the Duke, writing a cheque for that amount, and handing it to his visitor.

An anecdote of the late Duke of Wellington, connected as it is with some natives of the north, may not be inappropriate.

On the death of his Duchess, the Duke of Wellington requested the Marquis of Tweeddale to look out for a prudent Scotsman who might become his *major domo* or private secretary. Lord Tweeddale being reluctant to undertake the task, the Duke said to him, "Just select a man of sense and send him up; I'll take a look at him, and if I don't think he'll suit, I'll pay his expenses and send him home." Returning to Yester House, the Marquis sent for Mr. Heriot, who rented one of his farms, and asked him whether he would undertake the proposed secretaryship. Mr. Heriot consented to make a trial. Arriving at Apsley House, he was kindly received by the Duke, who explained that, while all private business would terminate at one o'clock, the secretary would afterwards be required to entertain visitors. The latter duties seemed formidable; but Mr. Heriot did not seek an explanation. That evening the Duke gave a dinner party. On the guests being ushered into the dining-room, the Duke said, "Mr. Heriot, will you take the end of the table?" Embarrassing as was his position, the new *major domo* acquitted himself well, evincing on the various topics of conversation, especially on questions of the day, much correct information. Some members of the company described him "as an intelligent Scotsman," which concurred with the Duke's own sentiments. He was soon in the entire possession of his Grace's confidence. Walking in the city one day, Mr. Heriot met an old acquaintance from Scotland. "Hollo! Heriot," said the friend, "what are you doing in London?" "I am secretary to the Duke of Wellington," answered Heriot. "You be nothing of the sort," said the Scotsman; "and I fear you're doing little good, since you would impose upon me in this fashion." Returning to Scotland, it occurred to Heriot's acquaintance that he would write the Duke, warning him that one Heriot "had been passing himself off as his secretary." From Apsley House he received a reply in these words:—"Sir, I am directed by the Duke of Wellington to acknowledge the receipt of your letter ; and I am, your obedient servant, J. Heriot, Private Secretary."

Maxton, the laird of Cultoquhey, in Strathearn, was one of the most eccentric of Scottish landowners. He was surrounded by four potent families, each of whom he conceived was anxious to appropriate his patrimonial acres. He prayed daily that he might be delivered—

> "From the greed of the Campbells,
> From the ire of the Drummonds,
> From the pride of the Grahams,
> And from the wind of the Murrays."

" If you mention my name any more in your prayers, I'll crop your ears," said the ducal chief of the Murrays to Mr. Maxton, one day they chanced to meet. " That's wind," replied Cultoquhey,—an answer expressed so imperturbably that the Duke's equanimity was restored.

"A stupid fellow," James Boswell writes in his "Note book," was declaiming that kind of raillery called roasting, and was saying, " I am sure I have a great deal of good nature, I never roast any." "Why, sir," said Boswell, "you are an exceedingly good-natured man, to be sure ; but I can give you a better reason for your never roasting any. Sir, you never roast because you have got no fire."

One of the most eccentric of old Scottish baronets was Sir John Malcolm of Lochore, who was reputed for his exaggerated details of personal adventure. The following verses, celebrating his peculiarities, have been parodied by Burns :—

> " Ken ye ought o' Sir John Malcolm ?
>   Igo and ago ;
> If he's a wise man I mistak him,
>   Iram, coram, dago.

> " To hear him o' his travels talk,
>   Igo and ago ;
> To go to London's but a walk,
>   Iram, coram, dago.

> " To see the leviathan skip,
>   Igo and ago ;
> And wi' his tail ding owre a ship,
>   Iram. coram, dago," &c.

Old Armstrong, Laird of Sorbietrees, in Liddesdale, had been attending one of those convivial meetings common in that district. He had drunk overmuch, so that in crossing the ford of the Liddell, he fell from his horse partially into the water. In the morning he was discovered by one of his people, his head resting on the margin of the current. As a ripple of the stream touched his mouth, he exclaimed, believing that he was still in the banqueting-place, "Nae mair, I thank ye ; not a drap mair !"

"A certain laird," remarks a writer in the *Quarterly Review*, "had quarrelled with his eldest son, and was believed to have made a settlement to disinherit him. The young man was in the army, and in process of time his regiment came to be quartered in a town near the residence of his father. The laird, as was his wont, invited the officers to dine with him ; and the son, by the colonel's advice, came to dinner with the rest of the officers. The old gentleman perceived during the evening that his son was a sound and fair drinker ; and when the officers took leave of their host, he said, 'That laddie,' pointing to his son, with whom he had not exchanged a word, 'may bide.' He abode accordingly for several days; and the father, finding him as much impressed by the duties of the table as himself, burnt some papers before his eyes, and said, 'Now you may go back to your regiment.' He went back, and in due time succeeded to the estate ; nor did he ever during a long life fall off from this fair promise of his youth."

Mr. Durham, of Largo, was noted for his curious stories of personal adventure, and a disposition to exaggerate. The following anecdote respecting Mr. Durham's unfortunate habit has often been incorrectly told. Mr. Durham was present among a party of gentlemen, when a bet was taken as to whether he or another gentleman of the company, also noted for bouncing, would tell the greatest untruth. Informed of the wager, Mr. Durham observed, that "it was singular he had the reputation of being a liar, since he was quite sure he had never told a lie in his life." "I've lost," exclaimed the gentleman who had been inclined to support the claims of the other bouncer.

A servant who had long been in Mr. Durham's employment informed him that he could no longer remain in his service. "Why should you leave, John ?" said Mr. Durham ; "have I not always treated you well?" "Oh," responded John, " I have nothing to complain of on that score. But there is a

reason." Mr. Durham insisted that he should state it. "Well,
then, sir," said John, "I must just tell you that the folks on
the street often point to me and say, 'That's the man that has
the leein' maister,' an' I dinna like this." "But, John, did
you ever observe that I told an untruth?" asked Mr. Durham.
"Weel, sir," responded John, "you sometimes gang a little
owre far." "I am not sensible of it," said Mr. Durham, "but,
John, when you are standing behind me at table, and think I
am going wrong, just give me a wee dunch on the back."
Soon afterwards there was a dinner party in Largo House, and
Mr. Durham, as usual, entertained his friends with his reminiscences of travel. In America he said he had seen monkeys of
prodigious size, with tails twenty feet long. There were
expressions of surprise. John gave his master a nudge.
"Well, gentlemen," said the laird, "if the tails were not quite
twenty feet long, I am sure they were fifteen." There were still
expressions of surprise. John administered another nudge.
"Certainly I did not measure the tails," said Mr. Durham,
"but they could not be less than ten feet long." There was
another nudge. This was too much for the laird's endurance.
He turned round and exclaimed, "What do you mean, John?
would you allow the monkeys no tails at all?"

When Mr. Durham died, a wag proposed as his epitaph,—

> " Here lies Durham,
> But Durham *lies* not here."

His son, Admiral Sir Philip Durham, inherited his father's
failing in relating stories of doubtful authenticity. His supposed exaggerations have led in the Royal Navy to the saying,
"That's a Durham," when an apparent falsehood has been
spoken.

Some capital anecdotes of old Scottish judges are related by
Lord Cockburn in his "Memorials." Lord Eskgrove was a
person of great eccentricity. In sentencing a tailor for mur-
dering a soldier, he used these words,—" And not only did you
murder him, whereby he was bereaved of his life, but you did
thrust, or push, or pierce, or project, or propel the lithal
weapon through the belly-band of his regimental breeches,
which were his Majesty's." While summing up evidence in a
case for the opinion of the jury, Eskgrove said, "And so,
gentlemen, having shown you that the pannel's argument is
utterly *impossibill*, I shall now proceed for to show you that it
is extremely *improbabill*."

Lord Hermand was noted for his irritability. When presiding at the Circuit Court at Inverness a wag, aware of his weakness, set a musical snuff-box a-playing on one of the benches. A pause in the business of the court immediately ensued. "Macer, what in the world is that?" exclaimed the irate judge. The officer looked about to discover the delinquent. "It's 'Jack's alive, my lord!'" exclaimed the unsuspected offender. "Dead or alive, put him out this moment," said the judge. "We canna grup him, my lord," was the reply. "I say," exclaimed the judge, "let every one assist to arraign him before me at once." The music having stopped, the macer stated to his lordship that the offender had escaped. The trial was resumed, when in half an hour another tune sprung up. "He's there again!" cried his lordship. "Feuce the doors of the court; let not a man escape." Search proved useless. "This is *deceptio auris*," said his lordship, somewhat subdued.

The most humorous of all Scottish lawyers were John Clerk, afterwards Lord Eldin, and the Honourable Henry Erskine, younger brother of the Lord Chancellor Erskine. A young advocate in pleading before the Court of Session had unwittingly expressed his "surprise and indignation" at the judgment of the court. To ward off the rebuke of their lordships, Mr. Clerk rose to the relief of his friend, and assured the court that no disrespect was intended by the expressions of his learned brother. He added, as a peroration, "Had my learned friend as long experience of your lordships as I have had, he would not have been surprised at anything your lordships said or did."

A professional brother, Mr. Maconochie, informing Mr. Clerk that he had the prospect of being raised to the bench, asked him to suggest what title he should adopt. "Lord Preserve us!" said Clerk. In pleading before the same learned senator, who assumed the judicial title of Lord Meadowbank, it was remarked to Mr. Clerk by his lordship that in the legal document submitted to the court he might have varied the ever-recurring expression "also" by *likewise*. "No, my lord," said Clerk, "there's a difference; your lordship's father was Lord Meadowbank, and you are also Lord Meadowbank, but, pardon me, you are not *like wise*."

When he was promoted as a Lord of Session, Mr. Clerk assumed the judicial title of Lord Eldin, from his family estate. Some one remarking that his title resembled that of the Lord Chancellor Eldon, he replied, "The difference between us is all in my eye" (i). In addressing a jury, Mr. Clerk was speaking freely of a military officer who had been a witness in the cause. Having frequently described him as "this soldier," the officer, who was present, could not restrain himself, but started up, calling out, "Don't call me a soldier, sir; I am an officer." "Well, gentlemen," proceeded Mr. Clerk, "this officer, who is no soldier, was the sole cause of the disturbance."

Henry Erskine was an inveterate punster, and never failed to set the table in a roar. "You cannot play on my name," said Mr. Dunlop to Mr. Erskine, as he was one evening exercising his gift. "Nothing more simple," was the answer; "*lop* off the last syllable and it is *done*."

On a change of ministry Erskine was appointed to succeed Henry Dundas as Lord Advocate. On the morning of his appointment he met Dundas in the Parliament House, who had resumed the ordinary gown worn by all practitioners at the Scottish bar, except the Lord Advocate and Solicitor-General. After a little conversation, Erskine remarked that he must be off to order his silk gown. "'Tis not worth your while," said Dundas, "for the short time you'll want it; you had better borrow mine." "I have no doubt your gown," replied Erskine, "is made to *fit any party;* but, however short may be my time in office, it shall not be said of Henry Erskine that he put on the *abandoned habits* of his predecessor."

Erskine was indifferent to the rules of pronunciation. In pleading before a learned judge, he spoke of a *curator bonis.* "The word is 'curātor,'" said his lordship. "Thank you, my lord," said Erskine, "I cannot doubt your lordship is right, since you are so learned a senātor and so eloquent an orātor."

Lord Kames was presiding at a justiciary dinner at Perth, at which Erskine was present. His lordship, who was careful of his money, had not produced the usual quantity of claret. The conversation turned on Sir Charles Hardy's fleet, which was then blockaded by the French. "They are," said Erskine, "like us, confined to port."

Erskine sent two of his sons to a private school in Edinburgh, which was lighted from the roof. At a public examination of the school he observed some drops of rain falling on the floor in consequence of a broken pane, on which he remarked to the teacher, "I perceive, sir, you spare no *panes* on your scholars."

Hugo Arnot, the historian of Edinburgh, was extremely emaciated. He was one day, in his usual eccentric manner, eating on the street a *speldin*, or dried fish. Erskine came up. "You see," said Arnot, "I'm not starving." "I confess," replied the wit, "you are very like your meat."

From Mr. Erskine's MSS. in the Advocates Library we have the following epigrams:—

> "The French have taste in all they do,
>   While we are quite without;
> For nature, which to them gavo goût,
>   To us gave only gout."

> "'That prattling Cloe fibs, forsooth,'
>   Demure and silent Cynthia cries,
> But falsely; for can, aught but truth
>   Flow from a tongue that *never lies!*"

Erskine was once outmatched by his friend Mr. Durham. They met accidentally in the capital, when Erskine remarked that he could not ask his friend to dinner, as he was *penting* (painting) his house for the reception of his second wife. "Weel, weel," said Durham, "*pent* awa', Harry, and ye may also *re-pent.*"

Patrick, afterwards Lord Robertson, was a noted humorist. "Pray, Mr. Robertson," said a lady, "can you tell me what sort of a bird the bulbul is?" "I suppose," replied the humorous judge, "it is the male of the coo-coo" (cuckoo).

A miner, who had lost his leg by a colliery accident, waited on Robertson to consult him regarding an action of compensation. "You have gone to the wrong man," said Robertson. "Go to York Place, and ask for one *Shank More.*" The humorist referred to his professional brother, the late Mr. Shank More, advocate.

Having with a large fee been retained as counsel in a heavy jury trial at Glasgow, a solicitor in Edinburgh who had a minor case at the same sittings, enclosed to Mr. Robertson a small fee, apologizing for the smallness by stating that he had heard the learned counsel was going to Glasgow *at any rate.* The characteristic reply was that his friend was misinformed as to his going to Glasgow "*at any rate*," as it was at the rate of £500. Nevertheless, he would accept the lesser fee, and do his best for it. He did, and won the cause.

Robertson was ambitious of fame in a department in which he did not excel. He published two volumes of poems which

are chiefly remembered on account of the epitaph which his
sarcastic friend John Gibson Lockhart proposed for him,—

" Here lies the Christian, judge, and poet, Peter,
    Who broke the laws of God, and man, and metre."

Macdonald of Staffa was for many years Sheriff of Stirlingshire. He held his magisterial office in great dignity, and
would permit no expression of feeling in reference either to the
debates or decisions. When any noise was perceptible, he proceeded in measured tones to call out, " If any person in this court
disturbs the court, the court will instantly order the court to
be cleared."

Sir John Hay, Bart., a late Sheriff-Substitute of Stirling,
was one of the most facetious members of his order. He had
fallen into the habit of *crooning*, or whistling in an undertone,
some of the more popular Scottish airs. A youthful panel,
whose Christian name was Charles, was, in his court, found
guilty of an act of larceny. After pronouncing a sentence of
imprisonment, Sir John added, " Take care you don't come here
again, or——," he closed the sentence by humming the tune,
" Owre the water to Charlie."

In sentencing a carter to a period of imprisonment, Sir John
asked him to send his donkey to Gartur, his place of residence,
till he had undergone his punishment. Owing to his benevolent habits he was often deceived by mendicants. He ceased
to give money. Even when he bestowed bread he found that
loaves were exchanged for whisky. At length he fell upon
an expedient. From every loaf he distributed he bit a portion ;
it was thus rendered useless for the market, and had therefore
to be eaten.

The magistrates of rural, and even of more important burghs,
were formerly most imperfectly fitted for their responsible
offices. A bailie of the Gorbals, Glasgow, was noted for his
simplicity on the bench. A youth was charged before him
with picking a handkerchief from a gentleman's pocket. The
indictment having been read, the bailie, addressing the prisoner,
remarked, " I hae nae doot ye did the deed, for I had a handkerchief ta'en oot o' my ain pouch this vera week."

The same magisterial logician was on the bench, when a case
of serious assault was brought forward by the public prosecutor.
Struck by the powerful phraseology of the indictment, the bailie
proceeded, " For this malicious crime you are fined half a
guinea." The assessor remarked that the case had not yet

been proven. "Then," said the magistrate, "we'll just mak the fine five shillings."

Bailie Auchan, of Glasgow, had some persons brought before him charged with being concerned in a riot. The evidence was circumscribed, and the prosecutor claimed time for further inquiry. "Then," said the bailie, "let the prisoners be reprimanded till to-morrow." He meant *remanded*.

The chief magistrate of a western burgh was dining with the late Lord Eglinton. His lordship requested his opinion of the wines. "My lord," said the magistrate, "I'm no *accoucheur*." He meant *coonnisseur*.

An Edinburgh bailie had visited London. On his return he expatiated to a friend on the attention he had experienced from one of the city members. Describing how the M.P. had procured free access for him to many of the public institutions, he reached the climax of eulogy by saying, "Why, sir, he got me a *blank cartridge* for every place in London." Probably he meant a *carte blanche*.

When George IV. made his state visit to Scotland in 1822, the Town Council of Dundee sent a deputation to the capital to pay homage to his Majesty. That the town might be suitably represented, the deputation were provided with a carriage and four. The carriage was adorned with the arms of the corporation, the box contained a highly decorated hammercloth, and the members of the deputation wore silk gowns and cocked hats. On the return of the deputation the provost suggested that the various *paraphernalia* should be preserved as a *memento mori* of the royal visit.

A late Provost of Bathgate, in presenting the parochial clergyman with a piece of plate, subscribed for by the parishioners, concluded his address to the reverend recipient in these words,— "In short, sir, we a' regard you as a soundin' brass and a tinklin' cymbal."

A Provost of Lochmaben had fined a stormy woman for being drunk and disorderly. The penalty, amounting to seven shillings and sixpence, was paid. In course of the afternoon the provost called at the shop of the village cobbler, and in an excited manner exclaimed, "Oh, now I'm juist real mad at our fiscal and town clerk, that am I. What d'ye think they've gane an' dune? They've drunk a' Tibby Johnstone's fine, that have they, an' nevir offered me a glass o' yill—did they nae."

Late in last century, the servant of a candidate for parliamentary honours waited on the Provost of Lochmaben with a letter from his master soliciting the provost's support. 'The magistrate, on opening the letter, held the document by the wrong end. The servant ventured to notice the fact. "What!" said the indignant magistrate, "d'ye think I wad be fit to be Provost o' Lochmaben gin I couldna read a letter at ony end?"

Legal practitioners in the provincial towns, who conduct pleadings before the local courts, are styled Writers or Procurators. About the beginning of the century, two sheep-farmers on the Braes of Balquhidder had disputed regarding a matter of boundary, and resolved to have recourse to the law. Unknown to each other they proceeded to Dunblane, the seat of the district Sheriff, with the view of employing a Writer of whose expertness they had a good report. The lawyer undertook the case of the first who presented himself; but shortly after, the other intending litigant sought his services. He offered him a letter of introduction to a brother of the craft. The farmer accepted the note, and proceeded to the residence of the other practitioner. He was from home, and not to return till the following morning. The farmer resolved to remain for the night, and in the course of a solitary evening at the inn gratified his curiosity by peeping into the note addressed to the proposed defender of his claims. He read,—

> "Twa fat sheep frae the Braes o' Balquhidder—
> Fleece you the ane—I'll fleece the ither."

The farmer left the hotel at dawn, and hastened to the abode of his antagonist. They were not *fleeced!*

THE YEOMAN AND THE COTTAGER.

OWING to the admirable system of long leases the Scottish yeoman is, in political and other matters, entirely unfettered by his landlord, and, on suitable occasions, is not slow in asserting his independence.

" Where are you going, Milton ?" inquired Mr. Lyell of Kinnordy, of an aged crofter, whom he met upon the turnpike. " I'm gaein, sir, to Fotheringham to pay my rent." " A long distance, Milton," said Mr. Lyell. " It is a pity I did not purchase your farm when it was in the market, as then you had not needed to walk so far on rent-day." " Deed, Maister Lyell," responded the crofter, I had rather travel twenty miles twice a year to pay my rent than tak aff my bonnet to my laird ilka day."

During the curling season the landowners, the yeomanry, and all the athletic males of the country-side meet on " the roaring rink." The late patriotic Earl of Eglinton was an enthusiastic curler, and when the ice was keen was seldom absent from the meetings of his club on the Kilwinning curling-pond. Cox, a farmer and innkeeper, was director of the Earl's party. When his lordship's curling-stone was moving in the right direction Cox would exclaim, besom overhead, " Come on, Eglinton, my boy ; I like ye, come on." If the stone made a decided hit, he would add, " Man, lord, that's graund." When the stone missed he would, unable to restrain himself, call out, " Dag on't, Eglinton, ye've spoilt a'." Such was Scottish life upon the ice twenty years ago.

Many of the Lowland tenantry are men of enlarged views, and well qualified to administer counsel to those whose educational advantages have not been tempered by experience. A farmer, the elder of a rural parish in Forfarshire, was suggesting to his lately appointed and youthful pastor how he should proceed in his parochial visitations. "To John," he

said, "speak on any subject save ploughin' and sawin'; for
John is sure to remark your deficiency on these; and if he
should detect that you dinna ken aboot ploughin' and sawin',
he'll no gie ye credit for understanding onything else."

A peculiar phraseology, which obtains among hill farmers,
will, in certain circumstances, provoke laughter. When the
Rev. Mr. C —— was appointed to his parochial cure on the
Braes of Angus, a hill farmer in the parish was desirous of seeing
him. After an interview with the reverend gentleman, he said
to a neighbour, " I've jist been seeing our new minister. He's
weel faured, and I maist think he'll be weel likeit; but waes
me, he's been ill wintered." The farmer meant that the pastor
was, though good-looking and agreeable, somewhat thin and
delicate.

The old country farmer was pawky, humorous, and full of
jocundity. A probationer of the Church, who had been officiating in his native parish in Haddingtonshire, was somewhat
lengthy in his services. "I gave you good measure yesterday,"
said he to one of the farmers, " and I know that you farmers
like that." " Ou ay," answered the farmer, "we like gude
measure, but we also like it weel dighted."*

When Sir James Matheson purchased the Island of Lewis he
caused his factor to read to the assembled tenantry at Storno-
way some fifty regulations for their guidance. The reader had
no sooner concluded than a white-haired veteran exclaimed,
" We've already ten commandments, and canna keep them;
how will we keep fifty ?" The regulations were unenforced.

Fifty years ago a northern presbytery had a respected member of the name of Honey. At a large convivial party sundry
conundrums were proposed for solution. A venerable member
of the court, anxious to contribute his share to the common
stock, propounded the following :—" Why is our presbytery
like a bee-skep ?" Silence was broken by an honest yeoman
exclaiming, " Because it contains drones." The riddle was
not repeated.

Dr. Guthrie relates the following :—A farmer came to Mr.
Linton, master of the Grammar School of Brechin, with his
son, a stripling, who was bent on attaining a better education
than his sires. The father said, " My laddie, Mr. Linton, is
unco fond o' lear [learning], and I'm maist resolved to mak a
scholar o' him." " Oh," said Mr. Linton, "an' what business

---

* Winnowed.

are you to put him to?" "If he gets grace we'll mak a minister o' him," answered the farmer. "But if he does not get grace," persisted Mr. Linton, "what then?" "In that case," said the farmer, with some warmth, "we'll just hae to mak him a schulemaister." The pedagogue was silenced.

The Scottish farmer, though generally shrewd, sometimes nods. A Kincardineshire husbandman, in expressing to his minister a favourable opinion of his personal virtues, concluded his eulogy in these words,—"An' I especially like your sterling independence, sir. I have always said, sir, that ye neither feared God nor man."

A person who had been employed in agricultural pursuits was appointed Bank Manager at Bo'ness. It was arranged with the local traders and country farmers that the usual bank holiday of Good Friday should not be observed on account of the weekly market falling upon it, but that, in its place, the Monday following should be observed. The bank agent accordingly posted up the following intimation :—"Good Friday will be kept on Monday next."

Referring to a descent from the martyr, Captain Paton, a zealous Presbyterian, remarked to a country farmer that he had an ancestor who was hanged. "I dinna misdoubt it, sir," said the farmer, who intended to be complimentary rather than embarrassing.

There was some shrewdness in the prayer of the Alloa crofter : "Keep our souls from the devil, our bodies from the doctor, and our purses from the lawyer."

Even among the most uneducated portion of the rural peasantry will be found striking examples of natural acuteness.

The Rev. Dr. R——h expressed himself loftily. In the course of pastoral visitation he called on an elderly female, who familiarly invited him to "come in an' sit doon." The Doctor, who expected a more reverential salutation, said, in stately tones, "I am a servant of the Lord, come to speak with you about your soul." "Then ye'll be humble like your Maister," rejoined the cottager. Dr. R——h did not forget the reproof, and afterwards conducted himself less loftily.

A geologist, more celebrated for his science than for his orthodoxy, was chipping rocks on a Sunday morning in Dura Den. A cottage matron asked him what he was doing. "Don't you," said the geologist, "see that I am breaking and examining these stones?" "You're doin' mair," said the matron, "you're breakin' the Sabbath."

L

The Countess of A——, with a laudable desire to promote tidiness in the different cottages on her estate, used to visit them periodically, and exhort the inmates to cleanliness. One cottage was always found especially untidy, and the Countess at length took up a broom, and having, by its use, made an improvement, said to the housewife, "Now, my good woman, is not this much better?" "Ou ay, my leddy," said the matron,

" an' will ye tak a blast noo?" The irate housewife meant that, as the Countess had stooped to sweep the cottage, she might also smoke a pipe with its mistress!

An elderly woman in Dundee, who sold fruit, was visited by the chief magistrate, who stated that he had received complaints as to portions of orange peel being thrown on the pavement near her shop. The woman expressed regret that her customers should be careless of the public safety, but quaintly added, "Deed, Provost, the streets have never been sae weel

keepit since your grandfaither sweepit them." That his grandfaither was a scavenger was an unpleasant reminiscence, so the
magistrate retired.

John Scott, the late keeper of Melrose Abbey, was a stanch
upholder of Presbyterianism, and held in utter abhorrence the
members of the Romish priesthood. There is a Catholic chapel
at Galashiels, and two priests connected with it were visiting
the abbey. John described the building to the visitors, com-
menting as usual on the evils of Catholicism and the irregular
conduct of the monks. The visitors heard John's stories
unmoved; but on giving him a *douceur* at parting, one of them
said, "I see, John, you don't know us." "Ou ay," responded
John, "I ken ye brawly; ye're twa emissaries o' the deevil."

Robert Flockhart, preaching at Edinburgh, was asked by a
High Church clergyman at what college he had studied. "At
John Bunyan's College; were you there?" answered Flockhart.

The celebrated General Scott, of Balcomie, M.P. for Fifeshire, was, along with Lord Boyd, riding from Balcomie
House to the neighbouring town of Crail. By the way they
encountered James Mitchell, a man in humble life, reputed for
his pungent repartee and skill in verse-making. The General,
as he saw Mitchell approaching, offered to bet a guinea with
his companion that any word he might address to the old man
would immediately be converted by him into verse. Lord
Boyd accepted the bet, and as Mitchell came up exclaimed
"Boo!" adding, "Old fellow, can you make verse of that?"
After a short pause Mitchell gave forth the following :—

> "There's General Scott and the Lord Boyd,
> Of grace and manners both are void ;
> For, like a bull amang the kye,
> They 'boo' to folk as they gang by."

Lord Boyd owned that he had lost, and General Scott handed
the guinea to the rhymer.

A country laird heard that his man-servant had in the neighbouring village been denouncing him as "no gentleman." On
being charged with the offence, the servant stoutly denied it,
adding emphatically that he "aye kept his thochts to himsel'."

Bauchie Lee, the boatman at Dalserf Ferry, on the Clyde,
was reputed for his ready sayings and curious expedients.
Bauchie was in the habit of receiving from the Earl of Hynd-
ford a shilling for rowing him across, instead of one penny, the
usual fare. One day the Earl walked off without tendering

the wonted gratuity. As his lordship had proceeded to some distance, Bauchie called out, " My lord, if you have lost your purse, it has not been in my boat."

An elderly gentlewoman had employed the village mason to execute some repairs. During his operations John repeatedly remarked that "it was a very stourie job, and that he might be the better of something to synd [wash] it doun." The bottle was at length produced, with a very small glass, which was filled a little way from the brim and handed to the mason. "Ye'll no be waur o' that, John," said the lady. "Atweel, no, mem," responded the artificer, holding up the dwarfish glass, " I wadna be the waur o' that, though it were vitriol."

In the course of his pastoral visitations, a clergyman came to a house, when his knock for admission could not be heard amidst the noise of contentions within. After a little he walked in, asking authoritatively, " Pray who is the master of this house?" "Weel, sir," said the husband and father, "that is just the question we've been trying to settle."

Reputed simpletons occasionally give smart answers. A stout English gentleman, a visitor at a watering-place on the west coast, was in the habit of conversing familiarly with Donald Fraser, a character of the place, who delighted to talk of his great relations. One day, as the gentleman was seated at the door of his lodging, Donald came up driving a fat boar. "One of your great relations, I suppose, Donald?" said the gentleman. "No," quietly retorted Donald, surveying the proportions of his interlocutor, "no relation whatever, but just an acquaintance like yoursel."

Professor John Hill, of Edinburgh, met in the suburbs of the city an inoffensive creature, who was regarded as an imbecile. Somewhat irritated by the creature's constant intrusion on the privacy of his walk, the professor said to him, " How long, Tom, may one live without brains ?" " I dinna ken," said Tom ; "how long hae ye lived yersel' ? "

A young man, deficient in judgment, was attending a university class, and when he came to be examined indicated absolute ignorance of the subject examined upon. Indignant at his stupidity, the professor said, "How, sir, would you discover a fool ?" " By the questions he would put," was the unexpected answer.

Bill Hamilton, the half-wit of Ayr, was lingering about a loch which was partially frozen. Several young ladies were deliberating as to whether they would venture on the surface, when one of them suggested that Bill should be asked to walk on it first. The proposal being made to him, Bill answered, " I'm daft, but no ill-bred ; after you, leddies."

Scottish youth, even in the humbler ranks, are not deficient in shrewdness. An old lady, relates Dr. Guthrie, was walking in Hanover Street, Edinburgh, with a large umbrella in her hand. A ragged urchin came up, without cap or shoes, and appealed to her for charity. She gave a grunt ; he persisted, and she gave him a poke. He now called out, "Jist oot o' the infirmary, mem, wi' the typhus." He had hit the proper chord at last. Apprehensive of infection, the ancient gentlewoman thrust a shilling into the boy's hand, and hastened off.

"Why don't you take off your bonnet to me?" said Mr. Stirling, an important landowner, to the small son of a cottager who was proceeding to his mansion, bearing a couple of fowls in each hand. "I'll tak aff my bannet," said the boy, "an ye'll haud the hens."

During the Voluntary controversy, Dr. John Ritchie, of the Potterrow Church, Edinburgh, was one of the foremost champions on the Voluntary side. At a public meeting held at Dundee, the reverend gentleman was descanting on the misrepresentations to which his opponents had subjected him. "They have," he said, "called me everything but a gentleman, everything but a minister ; nay, they have compared me to the devil himself. Now," he proceeded, coming forward to the front of the platform, and exhibiting a well-shaped limb, "I ask if you see any cloven foot there?" "Tak aff yere shae," (shoe), vociferated a youth from the gallery. The oratory was spoiled !

Scottish youth are prone to discover peculiarities in their seniors, and to bestow corresponding appellatives. Three reverend gentlemen, bearing the same patronymic, ministered in a western town. They belonged to different denominations, but it was difficult readily to distinguish in conversation which was meant. The young folks were at no loss: to them one was "Dirty D——," a second "Dainty D——," and a third "Dandy D——." Three successive tenants on the farm of Laws, parish of Monifieth, bore the surname of Peter. They were known as "Whisky Peter," "Ale Peter," and "Water Peter." A land surveyor in Fifeshire who lacked his right hand was known as "Handy Martin." My father, who wore

a large necktie, was styled "The British Linen Company," a
designation which he enjoyed.   An Edinburgh banker was,
owing to a crouching gait, known as " The Deerstalker." The
late Rev. John Mackenzie, of Lochcarron, bore the *sobriquet* of
" Potato John," on account of a foolish escapade practised in
his presence by a college companion, and which was erro-
neously ascribed to him.   It was alleged that he thrust a hot
potato in the hand of a college companion who was indiscreetly
expatiating in a long blessing while his associates were starving.
Thirty years ago there were two distinguished students at St.
Andrews, who each bore the name of John Anderson.   Their
comrades indicated their individuality by styling one *the Intellectual* and the other *the Profound.*   Two teachers in a well-
known seminary bore the name of Mill.   The one was the
antitype of Chesterfield, all suavity ; the other was the embo-
diment of discipline, and the rod was his sceptre.   The pupils
designated one *the Flour Mill,* the other *the Thrashing Mill.*   The
holders of pluralities were celebrated in rhymes more or less
doggerel.   The following are specimens :—

> "Sir Aulay Macaulay,
>   Laird o' Cairndhu,
>   Provost o' Dumbarton,
>   And Bailie o' the Row."

Sir James Strachan, Bart., minister of Keith, in Banffshire,
was celebrated in these lines :—

> "The beltit knicht o' Thornton,
>   An' laird o' Pittendriech ;
>   An' Maister James Strachan,
>   The minister o' Keith ! "

Mr. John Anderson, minister of Fochabers, had a turn for
business, and was accordingly appointed by the Duke of Gordon
his local factor and a county magistrate.   His pluralities were
thus rhymed upon :—

> "The Rev. John Anderson,
>   Factor to his Grace,
>   Minister of Fochabers,
>   And Justice of the Peace."

    Illustrations of juvenile stolidity may be found everywhere ;
but we have on the subject two anecdotes too humorous to be
omitted.   Mr. Nicolson, one of the Educational Commissioners,
was prosecuting his investigations in the Hebrides.   Examining

a class of young persons on the Shorter Catechism, he endeavoured to ascertain whether any ideas were associated with the words committed to memory. Putting the question, "What was the sin whereby our first parents 'fell from the estate wherein they were created ?" he obtained a 'ready answer in the words of the Catechism, "eating the forbidden fruit." Having changed the form of the question, he failed for a time to elicit any response, till at length a girl of fourteen said timidly, "Committing adultery, sir."

Dr. Guthrie relates the following :—"A boy, whose father and mother were dead, was taken on hand by a benevolent person. The gentleman began to ask the boy some questions, and among others, 'When your father and mother forsake you, Johnny, do you know who will take you up ?' 'Yes,' said he, 'I know perfectly well, sir.' 'Who will take you up ?' said my friend. 'The police!' said Johnny."

In his utterances the Scottish peasant frequently blends the Irish *bull* with native wit. An eloquent preacher was discoursing in a tent. His discourse was so extremely pathetic that the audience, with the exception of a solitary clodhopper, were moved to tears. The clodhopper, on being asked how he could listen to the discourse unmoved, made answer, "I dinna belang to this parish."

My friend Capt. D——, a member of the Episcopal Church, lately erected on his estate in Morayshire a place of worship in connection with his own communion. Soon afterwards, on inspecting a newly erected sheep-pen, he remarked to one of his hinds that it was too extravagantly ornamented. "Deed is it, sir," responded the hind, "its owre Episcopal chapel lookin'."

In one of his walks Sir Walter Scott was leaning on the arm of his attendant, Tom Purdie. Tom said, "Them are fine novels o' yours, Sir Walter ; they're just invaluable to me." "I am glad to hear it, Tom," said Sir Walter. "Yes, sir," proceeded Purdie, "for when I have been oot a' day hard at wark, and come hame tired, I put on the chimley a pint o' porter, an' tak up ane o' yere novels, and wad ye believe it, sir, I'm asleep directly !"

During cholera times, a Glasgow joiner was asked by a lady who was employing him at some household work, whether he would have a glass now, or wait till he had finished his job. "I'll be takin' the glass *noo*, mem," said the artisan, "for there's been a pour [vast number] o' sudden deaths lately."

A low-country hind was describing to Donald, his highland

cousin, how much enjoyment he had experienced at a recent wedding. " It's a' vera weel, Sawney," said Donald, " but let me hae a gude solid funeral, an' I wadna gie't for ten waddins." Donald alluded to the copious libations of whisky which usually attend death and burial in the highlands.

Social enjoyment among the Border peasantry formerly consisted in positive inebriety. John Anderson, blacksmith, in Ettrick, in passing through the hamlet late one evening, was heard by a bystander to be muttering, " I've spent half a crown, and, dash it, I'm not drunk yet " He was disgusted with his sobriety.

The Rev. Mr. G——, formerly of Stirling, remarked to one of his hearers that he had heard he was about to be married for the third time. The reverend gentleman added, " They say, John, you're getting money with her; you did so on the two last occasions ; you'll get quite rich by the wives." " Deed, sir," quietly responded John, " what wi' bringin' them in and putting them out, there's nae muckle made o' them."

The sexton of Dunino was visited early one morning by Alexander Bell, an aged labourer. " Gude mornin', Saunders," said the sexton, " I hope ye're a' weel." " Thank ye," said old Saunders, " we're a' weel, only the wife's dead." Saunders had lost his wife the previous evening.

The late Rev. Dr. Duncan, of Ruthwell, was early in the century delivering a course of week-day scientific lectures in his parish. The doctor one evening stated the discovery of Copernicus respecting the double motion of the earth. The lecture called forth severe strictures in regard to the Doctor's orthodoxy, and an old cobbler undertook to prove that not only was he theologically unsound, but scientifically erroneous. He *proved* the latter by appealing to the fact that he suspended a dried fish on a pin outside his door in the evening, and that he " found it in precisely the same position next morning, which would not have happened if the earth flew roun' like a ba'."

A Highland drover, who happened to be at Dumfries, was distressed to find one of the natives whistling a secular tune upon the Sunday. Having expressed his indignation to a bystander, who agreed with him in condemning the levity, he was asked by this party if there were no bad practices in the Highlands. The drover was at a loss to remember. " Don't they take rather much whisky," persisted the bystander, " and you know that is a very bad thing." " Very bad," responded Donald, " and especially bad whisky."

Mr. Boyd, in his "Reminiscences,"* presents the following:— His brother-in-law, Captain Robinson, had, in the course of surveying the west coast, received on board his steamer the Grand Duke Constantine of Russia. As the Duke could only remain a short time, the captain resolved to show him as much as possible during his brief stay. Accordingly, he steamed to Iona on a Sunday, believing that day especially suited for pointing out to his royal visitor remains associated with religion. Landing on the island, he waited on the custodian of the ancient church with the request that he would open it. "Not so," said the keeper, "not on Sunday." "Do you know whom I have brought to the island?" said the captain. "He's the Emperor of a' the Russias, I ken by the flag," responded the keeper; "but had it been the Queen hersel', I wadna gie up the keys on the Lord's day." "Would you take a glass of whisky on the Sabbath?" inquired the captain. "That's a different thing entirely," said the keeper.

The clergy were formerly debarred from every social recreation and personal amusement. One of the first to shake off these severe restraints was Mr. Ralph Erskine, of Dunfermline, one of the founders of the Secession Church. The following anecdote in connection with Mr. Erskine and a narrow-minded peasant has been often related, but not always correctly :—The jobbing gardener of Inverkeithing desired to have baptism administered to his child, but having differed with his parish minister, whom he accused of worldliness, he resolved to solicit the services of a neighbouring pastor. Reaching his manse, accompanied by his wife carrying the baby, he inquired whether the minister was at home. By the maid-servant he was informed that the minister was a-fishing, but that he would certainly return soon. "He may come hame when he likes," said the gardener, "but nae fishin' minister shall bapteeze my bairn!" The party proceeded to another manse, but the incumbent was, according to the story, "oot shootin'." "Nae shootin' minister" would suit the angry gardener, who, in his distress, proposed that his spouse should accompany him to "gude Maister Ralph Erskine at Dunfermline, wha," he added, "I'se warrant, will be better employed than in fishin' or shootin'." As the wanderers approached Mr. Erskine's residence, they heard the notes of a violin, and the gardener at once concluded that the reverend gentleman was from home. "The minister's no at

* "Reminiscences of Fifty Years," by Mark Boyd. London, 1871, 8vo., pp. 55—57.

hame, I see," said he, addressing Mr. Erskine's servant. "The minister is at hame," said the girl, "and dinna ye hear?—he's takin' a tune till himsel' on the fiddle; he taks a tune ilka e'enin'." The gardener was almost frantic. "Could I hae believed it," exclaimed he, "that Maister Ralph Erskine wad play the fiddle!" He was somewhat relieved by learning that Mr. Erskine did not use the ordinary instrument, "the wee sinfu' fiddle," but the violoncello, or "big gaucy fiddle." So he was content to accept baptism at his hands.

Janet Halliday was much distressed when she heard that her minister, the Rev. George Barclay, was removing from Hutton to the charge at Haddington. Meeting him one day, she said, "Oh, Maister Barclay, what for are ye to leave the folks o' Hutton, wha wud sae fain keep ye?" "I am obeying a call of Providence," said Mr. Barclay. "Aweel, aweel," said Janet, "and Providence is unco kind to ye a', for He never ca's ye to a waur stipend!"

No greater compliment was ever paid to the pathos of Christian eloquence than the following:—Dr. Carstairs, minister of Anstruther-wester, was remarkable for his thrilling utterances in exhorting Tables. He was in the habit of assisting at the communion at Dunino. My father, the incumbent, asked an elderly widow her opinion of the Doctor's services. "Deed, sir," said the widow, "I begin to greet [weep] when Dr. Carstairs begins to speak, for I ken I'll greet before he's dune."

Some forty years ago, the mother of Harry Johnstone, the famous humorist, invited a number of his cronies to supper, in honour of her son, who was on a visit to her at Edinburgh. At the supper table Harry told his drollest stories, exciting the greatest merriment. After a great explosion of laughter a dame rose up, and, holding a handkerchief to her face, said, addressing the humorist, "Maister Harry, excuse me for no laughin', for I hae got a sair mouth."

Dr. Andrew Bell, minister of Crail, was setting out for a drive with an invalid daughter, when a labourer called to seek baptism for his child. Mr. Bell promised that he would call on an early day to converse with him about the ordinance. He did so, and was met by the labourer's wife, who accosted him thus:—"The bairn's bapteezed by the bishop, and ye did vera ill to refuse baptism to my man; for if he hadna been a learnit man, Lord Kellie wadna hae employed him to brak' stanes."

A countrywoman was proceeding to church along a miry

road, when she was recommended by a neighbour pedestrian to select her steps more carefully. "Deed, I just tak it straught on, woman," was the reply; "ye ken we canna buy the Word owre dear."

The late Rev. William Ramsay, of Alyth, was visiting an old woman, one of his parishioners, who was especially zealous in her attachment to the Established Church. She informed him that she had completely silenced the wife of a neighbouring cottager who was advocating the cause of Dissent, by showing her the passage, Acts xvi. 5, "And so were the churches *established.*"

An agent of one of the religious societies entered a cottage in a Highland parish, and proceeding to exhibit his wares, announced himself as the *colporteur.* "Then gang awa, man," said the woman of the cottage; "we require nane o' yer gear, for we burn peats here." The matron mistook her visitor for a *coal porter.*

Mr. H——, a clergyman in Forfarshire, was visiting a cottar family in a sequestered portion of his parish. A girl of five years screamed most vociferously as he approached the cottage, nor would any gentle expedient induce her to be silent. Mr. H—— began to express regret that the child should have been led to regard the minister with alarm. "Hout na," said the mother, "that's no the reason ava'; it's no because ye're the minister; she thinks ye're to stick the soo." The butcher had been expected.

A country minister in Fife, who had been translated from one parish to another, was one Sunday exchanging pulpits with his successor in his former charge. At the close of the service an elderly woman asked him what had become "of her ain minister." "Oh, we're exchanging," he replied, "he's with my people to-day." "Indeed, indeed," said the matron, "they'll be gettin' a *treat* the day."

Lady Janet Sinclair, mother of the Right Honourable Sir John Sinclair, was much concerned in the welfare of her female dependents. During a serious illness she recommended her attendant to get married as the best means of rendering herself independent. The young woman hinted that she had already entered into an engagement, but was prevented carrying it out by a little impediment. "What is that?" said Lady Janet, anxiously. "Only just, my lady, that the man is married already, and his wife is not dead yet; but they say she's very near her end."

The Rev. Dr. Maclean, minister of the Gorbals, Glasgow, used to relate the following. In marrying a couple he failed to obtain any indication from the bridegroom as to whether he would accept the bride as his helpmate. After a considerable pause, the bride, indignant at the stolidity of her intended husband, pushed down his head with her hand, at the same time ejaculating, "Canna ye boo [bow], ye brute?"

Modes of expression are peculiar to the peasantry in certain localities. In the counties of Berwick and Roxburgh, tea is, by the peasantry, pronounced *toy*, a word which also denotes an old woman's *mutch*. Water is in the same district pronounced *waiter*, a name familiar to travellers. A friend being some years ago on a visit to Roxburghshire, established his head quarters in a town bordering on the Tweed. Walking out one morning by the margin of the river, he heard a fisherman say to his neighbour, "Lord John Scott last nicht was burnin' the waiter." "Burning the waiter!" ejaculated my informant; "and is he dead?" "Na," said the *piscator*, "there's naebody ony waur. They had fine sport." "Do you call burning a person sport?" asked my horrified friend. "There was naebody brent,". said the fisherman, "only a *waiter*." "And is not a waiter a man?" persisted my friend. "Oh, we mean *waiter*—watter—watter. His lordship was fishin' in a river wi' torchlicht, and that we ca' *burnin' a waiter*."

The kindly consideration evinced by the Scottish peasantry towards the domestic animals has frequently been remarked. Shepherds are most attentive to their dogs, which consequently become their attached companions. A clerical friend who formerly ministered in Roxburghshire was visiting a member of his flock. Before the fireplace lay three dogs, apparently asleep. At the sound of a whistle, two rose up and walked out; the third remained still. "It is odd," said my friend, "that this dog does not get up like the others." "It's no astonishin' ava," said the shepherd, "for it's no his turn; he was oot i' the mornin'."

A friend staying in the family of a sheep farmer in the south country remarked that daily as the family sat at dinner, a shepherd's *collie* came in, received its portion, and soon after disappeared. "I never see that dog," said the visitor, "except at dinner." "The reason is," said the farmer, "we've lent him to oor neebour, Jamie Nicol, an' we telt him to come hame ilka day to his denner. When he gets his denner, puir *beast*, he gaes awa back till his wark."

About twelve years ago the remains of a man named Gray, who lived in poor circumstances, were interred in the Greyfriars Churchyard, Edinburgh. His little terrier dog, "Bobby," accompanied the funeral party to the grave, where next morning he was found keeping affectionate watch. The keeper of the ground drove "Bobby" away, but next morning he was back again, and the third morning too, though it was cold and wet. At length the keeper's heart was moved, and he fed poor Bobby. Another benefactor arose in Sergeant Scott, of the Royal Engineers, in whose house Bobby dined daily for some years. When the sergeant went elsewhere, Mr. John Trail of Greyfriars Place succeeded him as Bobby's benefactor. Every day, as the castle gun signalled one o'clock, did Bobby leave his post for his daily meal; when it was finished he hastened back to the grave. For twelve long years, in all conditions of the weather, did Bobby maintain his watch. The faithful animal died in 1871, and was interred close by the grave of that master whom it had loved so well. By an eminent artist its portrait has been painted, and the Baroness Burdett Coutts has erected at Edinburgh a memorial fountain bearing Bobby's name, thereby commemorating the power and endurance of canine affection.

INDEX.

LIST OF STANDARD BOOKS

PUBLISHED BY

CHARLES GRIFFIN & COMPANY,

10, STATIONERS' HALL COURT, LONDON.

Aitken's (William, M.D., Prof. of Pathology in the Army Medical School, &c., &c., &c.) The Science and Practice of Medicine, in two vols., 8vo., bound in cloth, with a Steel Plate, Map, and nearly 200 Woodcuts. The Sixth Edition. Price 38s.

" *The Science and Practice of Medicine* must now be looked upon as the standard text-book in the English language."—*English Medical Journal.*

" The present work contains information that will not be found in any other manual of medicine."—*Athenæum.*

" The book is the most comprehensive of any that have in late years been published on the Practice of Medicine."—*British Medical Journal.*

" A more excellent work we really do not know."—*Lancet.*

" We most strongly recommend Dr. Aitken's work to every student and practitioner of medicine."—*Medical Times and Gazette.*

A Manual of Instruction for Attendants on Sick and Wounded in War. By Staff Assistant-Surgeon A. MOFFITT. Published under the sanction of the National Society for Aid to the Sick and Wounded in War. With numerous illustrations, post 8vo., cloth, 5s.

" A work by a practical and experienced author. After an explicit chapter on the Anatomy of the Human Body, directions are given concerning bandaging, dressing of sores, wounds, &c., assistance to wounded on field of action, stretchers, mule litters, ambulance, transport, &c. All Dr. Moffitt's instructions are assisted by well executed illustrations."—*Public Opinion.*

" A well written volume. Technical language has been avoided as much as possible, and ample explanations are afforded on all matters on the uses and management of the field hospital equipment of the British Army."—*Standard.*

Altar of the Household (The); A Series of Prayers, and Selections from the Scriptures, for Domestic Worship, for every Morning and Evening in the Year. Edited by the Rev. Dr. HARRIS, with an Introduction by the Rev. W. LINDSAY ALEXANDER, D.D. Royal 4to., cloth, gilt edges, 21s.; calf, gilt edges, 42s.; Levant morocco, antique, gilt edges, 50s.

.* Also, Illustrated with a Series of first-class Engravings on Steel, illustrative of some

Ansted's (Professor) Natural History of the

Inanimate Creation, recorded in the Structure of the Earth, the Plants of the Field, and the Atmospheric Phenomena. With numerous Illustrations. Large Post 8vo., 8s. 6d., cloth.

Applied Mechanics, by Professor W. J. Macquorn

Rankine. Sixth Edition. Cloth, 12s. 6d.

Beethoven. A Memoir. By Elliott Graeme.

With an Essay (Quasi Fantasia) "on the Hundredth Anniversary of his Birth," and remarks on the Pianoforte Sonatas, with hints to Students. By Dr. FERDINAND HILLER, of Cologne. Beautifully printed, and handsomely bound in cloth, gilt, 3s. 6d.

"This elegant and interesting Memoir....The newest, prettiest, and most readable sketch of the immortal Master of Music."—*Musical Standard.*
"A gracious and pleasant Memorial of the Centenary."—*Spectator.*
"This delightful little book—concise, sympathetic, judicious."—*Manchester Examiner.*
"We can, without reservation, recommend it as the most trustworthy and the pleasantest Memoir of Beethoven published in England."—*Observer.*
"A most readable volume, which ought to find a place in the library of every admirer of the great Tone-Poet."—*Edinburgh Daily Review.*

Biblical Cyclopædia; or, Dictionary of Eastern

Antiquities, Geography, Natural History, Sacred Annals and Biography, Theology, and Biblical Literature, illustrative of the Old and New Testament. By Rev. JOHN EADIE, D.D., LL.D. With Maps, prepared expressly by W. and A. K. JOHNSTON, and numerous Pictorial Illustrations. Just published, the Thirteenth Edition, embracing all the latest Discoveries and Explorations. Large post 8vo., 700 pages, handsome cloth, price 7s. 6d.

"It gives within a moderate compass a great amount of information, accurate and well put together. The article on 'Creation,' with its survey of the question as it stands between science and the Mosaic Cosmogony, may be cited as a specimen of the candour and liberality with which the Editor has done his work."—*Spectator.*
"We must regard this Bible Dictionary of Dr. Eadie's as decidedly the most adapted for popular use, and have always found it a reliable authority. To the clergy not possessed of large libraries, and to whom the price of books is important, we can cordially recommend the present volume."—*Clerical Journal.*
"We have no hesitation in recommending the work before us as the cheapest and best Bible Dictionary in a small form we have yet seen."—*The Rock.*
"The information given is condensed, yet clear, full, and accurate, exhibiting the results of profound and extensive research, though dispensing with the technical forms of learning and criticism."—*Scotsman.*
"Altogether, in arrangement, accuracy, judicious selection, and completeness, as well as cheapness, we consider Dr. Eadie's work one of the highest merit in its own department of literature."—*Glasgow Herald.*

Bookkeeping, a Complete System of Practical,

exemplified in Five Sets of Books, arranged by Single Entry, Double Entry in present practice, and a new method of Double Entry by Single. And an Appendix, containing a variety of Illustrations and Exercises, with a Series of Engraved Forms of Accounts. By C. MORRISON, Accountant. Ninth Edition, with valuable additions and improvements. 8vo., half-bound, 8s.

Brougham, The Life of Lord. His Career as a

Statesman, a Lawyer, and a Philanthropist, from Authentic Sources. By JOHN McGILCHRIST. Foolscap 8vo., with a fine Portrait on Steel. Cloth, 2s. 6d.

Bryce's Gazetteer and Johnston's Atlas. Comprising an Account of every Country and important Town and Locality in the World, from Recent Authorities. By JAMES BRYCE, LL.D., F.G.S. With numerous Engravings, and an Atlas of Twenty very beautiful Maps, engraved and printed in colours by Messrs. JOHNSTON, of Edinburgh. Roxburghe binding, 18s.

" We have examined this work with much care, and have derived both pleasure and profit from its perusal. We have, within a reasonable compass, a vast amount of solid, accurate information on Geographical subjects, written in a pleasant, readable style. We have every confidence in recommending it to the notice of our readers, and we can assure them that they will find in this portable volume more really valuable geographical information, combined with remarkable accuracy of facts and clearness of exposition, than in many Gazetteers costing *five* times the price."—*Educational Journal.*

" This volume contains a vast amount of useful information on the subject on which it treats. We have verified its correctness on several important topics, and can conscientiously recommend it as at once cheap, portable, and accurate."—*Leeds Mercury.*

" After a careful and rigorous examination, we must admit that, so far as it is possible to compress the whole world within the narrow limits of a single volume, Mr. Bryce has performed the task. As a work of reference this book is very valuable."—*Spectator.*

Bunyan's Pilgrim's Progress. With Life and Notes, Experimental and Practical, by WILLIAM MASON. Printed in large type, and illustrated with full page woodcuts, crown 8vo. handsomely bound in gilt cloth, gilt edges, price 3s. 6d,

Bunyan's Pilgrim's Progress. With Expository Lectures, by the Rev. ROBERT MAGUIRE, Incumbent of Clerkenwell. With Steel Engravings, second edition, imperial 8vo., cloth, 10s. 6d.

Burns and Scott. The Complete Poetical Works of Robert Burns and Sir Walter Scott. Lady of the Lake, Marmion, Lay of the Last Minstrel, &c., unabridged. Illustrated with fine Steel Portraits, and two fac-similes of an Original Letter and an Unpublished Poem of Burns' in his hand-writing, cloth, handsome, 5s.

Burns' Songs and Ballads. With an Introduction on the Character and Genius of Burns, by THOMAS CARLYLE. Carefully printed in antique type, and illustrated with beautiful Engravings on Steel. Foolscap 8vo., elegantly bound in cloth and gold, 3s. 6d. ; malachite, 10s. 6d.

Campbell's Pleasures of Hope, and other Poems: Including some Verses never before published. With an original Memoir by the Rev. CHARLES ROGERS, LL.D. Beautifully embellished with fine Portrait and several Steel Engravings. Just published. Cloth and gold, 3s. 6d.; morocco, 8s.; malachite, 10s. 6d.

" Well adapted for a choice present."—*Public Opinion.*

" A very charming edition of the poems of one who is deservedly a British Classic."—*Publisher's Circular.*

" The illustrations engraved on steel . . . . are very beautiful."—*Bookseller.*

" Dr. Rogers' memoir of the Poet is exceedingly well written, and contains several facts illustrative of Campbell's character and genius which are not to be found in any

Byron's Childe Harold's Pilgrimage. Illustrated with Engravings on Steel by GREATBACH, MILLER, LIGHTFOOT, &c., from Paintings by Cattermole, Sir T. Lawrence, H. Howard, and Stothard. Beautifully printed on Toned Paper. Foolscap 8vo., cloth elegant, 3s. 6d.; malachite, 10s. 6d.

Celestial Scenery; or, The Wonders of the Planet- ary System Displayed, including all new Discoveries. This Work is intended for general readers, presenting to their view, in an attractive manner, sublime objects of contemplation. By THOMAS DICK, LL.D. New Edition. Printed on Toned paper, handsomely bound, with gilt edges, price 5s.

Characteristics of Great Men, by John Timbs, bound in neat cloth, price 1s. (one of the Series, entitled "Griffin's Shilling Manuals," edited by JOHN TIMBS).

Chatterton's Poetical Works. With an Original Memoir. Beautifully Illustrated, and elegantly printed. Foolscap 8vo., cloth and gold, 3s. 6d.; malachite, 10s. 6d.

Christian Philosopher, The; or, The Connection of Science and Philosophy with Religion. By THOMAS DICK, LL D. Twenty-seventh Edition, revised and enlarged. Illustrated with 150 Engravings on Wood. Crown 8vo., cloth, printed on Toned paper, handsomely bound, with gilt edges, 5s.

Circle of the Sciences, by Owen, Ansted, Latham, etc., etc. Each Vol. 5s.

Vol.   I.—Organic Nature, Vol. 1—Physiology.
Vol.   II.—Organic Nature, Vol. 2—Botany, &c.
Vol.   III.—Organic Nature, Vol. 3—Zoology.
Vol.   IV.—Inorganic Nature.—Geology, &c.
Vol.   V.—Navigation, Astronomy, &c.
Vol.   VI.—Elementary Chemistry, Light, Heat, &c.
Vol.   VII.—Practical Chemistry.
Vol. VIII.—The Mathematical Sciences.
Vol.   IX.—Mechanical Philosophy.

The Treatises Separately.

	£	s.	d.
Ansted's Geology	0	2	6
Breen's Practical Astronomy	0	2	6
Bronner and Scoffern's Food and Diet	0	1	6
Bushman's Physiology	0	1	6
Gore's Electro-Deposition	0	1	6
Imray's Practical Mechanics	0	1	6
Jardine's Practical Geometry	0	1	6
Latham's Human Species	0	1	6
Martin's Photographic Art	0	2	6
Mitchell and Tennant's Mineralogy	0	3	0
Mitchell's Properties of Matter	0	1	6
Owen's Principal Forms of the Skeleton	0	1	6

Circle of the Sciences—*continued.*

	£	s.	d.
Primary Atlas of Geography	0	2	6
Primary Atlas of Geography, coloured	0	3	6
Scoffern's Light, Heat, &c.	0	3	0
Scoffern's Inorganic Bodies	0	3	0
Scoffern's Artificial Light	0	1	6
Scoffern and Lowe's Meteorology	0	1	6
Smith's Botany	0	2	0
Twisden's Trigonometry	0	1	6
Twisden on Logarithms	0	1	0
Young's Elements of Algebra	0	1	0
Young's Solutions of Questions in Algebra	0	1	0
Young's Navigation and Nautical Astronomy	0	2	6
Young's Plane Geometry	0	1	6
Young's Simple Arithmetic	0	1	0
Young's Elementary Dynamics	0	1	0

Civil Engineering, by Professor W. J. Macquorn

Rankine. Eighth Edition. Cloth, 16s.

"A work comprising much original research, as well as comprehensive study. Its pages contain a large amount of instructive matter, very clearly arranged and put into a shape readily available both to scientific and practical students."—*Civil Engineer and Architect's Journal.*

"Dr. Rankine has unquestionably carried out a great design in a most successful manner. It is quite impossible to give anything in the shape of a detailed notice of the contents of this last and best of Dr. Rankine's valuable professional works, but we are thoroughly convinced that it far surpasses in merit every existing work of the kind. As a 'Manual' (which it avowedly is) for the hands of the professional Civil Engineer, it is sufficient, and it is, as we have said, unrivalled, and even when we say this we fall short of that high appreciation of Dr. Rankine's labours which we should like to express."—*The Engineer.*

"The 'Manual of Civil Engineering' might without any impropriety be termed an *Encyclopædia* of the science, for it touches, and that with a master hand, every branch of it. We should imagine that the 'Manual of Engineering' is destined to become not only a monitor and guide to young engineers, but a friend and companion to those who, having advanced beyond their student days, are building for themselves names and fames which shall be imperishable as the granite upon which they work."—*Mechanics' Magazine.*

"A compact compression of the science of Engineering."—*Builder.*

Classified Bible, The: an Analysis of the Holy

Scriptures. By the Rev. JOHN EADIE, D.D., LL.D.,&c., Illustrated with Maps. Third Edition. Post 8vo., handsome, cloth antique, 8s. 6d. ; morocco, 16s.

"It is an attempt so to classify Scripture under separate heads as to exhaust its contents. The reader will find, under the respective Articles or Sections, what the Bible says on the separate subjects in relation to Doctrine, Ethics, and Antiquities."—*Preface.*

"We have only to add our unqualified commendation of a work of real excellence to every Biblical student."—*Christian Times.*

"This massive and valuable volume requires no notice at our hands."—*Edinburgh Mercury.*

"Professor Eadie, we have reason to think, is no bigot; and in preparing this work he doubtless felt that the interests of religion, founded upon a correct knowledge of the Scriptures, were dearer to him than those of any sect whatever. This work we recommend to the especial notice of clergymen, missionaries, and Sunday-school teachers."—*The Star.*

Cobbett's (William) Advice to Young Men, and

(incidentally) to Young Women, in the Middle and Higher Ranks of Life. In a Series of Letters addressed to a Youth, a Bachelor, a Lover, a Husband, a Father, a Citizen, and a Subject. New Edition. Foolscap 8vo., cloth, 2s. 6d. ; gilt, elegant, 3s.

Cobbett's (William) Cottage Economy; containing Information relative to the Brewing of Beer, Making of Bread, Keeping of Cows, Pigs, Bees, Poultry, &c.; and relative to other matters deemed useful in the conducting the affairs of a Poor Man's Family. New Edition, revised by the Author's Son. Foolscap 8vo., cloth, 2s. 6d.

Cobbett's (William) English Grammar. With an additional Chapter on Pronunciation. By J. P. COBBETT. Cloth, 1s. 6d.

Cobbett's (William) French Grammar. No better extant. Cloth, 3s. 6d. Thirteenth Edition.

"'Cobbett's French Grammar' comes out with perennial freshness. There are few grammars equal to it for those who are learning, or desirous of learning, French without a teacher. The work is excellently arranged, and in the present edition we note certain careful and wise revisions of the text."—*School Board Chronicle*, Feb. 18, 1871.

Cobbett's (William) Legacy to Parsons; or, Have the Clergy of the Established Church an Equitable Right to the Tithes and Church Property? With a New Preface by the Author's Son. Now ready, a New Edition. Cloth, 1s. 6d.

"The most powerful work of the greatest master of political controversy this country has ever produced."—*Pall Mall Gazette.*

Cobbett's (William) Rural Rides in Twenty-eight English Counties: with Economical and Political Observations. With Notes by J. P. COBBETT. 12mo., cloth, 3s. 6d.

Cobbett's (William) Poor Man's Friend: A Defence of the Rights of those who do the Work and Fight the Battles. Foolscap 8vo., limp, 1s.

Cook's Voyages. Voyages Round the World, by Captain Cook. Illustrated with Maps and numerous Engravings. 2 vols., super-royal 8vo., cloth, 30s.

Creation's Testimony to its God: the Accordance of Science, Philosophy, and Revelation. A Manual of the Evidences of Natural and Revealed Religion, with especial reference to the Progress of Science and Advance of Knowledge. By the Rev. THOMAS RAGG. Eleventh Edition, revised and enlarged. In handsome cloth, bevelled boards, 5s.

"We are not a little pleased again to meet with the author of this volume in the tenth edition of his far-famed work. Mr. Ragg is one of the few original writers of our time to whom justice is being done."—*British Standard.*

Cruden's Concordance to the Holy Scriptures.

By the Rev. JOHN EADIE, D.D., LL.D. With an Introduction by the Rev. Dr. KING. This has long and deservedly borne the reputation of being the completest and best edition extant, and the present reduction in price will also cause it to be by far the cheapest published. Thirty-second Edition. Cloth, 3s. 6d.; bevelled boards, antique, red edges, 4s. ; whole calf, 8s. ; whole morocco, 10s. 6d.

Curiosities of Animal and Vegetable Life. By

JOHN TIMBS. Neat cloth, 1s. (being one of a Series entitled "Griffin's Shilling Manuals," edited by John Timbs.)

Cyclopædia of the Physical Sciences; comprising

Acoustics, Astronomy, Dynamics, Electricity, Heat, Hydro-dynamics, Magnetism, Philosophy of Mathematics, Meteorology, Optics, Pneumatics, Statics, &c., &c. By Professor J. P. NICHOL, LL.D. Third Edition, revised and enlarged. With Maps and Illustrations, 8vo., bound in Roxburghe style, 21s.

"It takes its place at once, and of course among standard works. . . . . The ground of our opinion is the excellence of the matter, the freshness of the articles, and the attention which has been paid to bringing in the most recent views and discoveries."—*Athenæum.*

"Well printed and illustrated, and most ably edited."—*Examiner.*

"A most useful book of reference, deserving high commendation."—*Westminster Review.*

Dalgairns' Cookery: The Practice of Cookery,

adapted to the Business of Every-day Life. By Mrs. DALGAIRNS. The best book for Scotch dishes. About 50 new recipes have been added to the present edition, but only such as the Author has had adequate means of ascertaining to be valuable. Foolscap 8vo., cloth, 3s. 6d.

"This is by far the most complete and truly practical work which has yet appeared on the subject. It will be found an infallible "Cook's Companion," and a treasure of great price to the mistress of a family."—*Edinburgh Literary Journal.*

"We consider we have reason strongly to recommend Mrs. Dalgairns' as an economical, useful, and practical system of cookery, adapted to the wants of all families, from the tradesman to the country gentleman."—*Spectator.*

Dallas's (W. S.) Popular History of the Animal

Creation: being a systematic and popular Description of the Habits, Structure, and Classification of Animals. New Edition, with many hundred Illustrations. Crown 8vo., cloth, 8s. 6d.

1,000 Domestic Hints. By JOHN TIMBS. Cloth, 1s.

(being one of a Series entitled "Griffin's Shilling Manuals," edited by JOHN TIMBS).

"Domestic Hints" cannot fail to be appreciated by the housewife who is not above taking a hint. We cordially commend these Manuals to the attention of our readers."—*Aberdeen Herald.*

Domestic Medicine (Dr. Spencer Thomson's): a

Dictionary of Domestic Medicine and Household Surgery; with an additional Chapter on the Management of the Sick-room. Invaluable to Mothers. Ninth Edition, thoroughly revised, Illustrated. Large 8vo., 750 pages, cloth, 8s. 6d.

Rev. Professor Eadie's Commentary on the Greek

Text of the Epistle of Paul to the Ephesians. Second Edition, revised throughout and enlarged, 8vo., cloth, 14s.

"The book is one of prodigious learning and research. The author seems to have read all, in every language, that has been written upon the Epistle; it is also a work of independent criticism, and casts much new light upon many passages. Altogether it is a book itself sufficient to make a solid reputation."—APPOLODORUS *in Literary Gazette.*

Eadie's (Dr.) Dictionary of the Holy Bible;

designed chiefly for the Use of Young Persons. With numerous Illustrations. Eleventh Edition. Small 8vo., cloth antique, red edges, 2s. 6d.; gilt back and edges, 3s.; morocco, 7s. 6d.

"A carefully got up work; must prove of great use to the class for whom it is intended."—*Aberdeen Herald.*

"This is a most useful compendium of Bible lore. It is portable, yet comprehensive."—*Aberdeen Banner.*

"Parents and tutors will unanimously thank the author for this result of a labour of love."—*Critic.*

"A very good and useful compilation for youth."—*Literary Gazette.*

Rev. Professor Eadie's Ecclesiastical Cyclopædia;

a Dictionary of Christian Antiquities, Sects, Denominations, and Heresies; History of Dogmas, Rites, Sacraments, Ceremonies, etc., Liturgies, Creeds, Confessions, Monastic and Religious Orders, Modern Judaism, etc., etc. By the Rev. JOHN EADIE, D.D., LL.D., assisted by numerous Contributors. Third Edition, post 8vo., cloth, 8s. 6d.; morocco, 15s.

"This Cyclopædia will prove acceptable both to the clergy and laity of Great Britain. A great body of curious and useful information will be found in it; the aim has been to combine popularity with exactness."—*Athenæum.*

"We very warmly commend a book prepared with so much fullness of knowledge and conscientious care; and we especially press it on the attention of ordinarily educated persons in our general congregations, of Sunday School teachers, and of ministers not possessed of large libraries."—*Nonconformist.*

"Our readers will not need to be told that this is a 'comprehensive' work; and we may add that it is one that will be found useful and convenient to a large number of both clergy and laity."—*English Churchman.*

Earth Delineated with Pen and Pencil, The: an

Illustrated record of Voyages, Travels, and Adventures all round the World. Illustrated with more than 200 Engravings in the first style of Art, by the most eminent Artists, including several from the master pencil of GUSTAVE DORE. Demy 4to., 750 pages profusely Illustrated, very handsomely bound, price £1 1s.

English Literature, A Compendious History of,

and of the English Language, from the Norman Conquest. With numerous Specimens. By GEORGE L. CRAIK, LL.D. Now ready, a New Edition, in two large 8vo. vols., handsomely bound in cloth, £1 5s.; in tree calf, £1 17s. 6d.

"Professor Craik's book going, as it does, through the whole history of the language, probably takes a place quite by itself. The great value of the book is its thorough comprehensiveness. He is always clear and straightforward, and deals not in theories but in facts."—*Saturday Review.*

English Literature, A Manual of, for the Use of Colleges, Schools, and Civil Service Examinations. Selected from the larger work. By Professor CRAIK. Fourth Edition. Crown 8vo., 7s. 6d., cloth.

"A manual of English literature from such an experienced and well read a scholar as Professor Craik needs no other recommendation than the mention of its existence."— *Spectator*.

English Woman's Library : a Series of Moral and Descriptive Tales, by Mrs. ELLIS. Cloth, each 2s. 6d. ; with gilt backs and edges, 3s.

1.—THE WOMEN OF ENGLAND: their Social Duties and Domestic Habits. 39th thousand.
2.—THE DAUGHTERS OF ENGLAND : their Position in Society, Character, and Responsibilities. 20th thousand.
3.—THE WIVES OF ENGLAND: their Relative Duties, Domestic Influence, and Social Obligations. 18th thousand.
4.—THE MOTHERS OF ENGLAND : their Influence and Responsibility. 20th thousand.
5.—FAMILY SECRETS ; or, Hints to make Home Happy. 3 vols. 23rd thousand.
6.—SUMMER AND WINTER IN THE PYRENEES. 10th thousand.
7.—TEMPER AND TEMPERAMENT ; or, Varieties of Character. 2 vols. 10th thousand.
8.—PREVENTION BETTER THAN CURE ; or, The Moral Wants of the World we Live in. 12th thousand.
9.—HEARTS AND HOMES ; or, Social Distinction. 3 vols. 10th thousand.

Eventful Life of a Soldier in the Peninsula. By JOSEPH DONALDSON, Sergeant in the Ninety-fourth Scots Regiment. Foolscap 8vo., cloth, 3s. 6d.; with gilt sides and edges, 4s.

FINDEN'S FINE ART WORKS.

Gallery of Modern Art ; a Series of 31 highly- finished Steel Engravings, with Descriptive Tales by Mrs. S. C. HALL, MARY HOWITT, and others. Folio, cloth extra, gilt edges, 21s.

Beauties of Moore : being a Series of Portraits of his principal Female Characters, from Paintings by eminent Artists, engraved in the highest style of Art, by Mr. EDWARD FINDEN, with a Memoir of the Poet, and Descriptive Letter-press. Folio, cloth extra, gilt edges, 42s.

Drawing-room Table Book: a Series of 31 highly- finished Steel Engravings, with Descriptive Tales, by Mrs. S. C. HALL, MARY HOWITT, and others. Folio, cl. extra, gilt edges, 21s.

GRIFFIN'S EMERALD GEMS.

Just published, a new volume of this exqusite series. Beautifully printed on toned paper, with Portrait and other Illustrations. Cloth elegant, 6s. ; in malachite, 12s. 6d.

The Songs of the Baroness Nairne, authoress of
"The Land o' the Leal." With Memoir, from family papers and other original sources. Edited by the Rev. CHARLES ROGERS, LL.D.

*** Her Majesty the Queen has expressed her admiration of these beautiful Songs, the authorship of which is now for the first time made public.

Also, uniform with the above,

Gray's Poetical Works. With Life by the Rev.
JOHN MITFORD, and Essay by the EARL OF CARLISLE. With Portrait and numerous Engravings on Steel and Wood. New Edition. Elegantly printed on toned paper, foolscap 8vo., richly bound in cloth and gold, 5s. ; malachite, 12s. 6d.

Goldsmith's Poetical Works. With Memoir by
WILLIAM SPALDING, A.M. Exquisitely Illustrated with Steel Engravings. New Edition. Printed on superior toned paper. Foolscap 8vo, cloth and gold, 3s. 6d.; malachite, 10s. 6d.

Burns' Songs and Ballads. With an Introduction
on the Character and Genius of Burns, by THOMAS CARLYLE. Carefully printed in antique type, and Illustrated with beautiful Engravings on Steel. Foolscap 8vo., elegantly bound in cloth and gold, 3s. 6d. ; malachite, 10s. 6d.

Poe's Poetical Works, Complete. Edited by J.
HANNAY. Illustrations after WEHNERT, WEIR, &c. Toned Paper. Foolscap 8vo., cloth elegant, 3s. 6d. ; malachite, 10s. 6d.

Byron's Childe Harold's Pilgrimage. Illustrated
with Engravings on Steel by GREATBACH, MILLER, LIGHTFOOT, &c., from Paintings by CATTERMOLE, SIR T. LAWRENCE, H. HOWARD, and STOTHARD. Beautifully printed on toned paper. Foolscap 8vo., cloth elegant, 3s. 6d. ; malachite, 10s. 6d.

Chatterton's Poetical Works. With an Original
Memoir. Beautifully Illustrated, and elegantly printed. Foolscap 8vo., cloth and gold, 3s. 6d. ; malachite, 10s. 6d.

Herbert's Poetical Works. With Memoir by
J. NICHOL, B.A., Oxon. Edited by CHARLES COWDEN CLARKE. Foolscap 8vo., cloth and gold, 3s. 6d. ; malachite, 10s. 6d.

Campbell's Pleasures of Hope. With Introductory
Memoir. Illustrated with splendid Steel Engravings. Price 3s. 6d. Uniform with "GOLDSMITH," "GRAY," "POE," &c.

Other Volumes will be added from time to time.

Goldsmith's (Oliver) Poetical Works. With a
Memoir by WILLIAM SPALDING, A.M., and numerous Illustrations on Steel and Wood. Foolscap 4to., most elaborately gilt, cloth, 5s.

GRIFFIN'S SHILLING MANUALS.

Edited by JOHN TIMBS. Bound in neat cloth.

I. Popular Science.
II. One Thousand Domestic Hints.
III. Oddities of History.
IV. Thoughts for Times and Seasons.
V. Characteristics of Great Men.
VI. Curiosities of Animal and Vegetable Life.

"These additions to the Library, produced by Mr. Timbs' industry and ability, are useful, and in his pages many a hint and suggestion, and many a fact of importance, is stored up, that would otherwise have been lost to the public."—*Builder*.

"Capital little books of about a hundred pages each, wherein the indefatigable Author is seen at his best."—*Mechanics' Magazine*.

Henry's (Matthew) Commentary on the Holy
Bible. New Edition, 3 vols., super-royal 8vo., strongly bound in cloth, 50s., calf, marbled edges, 67s. 6d., levant morocco, antique, gilt edges, 84s.

Herbert's Poetical Works. With Memoir by
J. NICHOL, B.A., Oxon. Edited by CHARLES COWDEN CLARKE. Foolscap 8vo., cloth and gold, 3s. 6d. ; malachite, 10s. 6d.

Hogarth—The Works of William Hogarth, in a
Series of 150 Steel Engravings by the First Artists, with Descriptions by Rev. JOHN TRUSLER, and Introductory Essay on the Genius of Hogarth, by JAMES HANNAY. Small folio, cloth, gilt edges, 52s. 6d.

Horatii Opera. With copious English Notes by
JOSEPH CURRIE, Master of Sunderland Academy. Many illustrations. Fcap. 8vo., cloth, 5s.
Part 1. Carmina. With English Notes, cloth, 3s.
Part 2. Satires. With English Notes, cloth, 3s.

"The notes are excellent and exhaustive."—*Quarterly Jour. Educ.*, July, 1870.

Kitto's (Dr.) Holy Land. The Mountains, Valleys,
and Rivers of the Holy Land ; being the Physical Geography of Palestine. By JOHN KITTO, D.D., F.S.A. Just ready, new edition, fcap. 8vo., handsomely bound, 2s. 6d. ; in bevelled boards, red edges, 3s.

Leared (Dr.) On Imperfect Digestion. New
edition, post 8vo., cloth, 4s. 6d.

Lamb's (Charles and Mary) Tales from Shakespeare.
New Edition. To which are now added Scenes illustrating each Tale. With numerous Woodcuts from Designs by HARVEY. Edited by CHARLES KNIGHT. Small 8vo., cloth, bevelled boards, 2s. 6d. ; with gilt edges, 3s. ; morocco antique, 7s.

Language of Flowers, The ; or, The Pilgrimage of Love. By THOMAS MILLER. With eight beautifully coloured Plates. Just published, a New Edition. Small 8vo., cloth, gilt edges, 3s. 6d. ; handsomely bound in silk and in morocco, 8s.

Mackey's Freemasonry: a Lexicon of Free- masonry ; containing a Definition of all its Communicable Terms, Notices of its History, Tradition, and Antiquities, and an Account of all the Rites and Mysteries of the Ancient World. By ALBERT G. MACKEY, M.D., Secretary-General of the Supreme Council of the U.S., &c. Handsomely bound in cloth, price 5s.

Mangnall—Historical and Miscellaneous Questions, for the use of Young People. By RICHMAL MANGNALL. New Illustrated Edition, greatly enlarged and corrected, and continued to the present time, by INGRAM COBBIN, M.A., 12mo., bound, 4s. Forty-eighth thousand.

Many Thoughts of Many Minds: being a Treasury of Reference, consisting of Selections from the Writings of the most celebrated Authors. Compiled and analytically arranged by HENRY SOUTHGATE. Twentieth Thousand. Square 8vo., printed on toned paper, elegant binding, 12s. 6d. ; morocco, £1 1s.

"The produce of years of research."—*Examiner.*
"Destined to take a high place among books of this class."—*Notes and Queries.*
"A treasure to every reader who may be fortunate enough to possess it."—*English Journal of Education.*
"The accumulation of treasures truly wonderful."—*Morning Herald.*
"This is a wondrous book." —*Daily News.*
"Worth its weight in gold to literary men."—*Builder.*

Many Thoughts of Many Minds. Second Series.
By HENRY SOUTHGATE. Square 8vo., printed on Toned paper, and elegantly bound in cloth and gold, 12s. 6d.
The same, Handsome morocco antique, £1 1s.

"Few Christmas Books are likely to be more permanently valuable."—*Scotsman.*
"Fully sustains the deserved reputation achieved by the First Series."—*John Bull.*

Morison's (Dr. J.) Family Worship. Prayers for every Morning and Evening throughout the Year. 4to, cloth, gilt edges, 12s.

Nichol's (Professor) Cyclopædia of the Physical Sciences ; comprising Acoustics, Astronomy, Dynamics, Electricity, Heat, Magnetism, Meteorology, &c., &c. Third Edition, enlarged. Maps and Illustrations. Large 8vo. Half-bound, Roxburghe, £1 1s.

Pictorial Gallery of the Useful and Fine Arts,
Illustrated by numerous beautiful Steel Engravings, and nearly
Four Thousand Woodcuts. Edited by CHARLES KNIGHT. 2 vols.
folio, cloth gilt, 34s.

Pictorial Museum of Animated Nature. By
CHARLES KNIGHT. Illustrated with Four Thousand Woodcuts.
Folio, 2 vols. cloth, gilt, 34s.

Pictorial Sunday Book. Edited by Dr. JOHN
KITTO. Cloth, gilt, 25s.

Poe's Poetical Works, Complete. Edited by
J. HANNAY. Illustrations after Wehnert, Weir, &c. Toned
Paper. Foolscap 8vo., cloth, elegant, 3s. 6d.; malachite,
10s. 6d.

Poetry of the Year; or Pastorals from our Poets
illustrative of the Seasons. Embellished with a Series of Admirable Imitations of Water-Colour Paintings from the Drawings of
Birket Foster, Harrison Weir, Barker, Lejeune, E. V. B., Duncan,
Lee, Cox, T. Creswick, R.A., beautifully executed in Chromo-
Lithography, and mounted. 4to., handsomely bound in cloth and
gold, 16s.; morocco, £1 5s.

"One of the most admirable, as well as most original, contributions to the pictorial
literature of the season."—*Pall Mall Gazette.*
"Altogether, the book is a very attractive one."—*Times.*

PROFESSOR RAMSAY'S WORKS.

Ramsay's (Professor) Manual of Roman Antiquities.
With Map, numerous Engravings, and very copious Index.
Eighth Edition, revised and enlarged. Crown 8vo., cloth, 8s. 6d.

"'A Manual of Roman Antiquities,' by William Ramsay, M.A., is a useful work,
evidencing much thought in compilation and arrangement. Students of Latin literature
will find this volume handy in form and matter. There is a perfect index and numerous
illustrations, with a chapter on Roman Agriculture."—*School Board Chronicle.*

Ramsay's (Professor) Elementary Manual of Roman
Antiquities. Adapted for Junior Classes. Numerous Illustrations. Fifth Edition. Crown 8vo., cloth, 4s.

Ramsay's (Professor) Manual of Latin Prosody.
Fourth Edition, revised and greatly enlarged. Crown 8vo.,
cloth, 5s.

Ramsay's (Professor) Elementary Manual of Latin
Prosody. Adapted for Junior Classes. Crown 8vo., cloth, 2s.

PROFESSOR RANKINE'S WORKS.

Rankine's Machinery and Millwork: comprising Geometry of Machines, Motions of Machines, Work of Machines, Strength of Machines, Construction of Machines, Objects of Machines, &c., &c. Illustrated with nearly 300 Woodcuts. Crown 8vo., cloth, 12s. 6d.

"Professor Rankine's 'Manual of Machinery and Mill Work,' fully maintains the high reputation which he enjoys as a scientific author; higher praise it is difficult to award to any book. It is simply impossible, within the limits of a review of reasonable length even to indicate the multitude of subjects treated of, and well treated, by our author. We could wish to see such books as 'Professor Rankine's Manual' in the study of every engineer, aye, and to see it well thumbed, too, as books closely read and often referred to will be. The book cannot fail to be a lantern to the feet of every engineer."— *The Engineer.*

Rankine's Civil Engineering. Eighth Edition. Cloth, 16s.

Rankine's Applied Mechanics. Sixth Edition. Cloth, 12s. 6d.

Rankine's The Steam-Engine and other Prime Movers. Fifth Edition. Cloth, 12s. 6d.

Rankine's Useful Rules and Tables. Third Edition, *just ready.* Cloth, 9s.

" Undoubtedly the most useful collection of engineering data hitherto produced."— *Mining Journal.*

Religious and Moral Anecdotes. With an Intro- ductory Essay by the Rev. GEORGE CHEEVER, D.D. Tenth Thousand. Crown 8vo., cloth, 3s. 6d.

" Invaluable to those engaged in the instruction of the young."

Religions of the World (The). Being Confessions of Faith, contributed by eminent members of each Denomination of Christians, also of Mahometanism, the Parsee Religion, the Hindoo Religion, Mormonism, etc., etc. Cloth, 8vo., bevelled boards, 3s. 6d.

Senior's (Professor) Treatise on Political Economy: the Science which treats of the Nature, the Production, and Distribution of Wealth. Fourth edition. Crown 8vo., cloth, 4s.

Shakspeare's Dramatic and Poetical Works. Re- vised from the Original Editions, with a Memoir, and Essay on his Genius, by BARRY CORNWALL ; also, Annotations and Intro-ductory Remarks on his Plays, by R. H. HORNE, with numerous Engravings by Kenny Meadows. 3 vols., super-royal 8vo., cloth, £2 2s.

School Board Readers (The.) A New Series of

Standard Reading Books for Elementary Schools. Edited by a Former Her Majesty's Inspector of Schools. The Prices will be as follows :—

ELEMENTARY READING BOOK, Part I., containing lessons in all the short vowel sounds. Demy 18mo., 16 pages, in stiff wrapper, price 1d.

ELEMENTARY READING BOOK, Part II., containing the long vowel sounds, and other monosyllables. Demy 18mo., 48 pages, in stiff wrapper, price 2d.

STANDARD I., containing Reading, Dictation, and Arithmetic. Demy 18mo., 96 pages, neat cloth, price 4d.

STANDARD II. Ditto demy 18mo., 128 pages, neat cloth, price 6d.

STANDARD III. Ditto fcap. 8vo., 160 pages, neat cloth, price 9d.

STANDARD IV. Ditto fcap. 8vo., 192 pages, neat cloth, price 1s.

STANDARD V. Ditto crown 8vo., 256 pages, neat cloth, price 1s. 6d.

STANDARD VI. Ditto and Lessons on Scientific Subjects. Crown 8vo., 320 pages, neat cloth, price 2s.

Shakspeare's Works. Edited by T. O. HALLIWELL,

with a Series of Steel Portraits. 3 volumes, royal 8vo., cloth gilt, £2 10s.

Sidereal Heavens, The, and other Subjects con-

nected with Astronomy, as illustrative of the Character of the Deity, and of an Infinity of other Worlds. By THOMAS DICK, LL.D., author of the "Christian Philosopher," &c. New Edition. Printed on toned paper, handsomely bound, with gilt edges, price 5s.

Songs of the Baroness Nairne, authoress of "The

Land o' the Leal." With Memoir, from family papers and other original sources. Edited by the Rev. CHARLES ROGERS, LL.D. With Portrait and other Illustrations. Cloth elegant, 6s., malachite, 12s. 6d.

*** Her Majesty the Queen has expressed her admiration of these beautiful Songs, the authorship of which is now for the first time made public.

Spelling by Dictation : Progressive Exercises in
English Orthography for Schools and Civil Service Examinations.
By the Rev. A. J. D. D'ORSEY, of King's College. New Edition.
18mo., cloth, 1s. Thirteenth Thousand.

Student's Natural History : being a Dictionary of
the Natural Sciences. With a Zoological Chart, showing the
Distribution and Range of Animal Life. By W. BAIRD, M.D.,
F.L.S., British Museum. Numerous Illustrations. Demy 8vo.,
cloth, gilt, red edges, 10s. 6d.

"The work is a very useful one, and will contribute, by its cheapness and comprehensiveness, to foster the extending taste for natural science."—*Westminster Review*.

"We would well recommend this volume to students of natural history."—*Lancet*.

"Few men could be better qualified for such a task than Dr. Baird. . . . We can recommend it as a useful work of reference on the subject of natural history."—*Athenæum*.

"Edited with the utmost care, and deserves to rank among standard works of reference."—*Leader*.

"A most valuable work."—*Glasgow Herald*.

"Well worthy to be coupled with Nichol's *Physical Sciences*."—*Examiner*.

Thomson's (Spencer, M.D., L.R.C.S., Edinburgh)
Dictionary of Domestic Medicine and Household Surgery. Ninth
Edition. Thoroughly revised, and brought down to the present
state of Medical Science. With the addition of an Appendix and
a Chapter on the Management of the Sick Room. Illustrated
with 150 Engravings on wood. Post 8vo., cloth, 8s. 6d.

"The best and safest book on Domestic Medicine and Household Surgery which has yet appeared."—*London Journal of Medicine*.

"Dr. Thomson has fully succeeded in conveying to the public a vast amount of useful professional knowledge."—*Dublin Journal of Medical Science*.

Virgilii, Opera. With English Notes, Original
and Selected. By ARCHIBALD HAMILTON BRYCE, B.A., LL.D.
With numerous Illustrations. In three parts. Foolscap 8vo.,
cloth, 2s. 6d. each. 1. Bucolics and Georgics. 2. The Æneid,
Liber 1—6. 3. The Æneid, 7—12 ; or, complete in one volume,
6s.

"A credit to scholarship North of the Tweed. The illustrations are very well executed."
—*School Board Chronicle*.

Wanderings in every Clime ; or Voyages, Travels,
and Adventures All Round the World. Edited by W. F.
AINSWORTH, F.R.G.S., F.S.A., &c., and embellished with upwards of Two Hundred Illustrations by the first Artists, including
several from the master pencil of GUSTAVE DORE. Just
published, large 4to., 800 pages, cloth and gold, bevelled
boards, £1 1s.